Women's Studies

JULIA WATTS

Spinsters Ink
2006

This book is a work of fiction. All of the characters are entirely the products of the author's imagination, and any real locations mentioned in the work are used fictionally.

Spinsters Ink, Inc.
P.O. Box 242
Midway, Florida 32343

Printed in the United States of America on acid-free paper
First Edition

Editor: Christi Cassidy
Cover designer: Kiaro Creative Ltd.

ISBN 1-883523-75-3

Women's Studies

JULIA WATTS

Spinsters Ink
2006

Acknowledgments

My deepest thanks go to the terrific women at Spinsters Ink: Linda Hill for believing in this novel even when I had only twelve pages of it written, Christi Cassidy for being an inspiring editor as well as a cornbread enthusiast and Therese Szymanski for her typesetting and general swellness. As always, I want to express my love and appreciation to the family members who help me find time to write and then volunteer to read my drafts: Carol, Don, Mom and Dad. My love and appreciation also go to Ian and Alec, who are not allowed to read this book until they are at least as old as the characters in it.

About the Author

A native of southeastern Kentucky, Julia Watts is the author of the novels *Wildwood Flowers, Phases of the Moon, Piece of My Heart, Wedding Bell Blues, Mixed Blessings,* and the Lambda Literary Award-winning *Finding H.F.* Watts is a two-time recipient of grants from the Kentucky Foundation for Women and recently completed an M.F.A. in Writing from Spalding University. She lives, writes and teaches in Knoxville, Tennessee.

Part I:

Fall Semester, 1990

Liz

The first thing Liz noticed about Dr. Rivers was that she was wearing both pearls and Birkenstocks. This combination struck Liz as odd since she had always thought of pearl wearers and Birkenstock wearers as two separate groups. Barbara Bush was a pearl wearer, for instance, while the lank-haired girls in the dorm who stank of patchouli were Birkenstock wearers. If presented with a pair of Birkenstocks, Barbara Bush would no doubt wrinkle her nose in disgust and exchange them for a pair of matronly pumps. If presented with a string of pearls, the patchouli girls would pawn them and use the cash to buy weed.

Dr. Rivers took her place behind the podium and said, "Welcome to Women's Studies Three-Ten—Women in Literature. I assume you're all in the right place?"

Liz stifled a snicker as a terrified-looking frat boy, who apparently wasn't in the right place, made a beeline for the door.

Dr. Rivers smiled. "Well, now that we've scared off the only man in the room, I guess we can get started."

Liz tittered along with the rest of the women in the class.

"Well, let's see . . ." Dr. Rivers flipped back a tendril of blond-streaked-with-silver hair as she looked down at the podium. "This semester I have two Amys on the roll, two Melissas and, let's see, three Elizabeths. The first thing we need to do is figure out what to call the women with the same names so it won't be too confusing for your dotty, middle-aged professor. Then, I'll go ahead and call the names of the students whose parents had the good graces to name them more imaginatively."

One of the Melissas went by Missy, which solved that problem, but the only way to get past the Amy confusion was to call them by their first names and last initials. "And now our three Elizabeths," Dr. Rivers said, glancing down at the roll. "Where is Elizabeth Chamberlain?"

"Here," said a petite blond wearing a pink T-shirt celebrating her sorority's Spring Fling. She had a tan, Liz noticed, probably from summering at Hilton Head or Pawley's Island. The girl was, Liz supposed, pretty. But the sorority girls at William Blount U were like Persian cats. Sure, they were pretty, but they all looked alike.

"And what shall we call you, Ms. Chamberlain?" Dr. Rivers asked, emphasizing the "z" sound in "Ms."

"Beth, ma'am."

Dr. Rivers raised an unplucked eyebrow. "Let's drop the 'ma'am' and keep the 'Beth,' shall we? And where's Elizabeth Nelson?"

Liz raised her hand. "I'm Liz."

Dr. Rivers smiled. "And yet your shirt identifies you as Billy Ray. Clearly, you're a tricky one."

Liz aimed a rare smile back at Dr. Rivers. She was wearing a service station employee's shirt that she had picked up for a quarter at a thrift shop. A patch sewn over the breast pocket bore the name of the shirt's former owner.

"And now," Dr. Rivers said, "that leaves Elizabeth Ricketts."

"I'm here." The voice had come from a young woman who, Liz thought, would be quite pretty if she weren't so fashion-impaired. Her chestnut hair was much bigger than it needed to be, given that the eighties were over, and she was wearing those acid-washed jeans that made their wearers look like the victims of an industrial accident. Liz immediately pegged Elizabeth Ricketts as a small-town girl. Liz was able to identify her as such because she was a small-town girl herself, although she did try to avoid dressing like one.

"And what shall I call you, Ms. Ricketts?" Dr. Rivers asked, her pen poised over her roll sheet.

"Elisa, please."

"Elisa," Dr. Rivers said, stretching out the name's syllables. "That's rather nice, actually."

Elisa, to Liz's amusement, seemed to be blushing. "Thank you," she said. "I just started calling myself Elisa when I left for college. Momma and Daddy still call me Bitsy."

"Well," Dr. Rivers said, "college is definitely the time to cast off the old roles of childhood and adolescence and forge one's own identity. And between you and me, Elisa, the name 'Bitsy' is definitely something that needs to be cast off." Dr. Rivers looked back down at the podium. "Now, onto the rest of the roll, and then we'll take a look at the syllabus."

As Liz scanned the syllabus, she was relieved to see that she'd already read half the books required for the course: *Mrs. Dalloway*, *Their Eyes Were Watching God*, *The Handmaid's Tale* and *Beloved*. That left her with just three books to read. Assuming that Dr. Rivers wasn't psychotically picky when it came to grading papers, this class would be an easy A.

Liz considered herself a pretty good student, but not in the worrywart Phi Beta Kappa way. She had a knack for figuring out just how much work would get her a decent grade in a class. Once she'd determined how much was required of her, she'd do that much and no more. As a result, she tended to get all As in her major (English) and Bs in her other classes. She knew, because her parents were always telling her, that she could get straight As if she really applied herself, but somehow it didn't seem worth the effort. Keeping a 3.2 average instead of a 4.0 allowed her to go out and drink beer and have interesting conversations instead of staying holed up all night in the library's study lounge. And besides, at graduation, everybody got a diploma regardless of whether they were graduating summa cum laude or summa cum lazy.

By the time Dr. Rivers had finished talking them through the syllabus, it was time to go. Papers rustled, backpacks zipped and everybody shuffled toward the door.

Liz wasn't looking forward to her next class. For one thing, it was a horrifically long trudge across the hilly campus to get to the science buildings. For another, she suspected the class that awaited her once she got there—Geology 110, nicknamed Rocks for Jocks—would be totally devoid of interesting content. But like the jocks, with whom she rarely had anything in common, Liz was taking the class as an easy way to get her lab science requirement.

"Hey," a gravelly female voice called as she made her way through the crowded hall.

Liz turned to see a classmate from Women in Literature, a muscular, olive-skinned woman whose black hair had been clipped even shorter than Liz's in a military-style buzz cut. The woman was wearing a plain white men's T-shirt with no bra underneath, olive green cutoffs and black Doc Martens. It was the space between the cutoffs and Doc Martens that fascinated Liz, however. Liz had quit shaving her legs a year ago but had only grown a light dusting of pale-colored down. This woman had more leg hair than most men. Thick, black and curly, it was a bona fide pelt, and Liz found it strangely fascinating.

"Hi," Liz said, making herself look at the woman's face instead of her calves. "I'm Liz."

"I know," she said. "How could I not, after all that time Rivers spent trying to get y'all's names straight? I'm Thalia, which you probably remember from Rivers' five-minute gush-fest about how cool it is that I'm named after one of the Muses. Of course, I'm really named after my great-grandmother. I mean, my parents run a deli. I don't think they're literary enough to know that Thalia is the Muse of comedy. Rivers is cool, though. Have you had her before?"

Liz had gotten so caught up in Thalia's monologue that she found it jarring to be required to speak. "Uh . . . no."

"I had her for feminist theory in the spring, and it was great," Thalia said, "but I've got to tell you, some of those French feminist theorists come up with some crazy shit. Like there's this one, I can't remember her name—it's like Helene or Monique or something—who said that women are in a perpetual state of masturbation." A wholesome-looking guy passing by glowered at Thalia, but she ignored him. "I mean, can you imagine?"

Liz managed to squeeze in that no, she couldn't.

"Listen, anyway," Thalia said, digging into her backpack. "I wanted to give you something . . . I thought you might be interested." She rummaged around a few seconds more, then pulled out what looked to be a hot pink business card.

Liz took the card and read, "G.L.O.B.A.L.—the Gay, Lesbian or Bisexual Alliance—meetings Wednesdays at 7:30 p.m. in Room 213 of the University Center." *Here we go again,* she thought. But she said, "Thanks. That's really cool that you have an, uh, organization and everything. I totally support gay rights, but I'm straight."

Thalia's brow furrowed. "Really? Oh, well, my mistake. Pass the card on to somebody who needs it, okay?" She slung her backpack over her shoulder and disappeared into the human traffic of the hallway.

Liz stuck the pink card in the corner of a nearby bulletin board. *So,* she thought, *there goes the first time this semester I get mistaken for a lesbian.*

It happened all the time, even when she was out with her boyfriend, Dan. One time they were at one of the dive bars they frequented, and this masculine woman truck driver had kept talking to her and buying pitchers for their table. Finally, Liz had explained to the woman that Dan was her boyfriend, that she wasn't available. The woman had been flabbergasted. "You mean you're straight?" she had yelled over the Lynrd Skynrd on the jukebox. "But you don't understand; I'm never wrong about women."

But she had been wrong. People made such shallow assumptions based on appearance. Sure, Liz cut her technicolor-dyed hair short, wore no makeup and favored boys' Levi's and Converse Chuck Taylor All Stars. She was rebelling against the fascism of female beauty standards, but that didn't make her a lesbian. She and Dan had been together for a year and a half now, and all their friends said they were perfect for each other. Besides, Liz reasoned as she began the long trudge to Rocks for Jocks, she wasn't some kind of homophobe who would pretend to be straight out of fear and self-loathing. She was an open-minded, bohemian twenty-year-old. If she were really a lesbian, she would have figured it out by now.

Elisa

It was hard to make a card table in a dorm room look elegant, but Elisa was doing her best. She had covered the flimsy yard-sale special with a checked tablecloth from Walgreen's. It was the vinyl kind you bought for picnics, but it still looked pretty good. She placed a candle in the center of the table. Technically, candles were against the dorm's rules because of some stupid girl years ago who had fallen asleep with candles burning and set her curtains on fire. But Elisa figured lighting one candle on a special occasion wouldn't be too much of a violation. Besides, the girls across the hall smoked pot in their room all the time, and that had to be more of a fire hazard.

When Jo got back from softball practice, Elisa would take the two orders of spaghetti and meatballs she'd bought from the diner on the strip and warm them in the microwave. With the checked tablecloth and the candlelight and the spaghetti and meatballs, it would be just like that scene in *Lady and the Tramp*. Jo always said Lady and the Tramp were the movie couple she and Elisa most resembled. Even though the Disney characters were a straight couple and dogs, they did have the same kind of chemistry as Elisa and Jo. Elisa was Lady—a nickname Jo often called her. But Elisa didn't call Jo "Tramp" because it didn't sound right.

The table set, Elisa stretched across the bed to study. She had moved the room's two single beds together to form a double, although it was a double with a serious gap in the middle.

She picked up *Mrs. Dalloway* and started to read, but her anticipation of Jo's arrival made it hard for her to concentrate. Mrs. Dalloway was buying flowers for a party just like Elisa, using some cash saved from her awful summer job at Hardee's, had bought a tablecloth and candle and dinner for her and Jo's little party of two. A thrill ran through her. After a summer of sneaking kisses and nervous, furtive groping in the back seat of Jo's car, now they could finally settle back down to living together as lovers.

They'd been together since their sophomore year in high school. In their tiny hometown of Odessa, Tennessee, which consisted of a Hardee's, a grocery store, a school and more churches than you could shake a stick at, it was amazing to think that two girls could so easily fall in love with each other. But Elisa and Jo, who had adored each other since elementary school, fell into each other's arms as naturally as the head cheerleader and the captain of the football team.

The only difference was that Elisa and Jo had to be discreet. While football players and cheerleaders could practically do it against the lockers in the hall, Elisa and Jo knew that in public they could not hold hands, could not brush up against each other, could not even shoot each other a meaningful glance. They had heard the football players and cheerleaders spit their slurs about faggots and dykes, so they knew the dangers.

Back then, even their private moments hadn't been that private. Elisa always locked the door of her room when Jo was with her, but her family's house was tiny, and the living room where her parents and sister were watching TV was right next door to the room where she and Jo lay kissing. And at Jo's family's trailer, they didn't even try to grab any private moments. Jo's father had a volatile temper, had a pretty strong suspicion of "what" his daughter was, and Jo always feared that if they locked the door of her bedroom, her father would break it down.

A lot of Elisa and Jo's time in high school had been spent dreaming of the day when they would escape to William Blount University in the big city of Knoxville, where they could be roommates and spend every night in each other's arms. Because of Elisa's good grades and Jo's athletic talent, their dream had come true. This would be their third year of sharing the same room in McMillan Hall, a room that, despite its small size and institutional concrete block walls, felt more like home to Elisa than her family's house back in Odessa.

Elisa forced herself to focus on Virginia Woolf's words until she heard the click of Jo's key in the door.

"Hey, Lady." Jo was wearing her softball uniform. Even though it was maroon and yellow and synthetic, Elisa still loved the way it hugged Jo's muscles and calves.

"Hey yourself." Elisa stood on tiptoe to kiss her, running her fingers through her damp blond curls.

"I wouldn't be cozying up to somethin' that smelled like me," Jo said, holding her at arm's length.

"I like you sweaty." Elisa moved in closer to nuzzle Jo's neck.

"Well, that makes one of us. I'm gonna go hit the showers right quick."

"Do be quick. I've got supper for us." She nodded in the direction of the card table with the checked cloth.

"Well, would you look at that?" Jo grinned. "If I'd known you was gonna get all romantic on me, I would've stopped and bought you a rose or somethin'."

Elisa leaned her head on Jo's shoulder. "I bet you can make it up to me somehow."

Jo's ears turned red, as Elisa knew they would. "Yeah," Jo said, "I reckon I could think of somethin'."

"I just bet you can," Elisa said, grabbing a towel off the bureau and pressing it into Jo's hands. "Now, hit the showers, sport."

The spaghetti was warm and on the table when Jo returned from the shower wearing shorts and a William Blount U Lady Mountaineers T-shirt. "So what classes did my little bookworm have today?" Jo asked, hacking her spaghetti into tiny pieces with her fork—a habit that didn't lessen Elisa's affection for her, but did annoy her just a little. Of course,

Jo had grown up eating mayonnaise sandwiches she made for herself—bologna and mayonnaise was a luxury—so Elisa couldn't blame her for her lack of table manners. Elisa's family was poor, too, but her mother had made it a point of pride to cook supper every night, even if it was just beans and cornbread.

"I had human biology, which was as bad as I thought it would be. A hundred students in the class, and the professor didn't look up from his notes even once." Elisa twirled her spaghetti on her fork and hoped Jo would notice and follow suit. "But then I had that Women in Lit course, which is gonna be great."

Jo grinned. "You and your women's studies classes. So how many hairy-legged gals you got in this one?"

Elisa rolled her eyes. Athletic, assertive Jo was a walking poster for feminism in some ways, but in other ways she was disappointingly conventional. "Well, I didn't take a survey or anything, but I've got to say there's this one girl—uh, woman . . ." Elisa knew saying "girl" was sexist, and she was trying to break herself of the habit. "Her legs are hairier than my Uncle Ronnie's."

Jo dropped her fork. "Aw, man, that's just nasty!"

"No, she wasn't nasty at all. She was clean; she was just hairy. In Europe most of the women don't shave."

"Well, last time I checked a map Tennessee wasn't in Europe, and I'm glad of it. I like my girls soft and smooth."

Elisa raised an eyebrow. "Your *girls?*"

Jo grinned. "My *girl*. The only one I ever had and the only one I'll ever need."

Jo's blue eyes met Elisa's and just like that, Elisa melted like warm butter. It didn't matter that Jo called her *girl* instead of *woman* or that Jo insisted on dissecting her spaghetti before eating it. There was something between them that went deeper than words and that was pulling them away from the table and toward the bed.

After three months of quickies punctuated by paranoia—"You did lock the door, didn't you? What was that sound?"—it was bliss to lie back in this bed that was theirs, to kiss slowly, undress completely and relax into each other like a long, hot bubble bath. Jo's touch was no less exciting for being familiar. If anything, it was more exciting. Jo knew just how Elisa wanted to be touched, how Elisa wanted to be kissed, as though she had always known, had been born knowing. And now that they were alone for the first time in a long time, the knowledge in Jo's hands and mouth felt like it was waking Elisa, bringing alive the parts of her she had kept quiet and hidden when she was back with her family. Her long silence was broken by her cries, which came partly from physical pleasure and partly from the fact that for the first time in months, she felt glad to be who and where she was.

When she opened her eyes, she saw Jo propped up on one elbow, smiling down at her. "Now that," said Jo, "is my kind of women's studies."

Beth

The server brought their meal, a house salad with ranch dressing on the side for Beth and a bloody slab of meat with a sour-cream-sodden baked potato for Beth's father. "Is there anything else I can get you, Mr. Chamberlain?" the server asked.

"That's all for now, Brian," her father said. The Sequoyah Country Club had to be the name-dropping capital of Tennesee, Beth thought. Club employees always addressed club members by name as Mr., Mrs. or Miss So-and-So. Club members addressed club employees by name as well, but by first name only. "Here, sweetheart," he said, picking up his knife with a hand as big and meaty as the steak in front of him. "Let me cut off a chunk of this for you. You could use the iron."

"No, Daddy. The fall formal's coming up, and I've got to make sure I can squeeze my gigantic butt into a gown."

His laugh came from deep in his belly, the laugh of a confident man. "*Gigantic* butt? Honey, there's nothing gigantic about you. Why,

I could fit both my hands around your little waist, just like I could with your mother when she was your age. Of course, that was before she had three kids and lost her girlish metabolism." He looked down at his plate. "Here, let me give you half of my potato."

"Daddy, I'm fine." Beth speared a leaf of lettuce and let the very edge of it lightly brush over the little dish of ranch dressing. This struggle with food was typical of her twice-monthly "Dinner with Daddy." He always tried to push food at her, and she always rejected it. Lunches with her mother came with a different kind of food struggle. No matter how little Beth ate, her mother always insisted she could get by with less. Beth's mom's idea of a good lunch was going to her favorite tearoom, which served chilled wedges of iceberg lettuce. If Beth ate half of her lettuce wedge, her mother would start asking her if she was getting full and reminding her that bikini season was just around the corner, even if it was November.

"So I suppose Mike will be escorting you to this formal?" Her father stabbed a hunk of meat.

"Uh-huh."

Her dad smiled. "Well, I can't say I'm happy about anybody stealing my little girl away from me, but Mike is a helluva nice kid."

Beth pushed her salad plate away. "Daddy, nobody's stealing me. I'm not even thinking about that stuff yet."

"What's the matter?" Her daddy grinned. "Has that women's studies class you're taking turned you into some kind of bra burner?"

Daddy had already teased her plenty for signing up for a women's studies course. "The class has only met once, Daddy. That's not enough time to brainwash me." She pulled her salad back and picked at it. "I'm just saying that I'm not serious about Mike or about anything but school right now. I've got this year and one more to go, then three years of law school after that."

Beth's daddy was a partner in one of the most successful law firms in Knoxville. Her brothers had already finished law school, passed the bar and joined daddy at the firm. Beth's plan was to do the same.

"Well, sweetheart, you know your mother and I want you to graduate from college. And we'd be tickled if you went on to law school. But if you decided against law school, we'd be happy with that, too. Sometimes, for attractive young women, things come up that prevent them from getting professional degrees."

"What kind of things?" Beth asked, although she knew the answer good and well.

"Oh, you know . . . diamond rings, white gowns, maybe some maternity dresses. Those kind of things."

The few leaves of lettuce in Beth's stomach formed a bitter knot. As always, when Daddy talked about her future, she felt like there wasn't enough air in the room—that no matter how deeply she inhaled, there still wouldn't be enough. She couldn't speak, so she tried for a smile and failed.

"But just make sure," her dad said, reaching across the table to pat her hand, "that it's diamond ring, white gown and maternity dress . . . in that order." He let out one of his big belly laughs, then called for Brian to bring him another Scotch.

Beth had to go. She couldn't sit here anymore in this airless room where the men her father did business with and the ladies her mother played bridge with were all staring at her. "I hate to run off and leave you, Daddy, but I've got to be at a sorority meeting in half an hour."

"Stay until I finish this drink, and I'll drive you there."

"No, I'd . . . I'd rather walk. I could use the exercise."

"No time for dessert, even?"

"No, Daddy. No dessert."

"Ah, well." He reached into the inside of his suit jacket, pulled out a hundred-dollar bill and handed it to her. "There, little girl. Buy yourself some bubblegum."

Walking back to campus, Beth sucked in the fresh fall air and started to feel better. She had to figure out a way to get over these little fits or spells or whatever they were. She needed to keep reminding herself that she had no reason to be anxious. As her mom and dad and sorority sisters often reminded her, she was a very lucky girl. She made a list in her head of all the ways in which she was lucky: She had naturally blond hair and pretty blue eyes. Unlike some of her sorority sisters, who couldn't read *The Cat in the Hat* without Cliff's Notes, she was smart enough to do well in school. Her family had loads of money. She was a member of one of the top sororities on campus, and Mike was a member of one of the top—*Screech!*

Caught up in thinking about her good fortune, Beth hadn't noticed the blue BMW that she had stepped out in front of. She looked at the driver's face. He was a cute, Tom Cruise-ish type in a cap with frat letters on it. She was pretty sure she'd seen him at a party or two. He smiled at her and honked his horn teasingly, and she smiled back, with a shrug that established her as both ditzy and adorable.

Damn straight you're a lucky girl, Beth thought. You're lucky you didn't get yourself run over.

Liz

If they sat close together, hip to hip, thigh to thigh, all four of them could fit on the duct-tape-patched, snot-green couch. Liz sat on the far left side, Dan pressed up beside her, wearing his standard uniform of faded Levi's, a faded black pocket T-shirt and black Converse Chuck Taylor All Stars. Todd and Stu, whose apartment this was, were sitting on Dan's other side.

Usually you didn't see guys sitting this close together, Liz thought, but since the only other furniture in the room was a coffee table cluttered with overflowing ashtrays and pyramids of empty Black Label beer cans, there wasn't much choice but to sit right against one other. Nobody wanted to risk the diseases that could be contracted by sitting on the carpet, which, Liz was sure, had gone unshampooed and largely unvacuumed through many generations of slovenly college-boy tenants. Plus, if everybody sat together on the couch, it was easier to pass the bong around. The couch also offered the best view of the TV, and *Star Trek* was about to come on.

Watching *Star Trek: The Next Generation* at Todd and Stu's was Liz and Dan's Sunday night ritual. After a dismal dinner in the caf (the cafeteria's culinary efforts on the weekends were even more half-assed than during the week), they would walk to a deli on the Strip where they could buy beer without showing ID, on the condition that the deli owner was allowed to flirt outrageously with Liz and call her his "girlfriend." It was a running joke between Liz and Dan that Dan never referred to her as his girlfriend, while Moustafa at the deli did.

Beer purchased, they would trudge up the hill into Fort Sanders, the student slum neighborhood that had once been the site of a Civil War battle. Todd and Stu's apartment was in a run-down blue house at the crest of the hill—a house that, like most of the houses in the Fort, had been a single-family dwelling until it was purchased by a landlord and chopped up into student apartments with cheap paneling and oddly shaped rooms.

And so here they sat, just like every Sunday night, taking turns holding the bong in their hands while holding cans of Black Label between their knees. More Black Label was chilling in a fridge in which the only other contents were a bottle of ketchup and a bottle of mustard.

When Liz had been a little girl, her mother would wake her on Sunday morning to eat pancakes, and then they would all get dressed and go to Mass. It was Catholicism that had brought Liz's parents to the mountains back in the seventies when they were stringy haired, guitar-mass-loving, do-gooding lay missionaries. And though their missionary zeal faded somewhat and they found careers as secular social workers, they stayed in the mountains and kept sending Liz to the tiny missionary Catholic church.

Liz wouldn't have dreamed of setting foot in the door of a church these days, but in a way, she supposed this Sunday night ritual had replaced the old Sunday morning one. She had to say it was an improvement. You didn't have to get dressed up, for one thing, and there was beer and pot instead of communion wine and wafers. And instead of a sermon there was *Star Trek*. She wasn't as big a Trekkie as the guys were, but she had to admit the message of *Star Trek* was a positive one. On the *Enterprise*, people embraced diversity and cooperated with one other. And unlike on the old *Star Trek*, the new one gave women real positions of power, although Liz still couldn't figure out why Counselor Troy wore a cleavage-revealing uniform when everyone else's was high-necked.

"See, man, that's what I'm talking about." Todd used the bong to gesture toward the screen. "Captain Kirk would have totally smoked that dude, but Picard makes him a cup of tea and *talks* to him!"

"Which is why Picard is the superior captain," Dan said. "Kirk ran the ship with brute force, but Picard runs his ship with reason."

"Yeah, well, brute force makes better TV," Todd said.

"Brute force doesn't make for better anything." Dan's tone was calm and even. Liz smiled at him with his round, wire-framed glasses and keen nose. She had grown up listening to her parents' hippiefied music collection, and the Beatles had always been her favorite. Sometimes she thought being with Dan was what it must have felt like to be with John Lennon. She hoped that didn't make her Yoko Ono.

"Look, I accept that you guys are never going to stop having this argument," Stu said, "but could you at least pause it until the show's over? Liz and I can't hear."

Liz bristled a bit when Stu said "Liz and I" as though the two of them constituted a unit. She always felt comfortable around Todd. Sure, he was always wearing a heavy metal T-shirt with a leering skull on it, but his own face was never leering. Beneath his long mane of head-banger's hair, he looked like somebody's sweet kid brother. His bedroom in the apartment even matched the kid-brother image; the floor was littered with dirty clothes and comic books, and the walls were lined with shelves of neatly arranged *Star Wars* action figures.

Stu gave Liz the creeps, just a little. He was short but not bad looking, with tan skin and dark, curly, long hair, and yet he had never been known to have a girlfriend. Instead he obsessed over his friends' girlfriends and over the massive stash of porno magazines he kept in his room. Not the glossy, high-end pornos either—these were the kind with scrawny women splayed out on beds in cheap motels, women whose blue eyeshadow matched the bruises on their thighs. Stu's bed was always piled with these magazines, as though he wallowed in them, and once when Liz and Dan had engaged in a drunken contest trying to come up with the most disgusting thing imaginable, Liz had won by saying, "The sheets on Stu's bed."

"Now what?" Todd asked when the end credits started to roll.

"The eternal post-*Star Trek* question," Dan said, adding another empty Black Label can to the pyramid on the coffee table.

"Well," Stu said, standing up from the couch and stretching so that Liz could see the sweat stains under the arms of his Western-style shirt. "We could stay here and kill the rest of what's in the fridge, or we could head down to the Sagebrush." The Sagebrush Saloon was frequented by a bizarre mixture of bikers, Deadheads, rednecks and college students and was where Liz and Dan had had their first date, even though they were too cool to call it that.

"Well . . ." Dan nudged Liz. "What does my old lady want to do?"

Liz shrugged. "Whatever's cool with me."

As the daughter of two Catholics from a region locals referred to only as Up North, Liz had spent her childhood and adolescence in rural Southeastern Kentucky being The Girl Who Did Not Fit In. She spent her time reading or drawing or writing in her journal and was largely ignored by her peers, unless some of them grew bored enough to harass her. College was the first time she had had a group of friends who accepted her, let alone a boyfriend, and it was such a novelty to be accepted that she was content to drift along whichever way they wanted to go.

Elisa

The pink card advertising the meetings of the Gay, Lesbian Or Bisexual Alliance had been stuck in the frame of Elisa's dresser mirror for two weeks now. She had found the card on a bulletin board in the humanities building and had taken it back to the dorm to show it to Jo.

At first, they had been too nervous to go to the meeting, "What if it's some kind of a setup?" Jo had said. "I know that sounds crazy, but there's plenty of people out there who'd like to get a bunch of fags and dykes together just so they could beat up on them or get them in trouble some way."

"That's true, I guess," Elisa had said, but the more she thought about it she decided they were thinking like they were back in Odessa instead of here in Knoxville. In the city, people didn't have to hide, which was why, she reminded Jo, they came here in the first place.

It took a few days for Jo to process the idea, but finally in bed one night she said, "Okay, you're right."

"About what?"

"About that club for people like us. Next week we'll go."

Tonight was the night. Since they were going to present themselves as a couple in public, they wanted to look good. Jo had moussed her hair and put on a crisp white shirt with black pleated pants and freshly polished penny loafers. Elisa had spent a full hour on her hair and makeup, and after trying on three other outfits while Jo teased her, she had settled on the red dress that always made Jo call her "firecracker."

Elisa blotted her lipstick in front of the mirror as Jo hugged her from behind. "I don't know how I got so lucky," Jo whispered into Elisa's ear, then kissed it.

"I was just thinking the same thing about myself," Elisa said, leaning back into Jo's embrace.

When they walked into Room 213 of the University Center, there was no doubt that they were in the right place. As soon as they hit the door, they were approached by a tall black guy wearing a T-shirt that read, *How dare you assume that I'm straight?* "Welcome, ladies," he said with a friendly grin. "I'm Jamal, the president of GLOBAL."

Elisa shook his hand. "I'm Elisa." She looked over at Jo, who typically had been stricken shy. "And this is my girlfriend, Jo. I'm sorry if we're a little late."

"Late?" Jamal laughed. "Honey, you're early. These meetings always run on QPT." Elisa's ignorance must have shown on her face because Jamal quickly added, "Queer People Time."

Elisa smiled, although she wasn't that comfortable with the joke. She'd never heard "queer" used except as a word to put down people like her. But between Jamal's joke and the guy across the room in a T-shirt reading *Queer Nation*, she had to conclude that "queer" was a word people like her were using now.

Elisa and Jo took seats in the circle of folding chairs in the middle of the room. There must've been something to Jamal's statement about QPT because only three other people—Jamal, the Queer Nation guy and an older guy with a mustache—were there. Elisa and Jo sat in silence until the older guy made a beeline for them.

"Hi," he said with a toothy grin. "I'm Shaun. Are you ladies new here?"

"This is our first meeting," Elisa said.

"Well, congratulations on making it here," he said. "My first meeting was in the seventies back when I was an undergraduate here. I remember being terrified. I thought the meeting might just be an excuse to round up all the fags and shoot 'em or something."

"That's kinda what we thought at first," Jo said, to Elisa's embarrassment. "There'd never be something like this where we come from."

Shaun grinned. "I bet where you come from doesn't have more than three stoplights, does it, darlin'?"

Elisa felt her face grow hot. Odessa had gotten its third stoplight her senior year of high school, and its installation had been a big event.

"Hey, you mean old queen, you're not terrorizing these nice young women, are you?" a familiar gravelly voice called.

Shaun put his arm around the owner of the voice, the outspoken, hairy girl Elisa knew from her Women in Literature class. "I was being as sweet as pie, but thank you for asking, my hirsute little Amazon," Shaun said.

Elisa felt the girl's eyes on her. "Hi," she said. "Thalia, right?"

"Omigod!" Thalia whooped. "I would never have expected to see *you* here. I tell you, my gaydar's really been on the blink lately."

"Jo," Elisa said, "Thalia here's in my Women in Lit class."

Jo nodded and muttered, "Heyhowyadoin," but Elisa could see her staring at Thalia's leg hair and trying not to laugh.

When the meeting finally began, twenty-five minutes after its scheduled start time, Jamal introduced a guest speaker from AIDS Awareness Knoxville who talked about safe sex and passed around a goldfish bowl filled with condoms. Elisa half listened to the lecture, but she was too caught up in people-watching to give it her full attention. Of the twenty-two people present, seventeen were guys, several of them regular college Joe types in beer T-shirts and khakis—not guys she ever would have pegged as gay. The only women there were herself,

Jo, Thalia and one other couple—a pair of petite women with similar short haircuts, wire-framed glasses, jeans and hiking boots. This couple puzzled Elisa—what was the thrill of being with someone who looked just like you? If you were that self-centered, shouldn't you just spend a lot of time in front of a mirror?

After the meeting, Jamal issued an invitation for everybody to meet at Radar's for drinks. "It's not a gay bar," he said, "but the bartender's one of us, and he'll mix 'em strong and cheap."

At Radar's, they gathered at the umbrellaed tables on the patio. Thalia waved Elisa and Jo over toward an empty table. "Come sit with me."

"Setting up your own little island of Lesbos over there, are you, Thalia?" Shaun said.

"That's right," Thalia said, "but boys are welcome to visit. I may be a dyke, but I'm no separatist."

"You're too much of a fag hag to be a separatist," Shaun laughed.

Queer. Fag hag. Dyke. Separatist. Elisa felt like she was in a foreign country trying to keep up with a new language. Of course, most of those words she had heard before; she'd just never heard them spoken this way. They were words she'd only heard spoken in hate, and now, it seemed, she was hearing them spoken in love.

"So, what did you think of the meeting?" Thalia asked, digging a pack of Camels out of her duffle bag.

"It was good," Elisa said. "I kinda thought there'd be more women, though."

Thalia exhaled. "Yeah, well, the female population of our group goes up and down. When there are lots of single dykes, they'll come to meetings, but once they start pairing off, they get all domesticated and never leave their little nests. That couple that was here tonight—the Doublemint Dykes? Their names are Trish and Trina—God, they even *sound* alike! They hadn't been to a meeting since they paired off last winter, and of course, as soon as the meeting was over they had to scurry back to their little love nest. I'm not the nesting type, so I never miss a meeting."

A waitress in a white shirt and bow tie came to take their order. "Frozen margarita?" she said to Thalia.

Thalia grinned at her. "You know me so well."

Jo ordered coffee, and Elisa, who was not a drinker but wanted to be social, waffled for a moment before settling on a wine cooler.

"So what's with the coffee?" Thalia asked once the waitress had left.

Jo shifted in her seat, and Elisa wondered how truthful her answer was going to be. "My daddy's bad to drink," Jo said, "so I stay away from liquor."

"Huh," Thalia said. "Well, you've got more self-control than I have. Not like that's a major accomplishment or anything." She stubbed out her cigarette and gave the waitress a grateful smile when her margarita appeared. "You two interest me." She took a big gulp of her drink. "You're not the usual, garden-variety lesbians we tend to get at GLOBAL meetings. I mean, I'm just floored by how you look . . . like the perfect little lady and little gentleman. I don't think we've ever had a real butch-femme couple in GLOBAL before . . . not since I've been going anyway. But you know, I was in San Francisco this summer, and it seems like the whole butch-femme thing is coming back there . . . maybe with a little more irony and S and M flavor than what you two have going, but it's still there. I mean, if you read *On Our Backs*, it's full of butch-femme stuff."

"What's *On Our Backs*?" Elisa asked. She could've asked a lot of questions about what Thalia had just said, but she settled on this one.

"Omigod!" Thalia yelled. "It's only the best magazine *in the world!* Lesbian porno!"

"You're getting a little too excited over there, Thalia," Jamal said. "Don't make come over there and hose you down."

"Jamal, you know I've got no use for your hose." Thalia laughed. "Seriously, though, you've got to read it. Hey, wait a minute." She dug through her bag and produced a magazine with a pair of smiling, bare-shouldered women on the cover. "Here, why don't you borrow this? You can bring it back to me in class."

"Thanks."

"You'll want to look at it in private, though. We don't want to gross out the boys at the other table."

Back in the room, a little tipsy from the wine cooler, Elisa stretched out on the bed and said, "So do you think we're what Thalia called us—butch and femme?"

Jo flopped down beside her. "I don't know. I guess you could call us that. But I don't see much point in it."

"What about Thalia? Is she a butch or a femme?"

"Well . . ." Jo paused for a moment. "She looks like a butch, but she talks like a femme."

"And she drinks like a fish." Elisa giggled. "She'd knocked back three margaritas before you'd even finished your cup of coffee."

"You got that right," Jo said. "I ain't saying she could drink my daddy under the table, but for a little-bitty thing she sure can put it away. You reckon one of them hairy legs of hers is hollow?"

"Don't be mean," Elisa scolded, but she was laughing. "She's nice."

"She's all right. Everybody at that meeting was all right. Of course, some of them seem like they spend too much time thinking and not enough time just doing what's natural."

Elisa felt a prickle of fear. She, too, was a thinker, but Jo was a woman of action who'd once said that in life, like in softball, too much thinking would "psych you out." Jo had felt that same prickle when she had said that, too. "Hey," Elisa said, trying to shake off her anxiety, "let's look at that dirty magazine, want to?"

They lay stretched on the bed, peering at the pages. In one spread, a pair of wiry women wearing nothing but an assortment of studs and leather straps were doing things to each other with a dildo. It wasn't the dildo that shocked Elisa; she had heard of those before. It was—

"Good God a-mighty!" Jo hollered. "That woman's got an earring in her pussy!"

"And not just in her pussy," Elisa said. "It goes through her—her —"

"Ow!" Jo howled before Elisa could finish her sentence. Jo closed the magazine. "I believe we've seen enough for now."

"I don't know," Elisa said. "You can't say it's not interesting."

"It's interesting, all right," Jo said. "But looking at women doing things like that . . . It's like thinking you're a pretty experienced ball player because you've been doing it for years, and then you realize that all this time, you've just been batting for the Little League."

Beth

Beth poured a double shot of vodka into her plastic tumbler of Crystal Light lemonade. Quimby, Beth's roommate, leaned against the pile of teddy bears on her bed, sucking Crystal Light and Smirnoff through a Minnie Mouse bendy straw.

The sororities at William Blount hadn't been allowed to have their own houses since the sixties, when some girl had choked on her own vomit and caused a big scandal in the process. As a result, sorority houses on campus were banned, relegating sorority girls at WBU to regular dorms, where they usually arranged to have a sorority sister as a roommate.

Sorority meetings were held at the Panhellenic Building. Of course, there were fraternity houses, and the sorority girls spent way more time partying at fraternity mixers than they did attending meetings at Panhell. Beth couldn't see the logic in forbidding the girls to have sorority houses if the girls weren't also forbidden to attend frat parties, where a girl could get trashed and choke on her own vomit just as easily as she could in her own sorority house. But if girls weren't allowed at frat parties, it would mean the collapse of the whole Greek system.

Beth sipped her makeshift vodka collins. "Well, it doesn't hold a candle to the strawberry daiquiris at Radar's, but the price is right."

"And it's way lower in calories," Quimby said. Quimby was a brown-eyed brunette whose face wasn't as striking as Beth's, but from the neck down, Beth envied her. Quimby was a size two, and no matter how much Beth starved herself, she couldn't seem to get any smaller than a six. "The only calories are from the vodka," Quimby said. "Wouldn't it kick ass if somebody invented calorie-free alcohol?"

Beth flopped against the peach throw pillows on her bed. "The inventor of calorie-free alcohol would be totally worshipped by every college girl in this country."

"Totally."

Beth looked at her Benetton watch. "Shit. We'd better drink up if we're gonna make it to Panhell on time."

Quimby tossed her bendy straw on the floor, which was already strewn with various pairs of shoes, socks and panties. She chugged her drink, then came up for air. "There's no way I'm gonna get dressed up like a retard and sing to those guys if I'm all the way sober. I always feel like such a dork walking across campus in a little costume with everybody staring at me."

"Everybody's staring at the whole sorority, not at you in particular," Beth said, knocking back some more of her drink. She could never figure out how Quimby could be shy about going to sing to a fraternity, but then take her top off and dance on a table at a frat party. The girl seemed to have some bizarre ideas about when it was and was not okay to be the center of attention.

"I know, but it still feels like everybody's staring at me." Quimby stepped into her Tretorn tennis shoes. "But I am glad we're singing to Epsilon. That guy that pledged last spring . . . Chad? I would totally do him."

"I don't think I know him yet," Beth said. The truth was that Chad's status as a new member of Epsilon was the only reason Quimby hadn't done him already. Quimby went through boys like Madonna went through costume changes. Some of the other girls judged Quimby for her bed-hopping, but Beth thought their comments unfair and bitchy. Many of them were almost as promiscuous as Quimby; they were just better at keeping their activities secret. And besides, unlike those back-biting girls, Quimby was a genuinely kind person.

"You just haven't noticed Chad because you can't take your eyes off Mike," Quimby said. "But Mike is, like, the nicest guy in the whole frat. And cute, so I don't blame you. If I had a boyfriend like Mike, even I might be magnanimous."

Beth smiled. "Monogamous," she said.

In a dressing room in the Panhell Building, thirty girls, all of them slender, all of them white and most of them blond, crowded around the mirrors, painting on their mascara and lipstick and cursing their pimples and imperfections. Beth hung back and checked her face in her compact. The freckles she had painted on looked idiotic, but they were part of the country girl costume the sisters had chosen: fake freckles, pigtails, red-and-white gingham halter tops and Daisy Duke denim cutoffs.

"Beth, babe, would you help me with my pigtails?" one of the five girls named Amy asked. "They keep coming out lopsided."

"Sure." Beth took Amy's hairbrush. "Have a squat on the floor, and I'll fix you up fabulous."

"Fabulous, my ass," Amy said as Beth pulled the brush through her golden hair. "I can't believe I voted for these stupid outfits. I don't have enough boobies to fill out this halter top."

"You've got two. That's enough," Beth said.

"Not when a training bra would still fit 'em." Amy cupped her breasts and sighed. "I've got half a mind to stuff with Kleenex."

"Bad idea," Beth said, tying a red ribbon around the first pigtail. "Were you at the charity car wash last year when Jennifer decided to fill out her halter with Kleenex? This Epsilon she liked started teasing her and spraying her with the hose. He sprayed her boobs, and then all this wet Kleenex just fell—*splat!*—at their feet."

"I hear you over there telling tales on me, Beth," Jennifer called from her station at the mirror. "And I don't think it's fair for you to talk about girls who aren't lucky enough to have great big knockers like you've got."

"I'm not that lucky," Beth said, looking down at her legs and frowning. "I've got great big thighs to go with them."

Beth and her sisters walked across campus in a double line. Some of the guys they passed whistled. One said "nice tits" and looked right at Beth. She looked away, her face hot, and kept walking. They passed a dorm courtyard where three girls with hair dyed colors not found in nature were sitting on a bench, smoking. "Hey, look!" a pudgy girl with purple spiky hair hollered. "It's conformity on the march. Why don't you women go get your own personalities?"

"What, and be a dyke like you?" Ashley, the sister behind Beth, hollered back.

Beth's stomach clenched with that sick, panicky feeling she'd been having so often. She must have looked bad because Quimby touched her arm and said, "Are you okay?"

"Yeah, I'm fine," Beth said, telling herself it was true. "Just a little queasy. I probably drank that vodka too fast back in the room."

They lined up in front of the Epsilon house. Sarah, one of the senior girls, rang the doorbell and then ran back to join the line. Beth was still feeling sick and jittery, but she took a deep breath, and as soon as the frat brothers filed out on the lawn, she and her sisters sang out:

> *"We're just country bumpkins,*
> *We're as cute as pumpkins,*
> *But it's lonesome down here on the farm.*
> *So what would you say*
> *To a roll in the hay?*
> *It sure wouldn't do us no harm.*
>
> *So Epsilon misters,*
> *Come see these sisters,*
> *And you will quickly see*
> *That city girls tease you,*

But we will please you
When you visit our country!"

When the girls sang to a frat, they weren't supposed to pay special attention to any brother in particular, so Beth couldn't go talk to Mike. She did look right at him at the end of the song, though. He was wearing his red Polo shirt, and his dark, curly hair was trying to spring out from under his Epsilon baseball cap. He grinned at Beth and winked. She smiled, looked down at the amount of cleavage she was showing and mugged a look of shock.

Quimby grabbed her hand. "Come on now. We can't have you paying special attention to your boyfriend."

Beth let herself be dragged into line with the other girls.

"I swear to God, though," Quimby whispered, "Mike's eyes were on nobody but you the whole time we were singing, like the rest of us weren't even there. He doesn't even look at other girls, does he?"

"No," Beth said. "He doesn't."

Liz

When Liz's roommate wasn't invisible, she was beautiful. Most of the time, though, Martina was invisible because she, for all practical purposes, lived with her fiancé in his apartment. But, as Martina had explained to Liz, her mama and grandma would have a hissy fit if they knew she was shacked up with her boyfriend, so she kept up the appearance of living in the dorm room, mostly using it as a place to store her clothes.

Martina would pop by two or three times a week, always with her hair and makeup just so, and say hi to Liz as she grabbed a few outfits to take to her boyfriend's. Sometimes Liz felt like she had taken up residence in the glamorous woman's walk-in closet.

But last night Martina had actually slept in the room. Liz had staggered in about 2 a.m., fumbled drunkenly with the room key and had been startled to see her ersatz roommate actually sleeping in her designated bed. And now, at 7 a.m, two hours before Liz needed to get up to make it to her first class, Martina was up, standing in front of her dresser in a black lace bra and panties, ironing her hair. Martina's body was perfect—long legs, big boobs, slender waist, skin the color of toasted almonds. Liz's mouth was furry from last night's alcohol consumption, and she was sure her eyes were highlighted by red rims and dark circles. To see somebody like Martina, who looked better on a Tuesday morning at 7 a.m. than Liz would ever look in her life, was quite disheartening.

"I'm sorry I woke you up," Martina said. "I was trying to be quiet."

"No problem," Liz croaked as she reached for the water glass beside the bed. "With the hangover I've got, I could've been woken by the sound of an ant crawling."

Martina smiled. Her teeth were perfect. "I've had a hangover like that before. One night me and Antoine and my sister and her boyfriend went out to this club where they had all these different mixed drinks. They were all real pretty—pink, blue, green, like Easter eggs. I kept trying different ones, and I must have tried too many 'cause when I woke up the next morning, I thought, a person can't feel this bad and live."

"You would've been better off sticking to one kind of drink," Liz said, feeling quite the hangover guru despite her sorry physical state. Liz never drank mixed drinks, or "girl drinks" as she called them, in part because she knew Dan would disapprove if she did. He always said ice was the only acceptable mixer, and so if they were drinking liquor, she always took it straight. Last night they had split a fifth of Usher's—an act that, given how she felt this morning, she hoped they wouldn't repeat for a long time.

"That's probably true," Martina said, combing through her just-ironed hair. "Plus, I don't drink much usually, so I don't have a tolerance."

"Well, I'm just glad I didn't wake you when I came in last night. I was kind of surprised to see you here." Liz didn't want to be rude enough to ask why Martina had slept here—after all, it was her room, too—but she was curious.

"Yeah, me and Antoine had a little fight last night. I thought I'd spend a night away from him, make him realize what he's been missing," Martina made a goofy face to show she was kidding, but the sight of her body in only a couple of strategically placed scraps of lace made what Antoine was missing all too apparent. Liz hoped she wasn't staring.

"He'll come crawling back," Liz said, feeling relieved when Martina pulled a blouse from the closet.

"They always do, like the dogs they are." Martina sat on the edge of the bed and slipped a foot into her pantyhose. "You and your man doing all right—what's his name?"

"Dan. Yeah, we're cool."

"I bet y'all don't fight at all, do you?"

"Not really." She and Dan had never had an argument. They seemed to agree on most things. They were pro-choice and anti-apartheid and anti-war and marched in the same demonstrations. They liked the same books—*A Confederacy of Dunces*, anything by Kurt Vonnegut—and a lot of the same music—classic rock, especially the Stones. So basically there was nothing to argue about. There were some bands Liz liked that she knew Dan didn't like—the Cure and R.E.M., both of which Dan dismissed as artsy-fartsy, pretentious flashes in the pan. But with little differences like these, Liz just kept her mouth shut. Why get into an argument over something so inconsequential?

"That's what I thought," Martina said, tucking her blouse into her skirt. "Whenever I see you two sitting out in the courtyard or whatever, you just look so chilled out, you know. Anybody that was looking at you would know you're in love, you know what I'm saying?"

"Yeah." Liz made herself smile. She loved Dan, and she figured he must love her, or he would have dumped her by now. But he had never said, "I love you." Sometimes, her inhibitions washed away in a pitcher or two of beer, she had thought of saying it to him, but the terror of what he would or wouldn't say back always stopped her.

"Yeah, well, Antoine and me are in love, too. It just gets a little stormy every now and then." Martina blotted her lipstick. She looked polished enough to appear on TV. "But after the storm's over, the making up is *great*. Say, maybe you and Dan ought to fight once in a while just for the fun of making up after."

"Maybe we should." But Liz knew she wasn't going to generate any conflict with Dan if she could help it. Unlike Martina with Antoine, Liz wasn't sure Dan was devoted enough to her to want to make up after a fight.

"No lovin' like make-up lovin'," Martina said. "I'm heading over to the caf for some eggs. I don't guess your hungover self wants to join me."

Liz's stomach rolled in nausea. "I don't think I could even stand to smell an egg this morning. Thanks, though."

After the door closed—especially loudly, it seemed—Liz looked over at the alarm clock. 7:42. Women in Lit started at 10:10, so she usually didn't get up until 9:10. If she skipped breakfast, took an extra-quick shower and just threw on some clothes, she could be ready for class in fifteen minutes. She swallowed two aspirin, reset the alarm for 9:45 and fell back asleep.

Liz figured that Dr. Rivers must never take off her pearls. She had never seen her without that same pair of Birkenstocks either, but she assumed Dr. Rivers took those off at least to bathe and sleep.

"Between now and our next meeting," Dr. Rivers was saying, "I'd like you to turn your attentions to Rita Mae Brown's *Rubyfruit Jungle*. And as you read, keep this term in mind." She wrote the word *picaresque* on the board. "A picaresque, of course, is an episodic work of fiction centering on the adventures of a rogue or misfit. Most of the rogues whose adventures have been chronicled in picaresque fiction are male, Don Quixote and Tom Jones, for example. I'd like you to think about this as you read *Rubyfruit Jungle*: How is the picaresque structure affected when the novel is written by a woman, about a woman and for a predominantly female audience? And once you've chewed on that for a while"—Dr. Rivers smiled—"you can think about how the picaresque genre is affected by the fact that *Rubyfruit Jungle* was written by a lesbian, about a lesbian and for a primarily lesbian audience."

As she packed up her things, Liz wondered if several years down the road, after this degree and a couple of others, she might be doing what Dr. Rivers was doing—standing up in a college classroom, maybe even in Birkenstocks, holding forth on the subject of literature.

What Liz really wanted to do was write. She had the beginnings of two dozen different short stories in a file box in her room; she just could never seem to finish them. Inspiration would come in a quick burst, and she'd scribble down a couple of pages at top speed, but then the inspiration would disappear with a little *poof* and she'd have no idea where to go from there, except to stick the story fragment in the file box with all its siblings.

A hand grabbed her arm. "Hey," the hand's owner said.

"Hey, Thalia." Over the past couple of weeks, Thalia and Liz had turned into friendly acquaintances, in part because they both spoke up in class discussions when few others would.

"Listen." Thalia was wearing a black Dead Kennedys T-shirt with camouflage pants. "I'm starting up a women's group. We're gonna meet at my house the first and last Thursday of every month to talk politics and feminism and just to bullshit. Anyway, we start up next Thursday at seven thirty, and I thought you might be interested."

"I'll try to come." Liz sounded more tentative than she had intended to, but she couldn't help wondering if "women's group" might be code for "lesbian group."

"And just so you know," Thalia said, "there'll be straight women there, too. Dykes, straight women, bi women . . . any kind of woman is welcome." A giggling gaggle of sorority girls strolled past. "Though I doubt we'll be seeing many of their kind there."

"I'd think not," Liz said, her nose itching from the designer cologne that lingered after the sorority girls' passing. "But then, they wouldn't belong in a women's group, would they? That type stays girls as long as they can, then switch right over into being 'ladies.' They're never women."

Elisa

It was stupid to cry. Just because the book had been sitting untouched on Jo's dresser for over a week was no reason to cry.

Elisa had started reading *Rubyfruit Jungle* on Monday night after she'd finished her other homework. She had always been a reader, but *Rubyfruit Jungle* was the first book she literally could not put down. She felt like the only way you could've gotten the book away from her was to chop off her hands as she held it open. Jo finished her homework and beckoned Elisa to come to bed. Elisa said, "Just a minute," then read for another hour. Finally, feeling guilty for keeping the light on while Jo was trying to sleep, she had flipped off the switch, then sat out in the hall and read until morning.

The character of Molly Bolt hit her like lightning. Just like Elisa, Molly was a small-town Southern girl who wanted to see the world and do something bigger than settle for a life of marriage and babies in her hometown. The best part was that Molly was a lesbian—a happy, proud lesbian who didn't let anybody make her feel bad about being the way she was. Elisa had never read a book about women like her before, and the words felt so true that reading them was like looking inside her own heart. When she finally finished the book, it had been six in the morning. But she hadn't felt tired at all; instead she was full of energy.

When she opened the door of the room, Jo opened one eye. "Where you been?" she asked, her speech slurred with sleep.

"Reading." Elisa sat down on the edge of the bed. "I read out in the hall so I wouldn't bother you."

"You read all night?" Jo's tone was about the same as it would have been had Elisa announced that she had danced naked in the courtyard all night.

"Yep. This is the best book! I can't even begin to explain how great it is. It's about this girl who's poor and from the middle of nowhere like us, and she's a lesbian like us . . ." Words spilled out of her mouth, but they felt inadequate to illustrate how much the book meant to her. "Oh, I can't explain it . . . you've just got to read it."

When Elisa held out the book, Jo said, "Set it over there on my dresser, and I'll get to it one of these days. All this reading I've got to do for Human Performance is about to kill me."

And so there on Jo's dresser the book had sat for eight days. And even though it might be silly, Elisa's feelings were hurt that Jo hadn't so much as picked up the book and looked at it. When a person is in love with someone, shouldn't she at least try to show some interest in the subjects that fill her loved one with passion?

Elisa showed interest in sports for Jo's sake. She went to every home game during softball season and cheered herself hoarse. And she enjoyed herself. She liked to see Jo in her uniform, to watch the way her body moved.

But the other games—the ones Jo went to as a spectator—bored Elisa into a stupor. If it was a women's game, like basketball or soccer, she could get a few minutes' worth of entertainment out of looking at the cute girls in their shorts, but when it came to actually following the game, she was hopeless. She'd try to keep up with the score, but her mind would inevitably wander to the Virginia Woolf novel she was reading or the shoes at the mall she wanted to buy, and before long her thoughts were so far away that she didn't even know where she was. Sometimes the whoops that were the results of a particularly good play would startle her back into her surroundings, but more often, her thoughts were so far away from the playing field that she could sit through an entire game and have no idea who had won.

But she did try. She went with Jo when she would have rather been at the library or the movies. She listened to Jo talk at length about the finer points of the fast pitch, and when softball season started in the spring, she would be there for every home game.

So was it too much to ask that Jo read the book that had changed Elisa's whole life?

Elisa blew her nose and reached for the emergency stash of chocolate she kept in the drawer of the nightstand. This was ridiculous. How could she be brooding about how opposite she and Jo were when it was Jo's difference from her that was the basis for their attraction in the first place?

In grade school Jo was always the reliable home run during softball while Elisa was always among the last picked for the team. The only enjoyment Elisa ever derived from P.E. was from watching Jo knock the ball farther than any boy in the class could.

Ten-year-old Elisa didn't have the vocabulary to put her feelings for Jo into words, but she knew she thought about Jo a lot, stared at Jo during class and became instantly shy and idiotic whenever Jo talked to her. Jo was so different from the other girls. She didn't giggle, and she didn't wear hair ribbons to match her outfits. She played football with the boys at recess instead of jumping rope with the girls. Jo was fearless.

In fifth grade, Elisa's favorite T-shirt had pictured a girl baseball player hitting one out of the park with the caption, "Anything boys can do, girls can do better." After seeing Jo hit an especially impressive home run one day, Elisa decided that Jo deserved the T-shirt more than she did. The next day, shy to the point of tears, she had pressed the shirt into Jo's hands. She spent the next week waiting for Jo to wear the shirt to school. She never did.

It wasn't until seven years later, when they were lovers, that Jo told Elisa about the shirt. She had worn it only once. Her father had seen the shirt's caption, treated her to a drunken thirty-minute rant on the proper "place" of women (under men, literally and figuratively) and then made Jo take off the shirt and throw it on the trash heap, which he proceeded to burn.

Elisa figured that she and Jo had as much history to bind them together as any two people their age could have. What she couldn't figure out was why the same forces that had drawn them together now seemed to be pushing them apart. Unwrapping another Hershey's Kiss, she thought about Trish and Trina, the couple Thalia had called "the Doublemint Dykes." Two women who were so similar surely couldn't generate the same heat and energy that Elisa and Jo did. But Elisa also bet that neither of them spent much time crying alone.

Beth

Theta and Epsilon had rented out the whole second floor of Radar's. Tables and chairs had been cleared away to make a tiny makeshift dance floor, which was currently full of sisters and brothers bobbing up and down with beers in hand while a three-man band called Cover Me hacked their way through Jimmy Buffett's "Margaritaville."

The sisters and brothers who weren't dancing sat at tables loaded with pitchers of beer and baskets of Buffalo chicken wings, bleu cheese dressing and celery. The guys ate the chicken wings. The girls stuck to the celery.

Beth and Mike were sitting at a table with Quimby and her new victim, Chad, who looked sometimes intrigued and sometimes terrified by Quimby's increasingly drunken attentions. Jennifer and Amy were at the table, too. Seating was scarce, so Beth was sitting on Mike's lap, absent mindedly playing with the curls at the nape of his neck. Amy and Jennifer and Quimby were having some sort of shouted conversation, but Beth couldn't hear them for the band, which having dispensed with "Margaritaville" had now struck up a whining, discordant version of "Free Bird."

Mike leaned over to Beth's ear, giving, Beth imagined, the impression that he was whispering a sweet nothing. What he actually said was, "This band blows."

Beth leaned into his ear. "You're just mad they don't know any Cher songs."

Mike gave her butt a playful slap. She squealed, and everybody at the table laughed.

Another Amy came scurrying up with a camera. "Y'all look so cute I've just got to take your picture for the Theta scrapbook," she yelled over the endless guitar solo.

Beth and Mike cuddled close, pressed their cheeks together and smiled.

At 12:30, Mike whispered, "Do you think we've stayed long enough?"

Beth whispered back, "Definitely."

They made a circuit of the room, saying their good nights, with Mike getting winks and shoulder chucks from guys who believed he was leaving to "get some." Once they stepped out in the night air, Mike said, "It's a miracle. I can hear again!"

"Hallelujah," Beth said, laughing. She had drunk three beers over the past couple of hours, so she wasn't drunk, just happy.

After they were a ways from Radar's, Mike said, "I hate when we have parties at that place. There's a guy who works there that I know from . . . other circles. He wasn't working tonight, thank God."

"And how well do you know him?" Beth squeezed Mike's hand.

"Not that well, you dirty girl. I just talked to him a couple of times before I found out where he worked. He's kind of swishy, you know, so if we go to Radar's I'm always terrified he'll see me and try to talk to me."

"You could always pretend he was mistaking you for somebody else."

"Yeah, but still . . ." He shuddered theatrically.

Once they were a whole block away from Radar's, they stopped holding hands. The Merry-Go-Round, their destination, was one block ahead and another block to the left. They knew the location as well as if they walked there every night, even though they only did it once a month, twice at the absolute most.

For Beth, the walks to the Merry-Go-Round were always marked by a mixture of excitement and fear—excitement about what the evening would bring and fear that they'd run into somebody they knew.

Of course, they had things planned out so nobody would suspect anything. Whenever they left a Greek function early to go to the Merry-Go-Round, Mike's brothers always assumed he was leaving to spend the night in Beth's room. Beth's sisters assumed she would be spending the night with Mike at the frat house. Beth and Mike had decided that if anybody ever caught on to the fact that the two of them were in neither place, they could always say they had been feeling romantic and had sprung for a hotel room.

There was also the danger of being caught in the vicinity of the Merry-Go-Round. Fortunately, there was an all-night deli next door to the club, so if anyone saw them, they could always claim they were going to get a sandwich. If anybody saw them in the Merry-Go-Round itself, well, then, that person wouldn't have the right to say anything, would they? It would be like when Beth was a little girl in Sunday school, and some other kid had told the teacher, "Beth didn't close her eyes when we were saying the prayer." The teacher had said, "You don't have the right to judge because you were obviously doing the same thing she was."

Once they were outside the Merry-Go-Round, Mike said, "Okay, if Desiree Nicole is lip-synching to Taylor Dane again, then you buy the first round. If it's Lisa Stansfield, I buy."

Based on the drag queen's repertoire, the odds were 50/50. "It's a deal," Beth said.

They presented their fake IDs, which had been expensive but worth it for their realism, to the muscular guy at the door. Entering the Merry-Go-Round, Beth let the familiar assault on her senses wash over her—the loud thrumming of the bass as "Pump Up the Jam" boomed from the speakers, the smell of smoke and cologne and sweat, the flashing of the lights on the dancers on the sunken dance floor. They would come back to the dance floor later, but first they had to settle their bet.

The show bar was so packed that there were no free tables, so they stood in the back and watched a young blond queen in a silver showgirl costume do Madonna's "Vogue." Beth looked at Mike, whose mouth was moving slightly to the lyrics. After the obligatory Madonna number, the voice on the speaker boomed, "And now welcome to the stage, the statuesque Desiree Nicole."

Desiree, in a huge brown wig, her lips lined brown and painted pink so they looked like rare steak, stepped onstage to the strains of "Shelter" by Taylor Dane.

Mike nudged Beth. "A Corona with lime, please."

Beth excused herself through the crowd until she reached the bar where an older drag queen who looked startlingly like Beth's middle school music teacher was working. "Well, look at you!" the drag queen crowed. "We don't get too many girls in pink dresses around here . . . not real girls, anyway. What can I get you, straight girl?"

"Um . . . a Corona with lime and a vodka collins, please." She figured the queen's teasing was probably friendly, but she had no idea how to respond to it.

Beth and Mike drank their drinks and watched the show until Mike said, "Well, let me buy us another round, and then we'll divide and conquer."

This was the routine. They'd have one drink together, buy a second one and then go their separate ways. Mike always went to the dance floor, but Beth only did sometimes. Not all women danced.

Mike handed her a second vodka collins, kissed her on the cheek and said, "Good luck, girlfriend."

Beth sipped her drink and wandered over to the game room. Nothing doing there—two sets of couples shooting pool; there was no point in intruding on that. The problem was always that the ratio of men to women at the Merry-Go-Round was about 75 percent to 25 percent. And a lot of the women who did come were with their girlfriends.

She finished her drink quickly and ordered another one. Out in the disco, there was a Pet Shop Boys song she loved playing, so she danced to it. Mike was on the floor, too, already grinding up against some hot shirtless guy. Honestly, everything was so much easier for guys.

She went to the restroom to relieve herself of some excess alcohol. She was reapplying her lipstick in the mirror when a woman came up to the sink next to her to wash her hands—her long, strong hands. Hands were always the first thing Beth noticed. But there was more to this woman than just her hands—short, dark hair; lean, muscled form; liquid brown eyes. She looked like someone who used her muscles, not at a health club, but at her job.

The woman was looking at Beth, too. "Hey," she said.

"Hey." Beth's stomach fluttered with nervous excitement.

"Listen," the woman said, "if there's any justice in this world, you've already been told how beautiful you are a hundred times tonight. But I'm telling you again." She had a low, sultry voice, mellowed by an East Tennessee accent.

"Thanks." Beth felt her cheeks heat up. "And that was only the ninety-ninth time I've been told tonight."

"Just like I thought," the woman said, grinning. "There ain't no justice in the world." She looked down at the sticky bathroom floor, then back up at Beth. "So, can I buy you a drink?"

"It beats staying in the bathroom," Beth said.

At the bar the woman bought herself a Budweiser and Beth a vodka collins. "I know I've not seen you here before," the woman said. "If I had, I'd remember it."

Beth sipped her drink. "I don't come here very often."

"So, are you at student over at the college?"

Beth didn't want things to get too personal. So far she and this woman didn't even know each other's names. That was the best way. "Listen," Beth said, covering the woman's hand with hers. "There's no need for you to try to get to know me because I don't want to be your girlfriend."

"Is that a fact?" The woman sounded like she couldn't decide if her feelings should be hurt or not. "What do you want?"

"I want . . ." Beth stopped to knock back the rest of her drink like it was nothing but lemonade. "I want you to come outside with me for a few minutes."

"Uh . . . okay."

Beth took the woman's hand and led her out of the bar. She let her hand go once they were outside, though, just in case. "Do you have a car?"

"That's my truck over there." She nodded in the direction of a small, battered pickup.

The truck wouldn't do. The cab would be too cramped, and it was parked in too public a place. "Come with me," Beth said. She walked half a block up the street, stopping in front of a seedy Laundromat. "Come here," she said, stepping behind a Dumpster and into the alley that separated the Laundromat from a little grocery store.

"I don't think this is too safe," the woman said.

"You didn't strike me as the 'fraidy-cat type."

"And you didn't strike me as the alley cat type."

"Well, that's what I am." She put her finger on the woman's lips. "No more talking. We don't want to get caught." The fear of getting caught shot a thrill through her that went straight to her crotch.

She pulled the woman to her. There were no kisses and no preliminaries, only the woman's hot hands sliding over her breasts, cupping her ass, yanking down her panties and pushing her legs apart. And then a hand was inside her, and Beth was gasping "harder, harder" even as the woman did it so hard that Beth's shoulder blades were battered against the concrete block wall. But she liked the pain, too—the pleasure and the darkness and the pain and the hiding and how all of it exploded in her when she came.

After she caught her breath, Beth found herself staring at her twenty-dollar Victoria's Secret panties wadded up in a mud puddle.

"Sorry about your panties," the woman said. "I guess I kinda slung 'em."

"That's okay. It's not like they're my only pair. Would you walk me back to the door of the club?"

"Sure . . . okay." The woman's words sounded almost like a question, like she was confused about what was expected of her. But it was always awkward afterward.

They walked back in silence.

"So," the woman said, "I don't suppose I can have your phone number?"

"No."

"Can you at least tell me your first name?"

"No."

The woman shook her head. "Well, hon, I don't know what kind of game you're playing, but whatever it is, be careful, okay?"

"Okay." But the truth was, Beth spent 99 percent of her time being careful—careful about what she said and did, what impression she made. These occasional evenings at the Merry-Go-Round were a welcome break from all that carefulness.

But that didn't mean these evenings were carefree. The fear was always there. And while she and Mike, who, as a Republican state senator's son, stood to lose even more than she did, had everything planned out if they ever got caught en route to the Merry-Go-Round, what would she do if she got caught in an alley or the backseat of a car with a woman? This fear haunted her so much that she sometimes swore to give up her trips to the Merry-Go-Round, but her loneliness and desire always ended up overwhelming her. She always comforted herself with the fact that she was from one of the richest and most powerful families in town, so any lie she told would be believed. If a cop caught her in the alley, she could always say the other woman had been assaulting her and that she had been too scared to scream. She knew the cop would believe her. What she didn't know was if she'd be willing to go that far to protect herself.

Liz

A hand-scrawled sign on the door of the run-down, two-story house said, "Come on in," but Liz knocked anyway. She might have been able to cast off her mother's advice to always wear a bra and presentable-looking panties, but she couldn't cast off her mother's lessons in manners quite so easily. While Liz's parents may not have originally been Southerners, their time in the South had made them absorb the etiquette that reigned below the Mason Dixon line: Call older folks sir and ma'am. Don't interrupt when someone else is talking. Knock before entering.

And so Liz knocked. Even standing there with her spiky, recently dyed purple hair, wearing a thrift store army jacket with a peace symbol button on it and holding a forty-ounce bottle of Schlitz malt liquor, she still had some of the trappings of a well-brought-up Southern lady.

"Come on in!" a chorus of female voices hollered. Liz wondered if they figured she couldn't read the sign and so had decided to recite its words to her.

They were gathered in the living room, which was much cleaner than the guy apartments where Liz was used to hanging out. The couch and chairs were of the standard, college-issue, thrift-store variety, but some attempt had been made at decorating the place, unlike the guys' apartments, where towers of beer cans and strategically placed bongs were the decorative motif of choice. A print of a unibrowed Frida Kahlo hung on one wall; one of Georgia O'Keefe's vaginal-looking flowers hung on another. Liz was looking at the room instead of the people—something she had a tendency to do in social situations, especially when she had drunk no alcohol to soften the edges of her inhibitions.

"Hey, Liz!" Thalia called from her spot on the couch, where a beautiful yellowish Persian cat was curled up in her lap. "Glad you could come. I'd get up and give you a hug if Balthazar here would stop using me as his own personal recliner. I keep telling him he's screwing up the all-female vibe here, but he won't listen to me." She scratched the cat's ears. "He's a patriarchal pussy."

"Patriarchal pussy," the woman on the couch next to Thalia repeated. Her head was shaven as close as Thalia's, but her pretty face was decorated with makeup and with thin, silver hoops which hung from her nose, her lower lip and her left eyebrow. "Isn't that an oxymoron?"

"Not necessarily," the woman in the corner with the chic, European-style blunt haircut and cat's-eye glasses said. "I bet that's the kind of pussy Phyllis Schlafly has."

"That would be a kick-ass name for a band," the woman with long, blond hair who smelled of weed and patchouli said, her accent the classic stoner drawl. "Patriarchal pussy."

"Yeah, but Phyllis Schlafly's Pussy would be an even better name," the woman in the cat's-eye glasses said. She was wearing a super-short miniskirt with striped tights like the Wicked Witch of the East's and a pair of Doc Martens. Liz could tell she was the wisecracker of the group, and she liked her.

"Feel free to flop on a pillow, Liz," Thalia said, "and let me introduce you around. This is Chloe, my roommate." She indicated the pierced lip girl who, Liz noticed, had some tribal tattoos peeking out from the sleeves of the Dead Kennedys T-shirt she had seen Thalia wear before.

"Hey," Chloe said.

"And this is Dee Dee, my other roommate," Thalia said.

"It's D-E-E D-E-E, like Dee Dee Ramone," Dee Dee drawled.

"I wouldn't have pegged you for a Ramones fan," Liz said, cracking open her bottle of Schlitz.

"Yeah, she looks like a total Deadhead, doesn't she?" Chloe said.

"The Dead . . . fuckin' . . . blow." Dee Dee paused between each syllable for emphasis.

"Dee Dee is a punk in hippie's clothing," Thalia said. "My theory is she smokes so much weed it clouds her fashion sense." She ignored Dee Dee flipping her off and continued, "And over there in the corner is our sage graduate student, Audrey. She lives across the street with all those freaky theater people."

"You mean I live in Casa de Faggot instead of Casa de Lesbo," Audrey said. "You know, Liz, your hair is the same color as the plums I had for breakfast this morning. Very cool."

"Um . . . thanks." Liz wished she could think of a clever response. She usually could. What was wrong with her?

"This is kind of our core group," Thalia said, "but a few more women will show up."

"The token straight girls." Audrey laughed, and Thalia shushed her. There was that assumption again, Liz thought.

More women did show up—a couple of serious, bespectacled, unornamented studenty types and one wide-eyed, zealous petite woman named Bridget who had cut her hair short, Liz assumed, as a feminist statement but only looked like an adorable pixie as a result.

Once everybody was settled, some with beers, some with sodas, Thalia said, "So what's on everybody's mind?"

"Well," Chloe said, hugging her knees to her chin, "what's on my mind is how the fucking right-wingers want to stop me from being able to have an abortion, supposedly because they're pro-life, but meanwhile they think it's just fine and dandy to send full-grown people off to die in Iraq."

"Fuckin' A," Dee Dee said.

"And don't forget, y'all, about that big Planned Parenthood rally downtown next week," Thalia said. "You can bet the pro-lifers will be there with their crosses and their gory posters, so we've got to be sure there are plenty of us out there supporting choice."

"Last time I went to one of those things, some old codger hit me over the head with his big bloody fetus sign," Audrey said. "Pro-life, my ass. The old geezer just about gave me a concussion."

"Well, it's not women's lives they're for," Thalia said. "If you're viable outside the womb, you're on your fucking own. Okay, if we stay on this topic too long, I'm gonna get so mad I get out the castrating shears. Anybody got anything else?"

"I've got something," Audrey said, "and it's a lot more minor than Chloe's topic, but I'll bring it up anyway. I drove to Memphis to see my mom this past weekend. I hadn't seen her since back in the spring, and the first thing she asked me wasn't 'how's school?' or 'how was your summer internship?' or even 'how are you?' The first thing she asked me was 'how much do you weigh now?' Apparently, I've put on a few pounds, but I hadn't noticed till she told me. And you know, I ride my bike everywhere and eat vegetarian, so I'm pretty healthy. But her concern wasn't my health; it was my looks. And yeah, I know beauty standards are rooted in the patriarchy and yadda yadda yadda, but I still think women use these standards to beat up themselves and each other. I mean, every woman in this room who's drinking a soda is drinking a diet soda. And think about it . . . has anybody ever seen a straight guy drink a diet soda?"

"You're totally right," Thalia said. "My mother is the same way about me. It's gotten so bad that every time I go to see her, I stop at a store and pick up some kind of God-awful junk food—a Snickers bar or a big bag of Doritos—just so I'll be eating something really fattening when she sees me."

Wide-eyed Bridget, who, Liz noticed, had set aside her Diet Coke with a guilty expression, chimed in, "And I'd just like to add that anything we can do to free ourselves of these sexist beauty standards is just so liberating." Her eyes shone, and her smile was wide. She reminded Liz of those overzealous, Christian-to-the-point-of-creepiness girls who always used to invite her to Vacation Bible School at the Baptist Church. "As some of you know," Bridget said, "I cut my hair short recently, and I've never felt so free. And a month and two days ago"—she smiled even wider—"I quit shaving my legs."

A few women applauded politely.

"And I didn't think I would," Bridget said, "but I just love the way they feel . . . like fuzzy baby ducks!"

"Hell," Audrey said, "you could use Thalia's leg hair to *kill* fuzzy baby ducks."

The conversation zipped around, from date rape to pornography to favorite feminist authors. Liz listened and drank and thought. She had never been in a roomful of women discussing meaningful things before (and classrooms didn't count, since there was always a teacher to guide the discussion). Liz had always equated all-female gatherings with the one slumber party she attended in junior high, which had been marked by a riot of incoherent giggling and a game of Truth or Dare in which one girl had to stick her foot in the toilet because she wouldn't tell the name of the boy she liked.

Girls, Liz had decided then, made her uncomfortable, and she had resolved to hang out with boys instead. And that was what she had been doing up until now, she realized with a mixture of horror and amusement, carrying her anti-girl prejudices from junior high on into college. Despite her insistence that she was a feminist, she had spent a large portion of her life being sexist.

She still liked hanging out with the guys, of course. She loved Dan, and his friends were her friends as well. But being here in this room full of thoughtful women, most of whom (with the possible exception of Bridget, a born Truth or Dare player if there ever was one) had probably been as miserable in junior high as she had been, was good, too.

After the meeting, as she headed toward the Sagebrush to meet Dan, she heard a set of footsteps speed up to catch up with her.

"You were awfully quiet in there. We didn't scare you off, did we?"

It was Audrey, her face half-hidden by a sleek sheet of ash-blond hair. She was a tall, broad-shouldered woman. *Imposing* was the word that sprang to Liz's mind. Was that solid, imposing quality what Audrey's mother was dismissing as mere fat? "No. You didn't scare me. I'll talk my head off in a class, but in social situations it takes me a while to warm up."

"Well, there's no need to be shy with us. You're among friends. And don't spend too much time thinking about what you're going to say before you say it. Most of us are just throwing shit at the wall and hoping some of it sticks."

For some reason Liz felt shyer with Audrey than she had in the presence of the whole group, which was weird. She was usually comfortable with people one-on-one. "Well, uh, nice to meet you," she said while thinking, *Do you think you could have said anything more inane and socially inept?*

"Yeah," Audrey said. "Well, I'll see you, I guess the last Thursday of the month, then? And at that meeting, you *will* speak." She touched Liz's forehead like a faith-healing televangelist. "I have a feeling there are some interesting thoughts swirling around in that plum-colored head of yours."

Elisa

The paper didn't have a mark on it—no missing commas filled in, no corrections of her MLA documentation, no red-inked comments agreeing or disagreeing with the points she had made. But what was worse was that there was no grade, only "See me after class" scrawled on her Works Cited page.

Dr. Rivers had finished handing back the papers and begun her discussion of *The Golden Notebook*, but Elisa was too upset to follow what she was saying. What did "see me after class" mean? Did it mean she had a failing grade on this paper? But how could that be possible? This was her paper on *Rubyfruit Jungle*. She had been positively on fire when she wrote it, and she finished it with the confidence that it was the best paper she had ever written.

But apparently it wasn't, or Dr. Rivers would have slapped an A on it instead of writing a maddening little note. If Elisa had failed this paper, there was no way she could get an A in the class, which would blow her 4.0.

Elisa liked being an A student. Sometimes she had to work her butt off to get her A, but it was always worth it. She liked to please her teachers, and she liked to please herself. While Jo said she worked for her Bs and Cs out of fear that her athletic scholarship would be snatched if she didn't maintain a 2.5, Elisa worked toward her As for the pleasure they gave her. When it came to school, Elisa and Jo were two different workhorses—Elisa running toward the carrot, Jo running away from the stick.

Women in Lit usually zipped right by, but today it dragged. Once everybody was packing up to leave, Elisa approached Dr. Rivers' desk. The ball of anxiety in her stomach was growing like a snowball rolling down a hill.

"Hello, Elisa." Dr. Rivers smiled. Up close, under the fluorescent lights, Elisa could see details of Dr. Rivers' appearance that were invisible from the back of the classroom—the silver streaks in her blond hair, the lashes that were colored with mascara despite her otherwise makeup-free look.

"Hi." Elisa clutched her paper. "You wanted to see me about this?"

"I did, but you don't have to be so nervous about it. The guillotine is hardly waiting."

Elisa forced a smile.

"Do you have another class next period?" Dr. Rivers asked, shoving her dog-eared copy of *The Golden Notebook* into a tote bag that bore the name of a local bookstore.

"No, ma'am. I don't have another class until two-ten."

"Well, in that case, why don't you follow me over to my office and we'll talk about your paper?" She started toward the door. "And please don't call me ma'am. It makes me feel about nine hundred years old."

"Okay," Elisa said, resisting the urge to say "yes, ma'am" again.

The guillotine may not have been waiting, but as Elisa walked with Dr. Rivers across the breezeway into the humanities office building, she felt like a prisoner being escorted by a warden. Their walk was silent, and Elisa kept feeling like she should chat about the class or the weather or something, but she was too afraid that anything that came out of her mouth would reveal her ignorance.

Dr. Rivers' office door was plastered with cartoons from *The New Yorker* and picture postcards of famous women—sad-eyed Virginia Woolf, flower-bedecked Billie Holiday and a pair of homely old women Elisa did not recognize.

Dr. Rivers must have seen her looking because she pointed at the picture and said, "Gertrude and Alice—do you know them?"

"No," Elisa said, figuring it was better to admit her ignorance than to try to fake knowledge. "But I've got a great-aunt named Gertrude."

Dr. Rivers laughed, which made Elisa feel better. "I used to have a cat named Gertrude. I'm afraid it's a better name for a cat than a person." She pulled the postcard off the door. "Gertrude Stein and Alice B. Toklas—one of the great love stories of the twentieth century." She held the card out to Elisa. "Here . . . why don't you take this and put it up in your dorm room or something? It will serve as a reminder to read some of Stein's work. Which, if you wanted, you could do in my Women in Modernism course in the spring."

"Thanks." Elisa knew she sounded as confused as she actually was. If her paper was so bad that it required a one-on-one conference, then why was Dr. Rivers giving her a postcard and inviting her to take another class with her?

"And now," Dr. Rivers said, turning the key in the lock. "Let's get behind closed doors where we can discuss this paper." Dr. Rivers' office was cluttered with books and papers and little statues of naked women that Elisa tried hard to ignore. "Please sit," Dr. Rivers said.

Elisa obeyed, and Dr. Rivers grabbed the chair behind her desk and rolled it so it was right next to Elisa's. Dr. Rivers was so close that Elisa could smell her floral perfume and fruity shampoo.

"Now," Dr. Rivers said, taking the paper out of Elisa's hands, "had you ever written a paper about literature before this one?"

"I had to write a term paper my senior year of high school. And I wrote short papers for American Lit one and two." Elisa hoped she wouldn't cry. Clearly the paper was terrible, or Dr. Rivers wouldn't think she'd never written one before.

"Well, then, I have to tell you that often this paper achieves a level of sophistication that far surpasses your experience. You were the only student who chose to write about *Rubyfruit Jungle*, and as soon as I looked at your title—'Humor as Empowerment'—I thought, this student really gets what Brown was trying to achieve in this novel."

Elisa's brain was buzzing. "You liked it?"

"The majority of it was brilliant. You show real potential as a literary critic and as a feminist literary critic, which is, of course, the best kind." Dr. Rivers frowned down at Elisa's paper. "However, despite these flashes of brilliance, there are statements in the paper that are amateurish and juvenile."

Elisa's heart, which had been swelling, now began to deflate. "Oh," she said.

Dr. Rivers patted her arm. "Look at your little face. You look like I just decapitated your pet kitten." She held up Elisa's paper. "Look, what I'm trying to say is that most of the thought in this paper is above and beyond the abilities of most undergraduates. You just need to learn the discourse of criticism . . . you need to learn not to make statements such as"—she looked down at the page—" *Rubyfruit Jungle* is the best book I ever read.' These simplistic personal statements take away from the elegance of your argument. I'm giving you an A on this paper, Elisa, but in the next one I expect a consistently high level of discourse . . . none of these little detours into the land of the junior high book report."

"Yes." Elisa swallowed the "ma'am" and felt her anxiety level drop. She was getting her A.

"What I thought I might do," Dr. Rivers said, rising from her chair, "is loan you a few literary criticism texts. You could read some articles and get more of a feel for scholarly writing. Might that be helpful?"

"Yes, thank you." Elisa couldn't believe how nice Dr. Rivers was being. Why would such a sophisticated intellectual take an interest in an ignorant country girl like her?

Dr. Rivers pulled three paperbacks off her bookshelf and handed them to her. "So," she said, sitting on the edge of her desk and slipping off the clunky sandals she always wore, "tell me a little about yourself, Elisa. Reading your paper made me think there's a lot more to you than meets the eye." She smiled. "Apparently, you and Molly Bolt have a few things in common."

Elisa felt herself blushing. "Well, I do come from the middle of nowhere like Molly."

Dr. Rivers looked Elisa right in the eye. "And you're a lesbian?"

Elisa found herself looking down at the streaks and spots on her acid-washed jeans. But she whispered, "Yes."

"So were you the only little lesbian in whatever place you came from?"

"Odessa," Elisa said. She smiled. "No, there was one more. Jo, my girlfriend. We've been together since we were sixteen."

"My, you are a fast learner, aren't you?" Dr. Rivers tucked her legs under her, curling up like a cat. "You know, I already had my Ph.D. before I figured out I was a lesbian. It took me six years in a miserable marriage before I finally grasped the reason for my misery. I owe it all to Monique Wittig."

"Are you still with her?" Elisa asked.

Dr. Rivers knit her brow. "With whom?"

"Monique."

"Oh . . . oh!" Dr. Rivers laughed a little harder than Elisa was comfortable with, especially since Elisa couldn't figure out what was funny. "You misunderstood me. Monique Wittig wasn't my lover. She's a writer—a feminist theorist. She wrote a book called *Language and the Lesbian Body*. She awoke me to lesbianism the theory, which led me to embrace lesbianism, the practice."

"Oh," Elisa said, feeling as impressed by Dr. Rivers' intellect as she was ashamed of her own lack of sophistication.

"Are you an English major, Elisa?" Dr. Rivers asked.

"I'm an education major, but I'm specializing in English education," Elisa said. "See, me and Jo—" She winced at her grammatical slippage. "Jo and I came to William Blount together. She's majoring in phys ed, and I figure after we graduate we can get jobs teaching high school someplace. Maybe we can be the kind of teachers that make things a little easier for kids who are different."

Dr. Rivers looked at Elisa as if she had just confessed that her ultimate career goal was scrubbing toilets. "High-school teaching?" she said. "Oh, Elisa, that would be a terrible waste of a mind as fine as yours. It breaks my heart to think of you trying to share your passion for literature with a roomful of sweaty delinquents with nothing on their minds but fucking and football." Elisa must have shown her shock at hearing a teacher use profanity because Dr. Rivers said, "Forgive my language, but I feel I must speak bluntly with you. I don't think you appreciate how bright you are, and for a student with your aptitude to spend her college years in the stifling College of Education, taking courses in making up multiple-choice tests and using the overhead projector . . . well, it would be almost as bad as if you hadn't gone to college at all."

"Really?" Elisa was shocked. She was the first member of her family to attend college, and her custodian dad and cashier mom thought that being a high-school teacher was quite a lofty goal.

"Really." Dr. Rivers slid off her desk and leaned down to look into Elisa's eyes. "Change your major to English, Elisa. I could be your advisor and help you plan your classes and map out your goals. Then you could get your M.A., your Ph.D.—you'd be able to teach university students, to write and publish papers, to travel. You wouldn't be a glorified babysitter like a public school teacher. You'd be living the life of the mind."

"Do you really think I'm smart enough to do all that?" Elisa had always thought of herself as a good, dedicated student, but having been raised on *The Dukes of Hazzard* and Doritos, she never thought of herself as an intellectual.

"Absolutely. With the right guidance—and I am offering myself as your guide, if you'll have me—you could blossom into a true scholar."

"Wow. This is a lot to think about."

"So think. You're obviously good at it. And when you've decided, come back to see me."

"Who in the Sam Hill are these people?" Jo asked, looking at the postcard of Gertrude and Alice that Elisa had taped to her dresser mirror.

"Gertrude Stein and Alice B. somebody," Elisa said. "They were lovers."

"Hmm," Jo said, squinting at the card. "Were they women?"

Elisa laughed. "Well, yeah."

"I thought they might be from they way they dressed, but Lord, look at 'em! They look like a couple of old fellers in the Kiwanis Club who dressed up in drag on a dare."

Elisa laughed even harder and lobbed a pillow at Jo. "You're awful."

Jo threw the pillow back at her. "Well, I reckon it's a good thing the two of them found each other 'cause I bet nobody else—man or woman—ever looked at either one of them."

"Dr. Rivers says Gertrude Stein was a genius."

"Huh."

"And she thinks I should change my major to English."

"Well, you do love to read," Jo said. "But would you be able to get a job once you graduated?"

"Well, not with a bachelor's, but I could if I went on and got a master's and maybe even a Ph.D."

Jo's mouth dropped open. "You'd be willing to stay in school that long?"

"You know me. I love school." Elisa was nervous. If Jo said this was a bad idea—that she couldn't tolerate Elisa being a student six or seven more years—what would she do?

Jo plopped down on the bed beside Elisa. "I wouldn't have to get a Ph.D., too, would I?"

"Of course not."

"Well, then, genius girl, you go for it."

Her panic subsided, Elisa threw her arms around Jo.

Beth

Beth had skipped women's studies to get her nails done. This was the first time she'd missed Dr. Rivers' class, and given how pissed she was at Rivers for giving her a C+ on her short paper, playing hooky—especially for something so unapologetically girly as a manicure/pedicure appointment—filled her with vengeful glee.

Dr. Rivers had dismissed Beth's analysis of *Mrs. Dalloway* as "superficial." And, well, it probably was. Beth hadn't really felt like she understood the book, but what else was she supposed to write about? *Rubyfruit Jungle*? That wasn't exactly the kind of book you could sit around marking with your pink highlighter at your sorority study group. Besides, that Molly Bolt girl got on her nerves. Molly was too stuck on herself, and why did she have to go around stirring up trouble all the time? She just made things hard for herself and everyone around her. Beth bet that Dr. Rivers wouldn't have liked that analysis either.

Beth and Quimby were sitting in throne-like salon chairs while young Asian men squatted beneath them and snipped the cuticles of their toenails. "I don't know why we're getting pedicures along with our manicures," Beth said. "It's the *fall* formal. It's not like we're going to be wearing open-toed shoes."

"But you don't want gross-looking toes," Quimby said. "Mike might want to suck on them or something."

"Eww!" Beth squealed, play-slapping Quimby's arm. "You are a truly disgusting girl. I don't know how I can bring myself to live with you."

"You love me, and you know it," Quimby said. "And besides, you can't honestly tell me you've never let a guy suck on your toes."

"Yes, I can." Beth had had a testosterone-crazed high-school boyfriend who, much to her annoyance, was eager to suck on various parts of her anatomy. But he had never gotten down as far as her toes.

"God, Beth! You might as well be a virgin. Toe-sucking is fabulous— shrimping, some guy told me it was called."

"That's just nasty. I mean, haven't you ever heard of toe jam?"

"You know what your problem is, Beth? You're not sexually adventurous."

An image flashed into Beth's head. Her back against a concrete block wall in an alley, a stranger's hand between her thighs. "Oh, is that what my problem is?" She looked down at the man who cradled her left foot in his hand, and she whispered to Quimby, "You know, we probably shouldn't be talking about this stuff in front of these guys."

Quimby laughed. "Oh, come on, ditz brain, it's not like they speak any English."

But the smile on the face of Quimby's pedicurist said something different. *If he would stick one of Quimby's toes in his mouth,* Beth thought, *I would give him the biggest tip of his life.*

Getting ready was exhausting. After she and Quimby had gotten their nails done, they went to another salon for their hair and then to the mall to get their makeup fixed. At first, all the personal attention had been fun, but by the end of the day, Beth felt like she had been poked and prodded so much that she might as well throw in a dental exam and a Pap smear to cover her entire personal territory. Now that she was back in her room, though, sprawled on the bed in her bra and panties, halfway through her first Crystal Light and vodka, she could unwind a little before the formal.

Quimby was standing in front of the full-length mirror on her closet door, wearing only a pale pink strapless bra and matching bikini panties. Her collarbones and hipbones jutted, and her belly was concave. She frowned and tugged at her bra. "This thing doesn't push up like it's supposed to," she said. "Of course, it's not like there's much here to push in the first place."

"I'd trade my body for yours any day," Beth said, looking down at the little roll on her tummy that, for all her starvation and sit-ups, just wouldn't go away.

"Well, go ahead and trade, then," Quimby said. "I could do with a little cleavage tonight."

"But your boobs are so perky you don't even need a bra. Why don't you wear your gown without one?"

"Because," Quimby said, "if I wear a strapless gown without a bra, it might fall down while I'm dancing, and every frat guy at William Blount would see my tatas."

Nothing they hadn't seen before, Beth thought. But she kept her mouth shut—something real friends have to know when to do.

It was funny—Beth knew everything there was to know about Quimby, but when you got down to it, Quimby didn't know much about Beth. She knew what brands of tampons and vodka Beth preferred, but when it came to intimate knowledge, she had no clue. But that was how it had to be. If Quimby knew too much about Beth, she sure as hell wouldn't be hanging out with her in her underwear or asking Beth to help her get out a contraceptive sponge that was stuck, like that one time. Even though Beth was not at all attracted to Quimby, she knew that Quimby, if confronted with Beth's sexuality, would find this impossible to believe, and all those hours spent in their underwear, the fishing expedition for the contraceptive sponge, every hug or sisterly kiss on the cheek would take on a different, even sinister meaning.

"Zip me up?" Quimby stood with her back to Beth.

"Sure."

"Then I'll do you. The boys'll be here in, like, ten minutes."

When they walked into the lobby, Beth in her fuchsia gown and Quimby in her emerald one, Beth could feel everyone's eyes on her: the front desk receptionist; the chunky, sweatpanted girls in the TV lounge; the study group gathered around the coffee table. Beth had felt stares like this for as long as she remembered, stares that told her she was pretty, popular, envied.

"Omigod, aren't the boys *cute*?" Quimby squealed as if she were looking at puppies in a pet shop window.

Mike was handsome in his beautifully tailored tux, and Chad, who was looking at Quimby with a mixture of lust and fear, was, Beth supposed, cute.

"Hello, gorgeous," Mike said, pecking Beth on the cheek.

"You look . . . uh . . . real nice," Chad said to Quimby, who giggled and called him sweet.

Arm in arm with their dates, the girls departed for the fall formal. Outside in the moonlight, Quimby stretched out her arms and sighed. "I feel like Cinderella."

Beth also felt like Cinderella. She was giddy from the excitement of being the center of attention in her fancy dress, but a sharp pinprick of fear was threatening to penetrate the balloon of her giddiness. Cinderella, too, must have been terrified that someone at the ball would discover she wasn't who she pretended to be. How could she have been carefree, knowing that there was always the danger that her coach would be revealed to be a pumpkin, that her footmen would shrink back into rodents, that the whole illusion she was creating could shatter as easily as a glass slipper?

Liz

"Draft George Bush!
Draft Dan Quayle!
Draft Neil Bush when he gets out of jail!"

Liz's energy surged as she stood chanting along with the protesters outside the student center. All her conscious life she had felt like she had been born too late. Her parents' generation had protested Vietnam, founded the women's movement and listened to the Rolling Stones before they metamorphosed into "classic rock." What did Liz's generation have to call its own? Video games, MTV and a bunch of sound-alike hair metal bands.

But here at the protest, she felt like she was part of something that mattered. Sure, a bunch of college students in Tennessee weren't going to put a stop to this farce of a war, this ridiculous trade of human life for big oil. But they were making their voices heard—a fact that made Liz feel patriotic, though not in a way that the student Republicans could ever understand.

She was glad, too, that Dan was there beside her. He had even held her hand as they marched across campus. Demonstrating for peace seemed to make him more affectionate than usual, perhaps because of the connection between peace and that other word he had never said to her.

As the chanting died down, a carload of frat boys drove by, slowing down to yell such incisive remarks as "Fucking freaks!" and "Support our troops!"

"You know," Liz said, "I can accept being called a freak, but I just don't get how demonstrating for peace isn't supporting the troops."

"Yeah," Dan said, lighting up a Kool Mild. "As if the fact that we don't want them to get their asses shot off isn't supportive."

"Hey, guys." Stu appeared before them wearing a floppy trench coat—not exactly the fashion choice to contradict his sleazy, porn-hound image, Liz thought. "I just lifted three bottles of Robo from Walgreen's. You guys interested?"

"Sure, I'd Robo. Why the hell not?" Dan looked down at Liz. "How about you?"

"I think I'll pass." When it came to recreational drugs, Robo was one of the substances at which Liz drew the line. Stu had turned Dan and Todd on to Robo-ing, a practice which consisted of drinking the entire contents of a bottle of Robitussin DM, spending the next thirty minutes trying not to puke it back up and then passing the ensuing hours enjoying the Robo buzz, which Dan described as like being really drunk while tripping on half a hit of acid.

As happy as Liz was to be one of the guys, she held firm to her decision to avoid Robo. For one thing, she hated the taste of cough syrup to the point that when she was sick, she would rather cough up her lungs than swallow a spoonful of the stuff. She could almost induce vomiting by just the thought of drinking a whole bottle.

Liz liked her drugs to have a certain glamour. When she was hunched over a bong, she felt like a cool hippie chick—like she could be hanging out in Haight-Ashbury with Janis Joplin. With a gin and tonic in her hand, her wit sharpened and her tongue loosened by alcohol, she felt chic and cynical, an heiress to the legacy of Dorothy Parker.

But there was no glamour to chugging down a whole bottle of cough syrup. It seemed desperate, like the old derelicts her grandfather had told her about who used to buy bottles of hair tonic, strain them through a slice of white bread, and then drink the alcohol.

"You wanna hang out with us while we do it?" Stu asked.

"Man, I don't even like to smell that stuff," Liz said. "Maybe we could hook up later."

"Why don't we meet up at the Sagebrush about nine or so?" Dan said.

"That's cool."

Dan and Stu scurried off while Liz decided what she was going to do in the forty-five minutes it would take them to consume the cough syrup and hold it down.

"Hey, you," a smoky female voice said.

Liz turned around to see Audrey from the women's group meeting, holding a poster that read "Lesbians Against Bush" and pictured the President's face on the crotch of a pair of panties. "Oh, hey," Liz said, feeling shy all of a sudden. "Great poster."

"Yeah," Audrey said. "I have the feeling this is the closest ol' George's face has been to a pussy in quite some time." She grinned, making Liz notice her dimples. Liz could scarcely imagine the amount of cheek-pinching Audrey must have endured as a toddler.

Liz laughed. "No, I don't imagine Barbara lets him visit that neighborhood too often." She eyed the skimpy undies on the poster. "Nor do I imagine she wears panties that look like that."

"Nope. Ol' Babs is definitely the voluminous white cotton type, where panties are concerned. You can tell a lot about a woman from the kind of underwear she wears."

"Really?" It was a logical statement in an off-the-wall way, but Liz had never given the connection between panties and personality much thought.

"Sure." Audrey narrowed her eyes. "What color panties do you have on, Liz?"

Liz didn't embarrass easily and couldn't figure out why she was embarrassed now. "I don't remember."

Audrey grinned. "Check."

"What?"

"Check. I'm a grad student, damn it. I'm conducting research here."

"You're a grad student in *theater*."

"Humor me."

Liz peeked down the front of her baggy carpenter's pants, noting with disappointment that on today of all days, when she was going to be called on it, white cotton was the panty du jour. "Just white." She should have fabricated something more interesting, but she was a terrible liar.

"So disappointing." Audrey clucked her tongue. "Good-girl panties are a step down the road to Republicanism." Her eyes narrowed. "Unless you're wearing them with irony."

"Oh, I am. It's the only way I ever wear my panties." Liz thought about the contents of her underwear drawer. "And sometimes I wear boxers."

"See, that's much, much better." Audrey smiled.

"And what about you?" Liz asked. "What kind of subversive underwear are you sporting?"

"Today?" Audrey looked down at her black mini-skirt and thigh-high fishnet stockings. "I'm not wearing any underwear. And I shaved my pubes. 'Lesbians Against Bush,' get it?"

Even as Liz laughed, she felt like her face was going to spontaneously combust from embarrassment. If there was a witty comeback to be made, she surely couldn't think of it.

The clientele of the Sagebrush could best be described as eclectic. Half a dozen Harleys were usually parked out front, and the pool table was generally surrounded by the bikes' burly, bearded owners. And yet the Sagebrush wasn't a biker bar. On any given night, one might see a table full of black-clad, eyeliner-wearing female, male and confusingly androgynous art students sucking down dollar longnecks. Another table might be full of activist types—Earth First-ers or the Anti-Apartheid Coalition folks—engaging in passionate dialogue and gesturing wildly. The next table might be occupied by garden variety good ol' boys, singing along with Hank Williams Junior's "Family Tradition" on the jukebox—a jukebox which could also play "Three Little Birds" by Bob Marley and "Tainted Love" by Soft Cell.

Liz loved the Sagebrush. Maybe because she had spent so much of her life feeling like she didn't fit anywhere, it was a welcome break to be in a place where everybody fit, no questions asked. Even though the décor consisted of neon beer lights hung on cheap paneling, the draft beer was tepid and the floor was sticky, the Sagebrush filled her with a sense of well-being—a sense that was enhanced by the numerous beers she consumed there.

Tonight a bunch of rugby players, in T-shirts proclaiming "Rugby Players Eat Their Own Dead" were gathered around the bar, whooping and high-fiving. A lank-haired hippie chick was dancing barefoot to the Dead's "Sugar Magnolia" on the jukebox—no matter how much Liz loved the Sagebrush, she wouldn't walk on its floor barefoot for any amount of money—and the black-clad, heavily tattooed and largely toothless members of a local hard rock band were engaged in a game of pool with the bikers.

Liz spotted Stu and Dan at a table in the corner. Stu was grinning, and his dark, beady eyes had a manic gleam, but Dan showed no signs of being in an altered state. Liz knew it was a point of pride with him never to let people see how fucked up he was. Whether he was stoned, drunk or tripping, he never giggled or slurred or did anything that might reveal the bubbling, fizzing chemistry project that his brain had become. To show signs of his intoxication, he once told Liz, would be giving too much of himself away.

Stu saw Liz, waved, and smiled a little too enthusiastically. Liz waved back and made her way to the booth, where she slid in next to Dan.

"I don't know if I've ever been so glad to see you," Dan said. "We're in desperate need of someone to help us finish this pitcher."

"Happy to be of service," Liz said, grabbing a mug.

"There's a distinct limit to how much one can drink while on Robo," Dan said, lighting a Kool Mild. "If you hadn't appeared, we would have exceeded it out of sheer testosterone-induced stupidity."

"Well, thankfully I'm here to save you from your own testosterone." Liz poured the beer from Dan's mug into her own.

"I wish a girl would come save me from my testosterone," Stu said, his eyes glazed. "Estrogen, testosterone, testrogen, estosterone." Stu did not possess Dan's ability to hide his altered state.

"Liking that Robo, Stu?" Liz grinned.

"I am now, but about an hour ago it wasn't liking me. I had to lie down in Dan's room to keep from blowing chunks." A goofy smile lit up his face. "You're pretty."

"Pretty is as pretty does," Liz said, draining her beer in one gulp and letting out a gigantic belch, much to Dan's seeming amusement. She wasn't really sure how to handle being called pretty. It was like when someone said "God bless you" when you hadn't sneezed—it was hard to think of an appropriate response. If she said "thank you," it would sound like she was agreeing with Stu's statement, and while she wasn't one of those girls who went around saying "I'm so fat, I'm so ugly," neither did she think of the word *pretty* as describing her. It was too girly and frilly-sounding; it made her think of a little girl's bedroom with a French provincial canopy bed and pink bedspread. Liz knew she was smart. She knew she was funny. And with Dan's help, she was learning how to be cool. But pretty? Pretty was rainbows and butterflies, not her with her purple crew cut and earrings shaped like handcuffs.

"You're not pissed, are you, Dan, that I said your girlfriend is pretty?" Stu slurred.

Drop it, creep, Liz thought.

"Why should I be mad at you for simply stating a fact?" Dan offered Liz a rare smile. "Besides, it's not like Liz and I own each other. We don't go in for that reductive boyfriend/girlfriend labeling stuff. Liz isn't *my* anything; she's this cool chick I sometimes happen to fuck."

Liz looked away from Stu's leer. Dan might not be showing outward signs of fucked-upness the way Stu was, but his inhibitions had definitely been lowered, or he wouldn't have made a sexual comment in Stu's presence. But even if Stu hadn't been there, she wasn't sure how she would have felt about Dan's comment. True, she didn't like the boyfriend-girlfriend labels and the formality of going out on planned "dates," but it would be nice if after two years of being together, Dan could find a more intimate and, she hoped, accurate way of describing her relationship to him. But what word would describe their relationship? *Companions* addressed their friendship but not their physical relationship. *Lovers* covered the physical, but was too gushy for either of them, especially Dan, to use.

"You went away for a minute," Dan said.

"Sorry. I was just musing on the inadequacy of language."

"Yeah," Dan said. "I know what you mean. There are just some things there are no words for . . . to describe how food tastes, for example. You bite into an artichoke, and it's delicious, but how to describe its particular deliciousness? Tangy? Piquant? Words don't do justice to the complexity of the flavor."

"I've never eaten an artichoke," Stu said.

Dan looked as if Stu had just admitted he had never breathed air. "Never? Seriously? Well, you must. You're missing out."

"You really are," Liz said, although she had never tasted an artichoke either.

And then they were talking about food, and food gave way to talking about the Mr. Creosote scene in Monty Python's *The Meaning of Life*, which led to the exchange of various Python lines in fake British accents. Then Todd showed up, fresh from his shift delivering pizzas, with a couple of Deadheads who also worked at Mario's, and they and Liz ordered another pitcher. And then it was 1 a.m., and Liz was drunk.

Dan leaned over the table, which was cluttered with drained mugs and an overflowing ashtray. "Liz," he said in a measured tone, "if it's acceptable to you, I'd really like to jump your bones tonight."

"Yeah, okay," Liz said with careful casualness. But inside she sang, *he wants me.*

Sex with Dan didn't happen very often. Her chances really depended on what substance he was using that evening. If he was just drinking, her chances of getting laid were at their highest. Pot usually made him more interested in Krystals than sex, and on acid, sex was of less interest than contemplating the glowing light of his cigarette. With Robo, things could go either way, but they appeared to be going her way tonight.

Dan's room was on the honors floor of Bennett Hall, which meant he had open visitation. Apparently, the powers that be had decided that honors students would not deign to use open visitation for prurient reasons; they would just use the opportunity to form mixed-sex study groups.

Dan's single room was shaped like a shoebox, and a poster titled "Great Irish Writers" hung over his narrow bed. It had taken Liz a while to adjust to looking up during sex and feeling that Samuel Beckett was staring at her judgmentally. They wedged their bodies together on the single bed and kissed. Dan tasted of cigarette smoke and beer and, faintly, Robitussin. He held and squeezed her breasts and helped her pull her Bettie Page T-shirt off over her head.

As always, Liz was interested in what was going on—in the texture of skin touching skin, tongue touching tongue. But also as always, there was a distance between her and the activities, as if she were sitting in a dark movie theater, watching Dan and a girl who looked like her on the screen. It was entertaining and enjoyable, but physically, she wasn't a part of it. It was strange. Whenever she and Dan would decide to have sex, she always felt a great rush of arousal that lasted for the whole walk to his dorm room. But once they actually got down to business, she was reduced to being a voyeur to her own sex life.

She pulled off her pants and the white panties that had caused her embarrassment earlier in the evening, then leaned over Dan and kissed him. When she pulled away from his lips, he placed his hand on the back of her head and gently pushed it downward.

Maybe because of the Robo, it took a while. Her jaw ached, and the repetitive head-bobbing made her think of the glass "drinking bird" she had bought as a kid on vacation in Florida. The bird had googly plastic eyes and a little top hat, and it balanced on the side of a glass, then dipped down, then came back up, then down, then up . . .

Liz spat into a Kleenex she grabbed off the bedside table. When she looked up at Dan, his eyes were glassy and staring, like Janet Leigh's at the end of the shower scene in *Psycho*.

After a minute or two, he spoke. "The Robo's starting to wear off now. You should probably go so I can get some sleep."

Liz felt a pinprick of pain but chided herself for acting like somebody's girlfriend. Of course she couldn't spend the night with him in that tiny bed. One of them would fall out and break an arm or something. "Yeah, it is pretty late."

She got up to dress, and Dan fluffed his pillow, pulled up the covers and closed his eyes. She pulled on her pants and her shirt and sat at Dan's desk to lace her Converse high-tops. His breathing was steady, and she thought he was already asleep, but as she walked toward the door, he whispered, "Liz?"

"Hmm?" Anticipation tickled her stomach.

"Turn out the light as you go."

Elisa

Elisa tapped lightly on the half-open door of Dr. Rivers' office. When Dr. Rivers said, "Yes?" she sounded gruff and a little distracted, but when she looked up from her pile of papers and saw Elisa, she smiled. "So," she said, "have you thought about leaving the field of education for more enlightening pastures?"

Elisa wished she could sound as sophisticated as Dr. Rivers. "Yes," she said. "I've decided to change my major."

"Brava!" Dr. Rivers said, applauding. "And have you given any thought as to whom you might choose as your advisor? Hint, hint."

Elisa grinned and looked down at her Candies ballet flats. "I was thinking of you, if that's all right."

"Elisa, it's much better than all right." Dr. Rivers stood up and flipped back her hair. "I'll tell you what. Why don't we go to lunch and celebrate? We can celebrate our working together and your change in your life's path."

Elisa felt like she was riding the Tilt-a-Whirl at the county fair, elated but a little sick. "Um . . . okay. That's real nice of you."

"Well, even budding intellectuals have to eat. And it can be a working lunch. We can talk about your plans for the rest of your college career."

Elisa expected Dr. Rivers to walk in the direction of the cafeteria, but she walked toward the faculty parking garage instead, where she unlocked the door of a silver Mercedes.

"This is a beautiful car," Elisa said, running her hand over the leather interior.

"It's a souvenir of that wretched six-year marriage I was telling you about," Dr. Rivers said, starting the engine. "This car was the only good thing that came out of that marriage . . . besides me, of course."

Elisa smiled but didn't say anything. She had no idea why Dr. Rivers seemed to like her, but she certainly didn't want to say anything ignorant that would make her change her mind.

Dr. Rivers drove past all the restaurants on the strip: the chain fast-food places, the delis, the pizza joints. "You have to drive a bit if your food tastes go beyond the usual burgers, beer and Buffalo wings," she said. "You don't have anything against Japanese food, do you?"

Elisa had never even tried Chinese food before she came to college. She wondered if Japanese food was about the same thing. "Well, I don't know anything about it, so I guess I can't have anything against it, right?"

Dr. Rivers looked away from the traffic light to smile at her. "The world would be a finer place if more people adopted your point of view, Elisa. But the primary reason people decide they're against something is because they don't know anything about it."

Elisa was so amazed by Dr. Rivers' comment that she couldn't help talking. "That's so true. In Odessa, lots of people are racist—people in my family, too, I'm ashamed to say. But once I came here I realized the reason people back home are racist is because most of them have never been around any black people before, so they don't know they're just regular people like anybody else."

"It's the nature of prejudice," Dr. Rivers said. "Fear of the unknown—of the other."

"And it's the same when people are going on about gay people, too.

They don't know what they're like, so they come up with all this ignorant stuff—like this guy back in high school who always went on about how gay men had sex with gerbils. He also said he could always spot a lesbian because they all had the fuzzy little mustaches and were mannish-looking."

"He said this in your presence?" Dr. Rivers asked.

"Yes."

"Well, you're not exactly mannish-looking, are you?"

Elisa smiled. "No, and for all of his talking about being able to spot a lesbian immediately, he never spotted me."

Dr. Rivers pulled into the parking lot of a squat, tiny restaurant called Rashomon. A pretty little fountain surrounded by rocks bubbled outside the entrance, and Elisa couldn't help but be charmed, even though she was nervous about eating unfamiliar food in an unfamiliar setting while still managing to make a good impression on her mentor.

A smiling woman whose tiny waist Elisa envied led them to a low table with two big cushions on either side of it. Dr. Rivers slipped off her clunky sandals and sat right down on the floor, looking as comfortable as a little kid sitting in front of the TV.

For Elisa, sitting on the floor was a problem. While Dr. Rivers had on one of the long, flowing, floral-print skirts she seemed to favor, Elisa was wearing a tight, acid-washed denim mini. If she sat on the floor "Indian-style," as Dr. Rivers was doing, her skirt would hitch up to the tops of her thighs, and the crotch of her black lace panties would be on display to the waitress and any other passersby. Finally, she settled on lowering herself to the cushion so that her legs were pressed together and turned to the left, like an old-fashioned lady riding a horse sidesaddle. It wasn't comfortable, but at least she wouldn't be arrested for indecent exposure.

The woman who had seated them set a teapot and two small cups on the table. "This is all so cute!" Elisa exclaimed, carried away by the object's delicate perfection. "It's like a little girl's tea party. I feel like we should have dolls and teddy bears sitting around the table, too."

Dr. Rivers did not smile. "I know you meant that with all the kindness in the world, Elisa, but we have to be careful about dismissing the mores of another culture as merely cute or quaint. Condescension, no matter how affectionate, is still a form of prejudice."

Elisa stared down at her teacup, her face burning. They hadn't been here five minutes, and already she'd said something wrong.

"Look up at me, Elisa." Dr. Rivers' tone was so gentle it was almost a whisper. "I wasn't scolding you. I was simply using the statement you made as a teaching opportunity. There's a lot I can teach you, Elisa . . . about literature, about culture, about being a citizen of the world. You want to learn, don't you?"

"Yes." Elisa looked into the wise bluish-gray eyes of the woman who, for some unknowable reason, was offering to open up new worlds to her. "More than anything, I want to learn."

"I sensed that about you the first time I saw you." Dr. Rivers did not break Elisa's gaze. "I could feel your hunger." A smile darted across her lips, and she picked up her menu. "Speaking of hunger, shall we order some sushi?"

Elisa picked up her menu, too. "Sure."

"The yellowtail is very good," Dr. Rivers said. "And I like the uni, though I realize it's not for everyone. But whatever you do, don't order the California roll, like so many of the uninitiated. It's the sushi cop-out—cooked crab, avocado and cucumber—the sort of thing for people whose idea of fine dining is Red Lobster."

Elisa tried not to show her shock. She and Jo had gotten dressed up and gone to the Red Lobster for their anniversary last year.

She scanned the menu, but it looked more like the chapter headings in a marine biology textbook than a list of lunch choices. Octopus, sea urchin, eel . . . the California roll was the only thing that jumped out as an edible option, which just showed how unsophisticated she was.

She saw the salmon on the menu. She had always liked salmon when her mamaw had made it, mixing the canned fish with egg, flour, salt and pepper; forming it into patties; and frying it. She wasn't so ignorant that she thought the salmon here would be like her mamaw's, but at least she knew what it was.

After they ordered, Dr. Rivers ran her finger around the rim of her teacup and said, "While we wait for our lunch, I'd like to talk a little about what it means to have me as your advisor."

"Okay."

"For many faculty, being an advisor means nothing more than

seeing your advisee once a semester and signing off on her schedule. It means much more than that to me, Elisa. Just as most learning takes place outside of a classroom, most advising should take place out of the confines of your advisor's office. I feel I would be doing you a disservice if my only advising duties were telling you what classes to take. I want to advise you in a fuller sense—to help you find your identity and shape your future."

Elisa felt as if she might cry. "But why . . . why would a busy, successful person like you want to take that trouble?"

"Because you, Elisa, are a deep, untapped well of potential." She smiled. "And I want to see that potential realized—to see all that undiscovered brilliance burst forth like a geyser."

Elisa suppressed a giggle, but it bubbled out anyway. "Sorry . . . it's just funny to hear somebody like you talking about somebody like me being smart."

"That's because you don't know what you have yet. But I'm going to teach you." The waitress came with their food, and Dr. Rivers said, "How lovely!"

The little black rectangular dishes were indeed lovely, but Elisa didn't see how that word could describe what was on Dr. Rivers' plate, which looked as though it might crawl across the table and spring for Elisa's throat. The items on Elisa's own plate were less disturbing to look at, but they still didn't resemble anything she'd normally think of as food. A far cry from Mamaw's salmon patties, the round, flat rolls of rice with a glistening red chunk of fish in their centers looked more like votive candles than lunch. She watched Dr. Rivers capture a tentacle between her chopsticks.

"If you don't care for chopsticks," Dr. Rivers said, "it's perfectly acceptable to use your fingers. Just never use a fork; it destroys the integrity of the roll."

Elisa picked up a piece of sushi and bit into it. The seaweed was strange but not unpleasant, and while the taste of the salmon was okay, the texture—like fish-flavored Jell-O—was going to take some getting used to. The rice helped with the texture some, but she wished she had something to put on the sushi, like ketchup or tartar sauce. It was then that she noticed on her plate a little scoop of something bright green and slightly lumpy. She remembered Dr. Rivers saying that avocado came with the California roll, so maybe this was some smooshed-up avocado, like the guacamole she had tried once in a Tex-Mex place. She dipped her sushi roll into a generous amount of the green stuff.

"Be careful with the wasabi," Dr. Rivers began, but it was too late. The sushi roll was already in Elisa's mouth, and she might as well have chomped down on a pack of lit matches. Her tongue was melting like candle wax, her sinuses opened, and her nose and eyes poured. She grabbed her just-refilled cup of hot tea, which offered all the comfort of pouring boiling water on a second-degree burn. Somehow, though, while Elisa gasped and choked and sobbed, Dr. Rivers had managed to get a glass of ice water, which she poured between Elisa's burning lips.

Elisa grabbed the glass and guzzled its contents. When it was empty, she managed to gasp, "Oh . . . my . . . God. What *was* that?"

"Japanese horseradish," Dr. Rivers said. "It's a little hot."

"A little hot? I thought I'd burnt my tongue off! Can you imagine going through life as a lesbian without a tongue?" Her senses coming back, Elisa remembered who she was talking to. "I can't believe I just said that to a teacher."

To Elisa's relief, Dr. Rivers was laughing. "That's quite all right . . . especially given your recent trauma. I am sorry that happened, Elisa. I tried to warn you, but by the time the words were out of my mouth, it was too late."

Elisa wiped her eyes. She hated to think what her mascara probably looked like. "Well, if you wanted me to have a learning experience, I reckon I just had one."

"True, but it wasn't quite what I had in mind." Dr. Rivers patted Elisa's arm with surprising warmth. "In the future, I will try to dispense my advice in a more timely manner."

Beth

The girls always dressed up more than the guys did for the Halloween Howl. Beth's sisters were decked out in a variety of elaborate costumes, most of them revealing: a horned devil girl in red fishnets, a red vinyl bra and matching miniskirt; a would-be Playboy bunny; a naughty nurse. Quimby was wearing a huge, blond curly wig and gold hot pants and had declared herself a hooker. This, Beth thought, didn't constitute much of a lifestyle change for Quimby, except for the fact that her services would no longer be provided on a pro bono basis.

Beth's outfit was a little sexy but was positively nunlike compared with those of her sisters. She wore a black spandex unitard (and was thankful for the tummy-flattening powers of spandex), along with a black sequined kitty-cat mask that covered the top half of her face. She liked the way the costume made her feel, and the more she drank, the more she liked it. She had always liked Catwoman from *Batman*—liked her more than she could ever admit to the sisters and brothers around her—and now she felt like Catwoman: slinky and a little dangerous.

The guys had made some effort to make the house look Halloweeny by putting up some fake spiderwebs and screwing black-light bulbs into all the lamps. But in terms of looking Halloweeny themselves, they were a sorry bunch. Most were dressed in their usual T-shirts and shorts. A couple of guys had started off the evening wearing rubber monster masks but had tossed them aside because they interfered with their drinking. Chad, who, as Quimby explained it, had broken up with her although they still had sex sometimes, was wearing a T-shirt that read, *This is my Halloween costume.*

Mike was the only guy who had put any effort into his costume, and even he was clad in his usual Levi's and Nikes. Above the waist, though, he sported a loose-fitting white shirt, a red bandana on his head, a gold hoop earring and an eye patch. Beth stood beside him with her paper cup of what she had been told was Dead Man's Punch, which tasted suspiciously of orange Kool-Aid and pure grain alcohol.

"Hey, man," a beefy brother named Chris said, slapping Mike on the back and leering, "Looks like you'll be getting some *pussy* tonight!"

Beth smiled, though she was growing tired of this joke. If she had thought that every guy at the party was going to make it, each one of them thinking he was really clever for saying it, she would've picked another costume.

"Yeah," Chris's skinny sidekick, whom Beth didn't recognize, said, "can you make that pussy purr, man?"

"I don't think she has any complaints," Mike said. His tone was light and joking, but Beth could tell he was squirming inside.

"I sure don't," she said, leaning into Mike and putting her arm around him, "unless I was going to complain about what nasty minds you two have." She put on her sunniest smile so they'd know she was joking.

"Hey now, Amy never complains about my nasty mind, do you, Amy?" Chris said as Amy in her devil costume sidled up to him and giggled. "Just look at how horny she is!" He tugged on her headgear, and she giggled again.

"So what are you, man?" Chris's sidekick asked Mike. "A pirate?"

"Arrgh, that be right, matey," Mike growled.

"Well, man, as long as you're not a butt pirate, I guess that's all right," Chris said, and he and Amy and the skinny guy broke up laughing.

Beth made herself laugh, too, but she saw that Mike was frozen. He wasn't laughing, frowning or showing any emotion. He had, it appeared, mentally left the building. She had to help him because she knew he would do the same for her.

"Not unless it's my butt you're talking about, right, baby?" Beth stood on tiptoe, pulled Mike toward her and gave him a long, open-mouthed kiss.

To her relief, Mike had snapped out of it enough to kiss back, and Chris and Amy and a chorus of others cheered, "Woo-hoo!" and "Gettin' some pussy!"

Kissing Mike didn't feel gross. It didn't feel like anything. Kissing boys was like eating one of those styrofoam-textured rice cakes. It didn't make her want to gag or anything, but she couldn't fool herself into thinking she was experiencing the height of deliciousness like a hot fudge sundae or another girl's kisses.

"You saved my ass tonight," Mike said. They held hands partly to appear straight and partly to stand up straight as they staggered toward Beth's dorm.

"No problem," Beth said. "You would've done the same for me."

Mike looked around to make sure the sidewalk was as deserted as it appeared. "Butt pirate!" he said. "Fucking butt pirate . . . I had never heard that one before! If I had, you can damn sure bet I wouldn't have worn this costume!"

"Well, if it's any consolation, I wish I'd worn something else, too. All those pussy jokes . . ."

"Yeah, but those were just because you're a cute girl. Not because you're a—"

"Chris didn't say butt pirate because he thought you *were* one. He was just playing with you. You know how Chris is."

"Yeah, how he is tonight is high on coke. That little twitchy guy with him is his dealer. Sometimes, especially when he's fucked up, it's like Chris can *smell* that I'm different."

"With all the coke he snorts, Chris couldn't smell a skunk if it was sitting in his lap, and you know it. You're just paranoid when you're drunk."

"I probably am," Mike said. "I mean, I'm probably paranoid, but I'm definitely drunk." He let go of Beth's hand. "Hey, let's go up to the place."

"The place" was always the Merry-Go-Round. Beth looked at her watch. "It's almost one thirty."

"So? They're open till three, and you know it's gotta be wild on Halloween. And besides . . ." He leaned in close. "Some lovely lezzie might want to pet this pussy."

Beth rolled her eyes. "If I go, do you promise that's the last pussy joke I'll hear tonight?"

Mike arched an eyebrow. "I promise that's the last pussy joke *I'll* tell tonight. I can't speak for the lesbians of Knoxville."

Even though it was almost two, the Merry-Go-Round was packed. Here, though, the devil girls and naughty nurses were boys. A drag queen in full vampire regalia—"Count Dragula," Mike whispered to Beth— swooped across the stage lip-synching "Total Eclipse of the Heart." Celebrity costumes were also popular. Looking around, Beth spotted a Marilyn Monroe, a Janet Jackson, a Tina Turner and two Madonnas. But where were the real women? She didn't have much time to find one.

Drunkenly trying to maneuver her way through the press of partiers, she bumped into a drag queen who was at least 6'5" and dressed as Cruella de Vil. "I want puppies, not pussy!" he screeched when he got a look at her outfit.

"It seems that your frat brothers and drag queens have a similar sense of humor," she shouted to Mike over Cher's "Bang Bang," which was being performed by a queen in a Cher-like wig, chaps and buttfloss.

"God, I love Cher!" Mike said, staring at the stage. "What did you say, hon?"

"Nothing," Beth shouted back. It was so loud and she was so drunk it didn't seem worth the effort to repeat herself. "What do you want to drink?" she said instead.

"I don't know. I want to keep my buzz going, but I don't want to make myself puke, you know?"

Beth did know. She wanted to stay drunk but wasn't sure how her body would react to more alcohol after an evening of PGA and Kool-Aid. "How about just a beer?"

"Perfect. Corona and lime."

She pushed past the Marilyns and Madonnas to place her order with the bartender, who was dressed as a nun. As Beth turned around with a beer in each hand, she saw, through a parting of the crowd, a black-cloaked figure. It was an opera cloak draped over a slim pair of shoulders. The figure wore a black suit with a white sash, white gloves and, on its face, a white mask that obscured its features on one side. The Phantom of the Opera.

Mother and Daddy had taken Beth to see *The Phantom of the Opera* in New York for her high school graduation present. It had been the most incredible experience of her life. She had sat, rapt, engrossed in the music and the spectacle and the darkness of it all, even though her father kept shifting in his seat and checking his watch. For the whole show, Beth had felt her heart pounding, and when the chandelier fell, she had screamed. The phantom himself made her swoon—true, he was male, and she had already figured out that males were not her preference—but everything else had been perfect: the dark, brooding mystery; the beautiful suffering of being a misunderstood outsider.

And now the phantom was standing only a few yards away from her. But this phantom was quite possibly female. Beth had to find out.

The phantom turned, its cape billowing as it descended the spiral staircase that led to the lower level of the club. Beth handed Mike his Corona, saying only "Here," and followed the phantom.

Downstairs she found the phantom standing near the bar, a Rolling Rock in one white-gloved hand.

Beth knocked back half her beer, sucked in her tummy and approached. "Um . . . hi," she yelled over the pounding disco.

"Hey." The phantom's voice was low, but definitely female. "This beer doesn't quite work with this outfit, does it? I need a glass of champagne or something. Actually, my roommate told me I shouldn't wear this costume at all. She said it was totally lame, but then she can't understand how I can love punk rock but love musical theater, too. I tell her I'm just exploring my inner faggot. So . . . you're about the last person I'd expect to see here."

"What do you mean?"

"You're just not the type, that's all. Usually if you see long blond hair and a beautiful, made-up face around these parts, then you're not looking at a biological woman. But I bet you're here as somebody's fag hag, am I right?"

"No." Beth couldn't quite wrap her mind around how she was feeling. Drunk, yes, but the energy buzzing through her was more than the alcohol. When she opened her mouth, she was shocked by the words that spilled out: "I'm here because I want you."

The phantom choked on her beer. "Whoa! Well, that was certainly direct."

Heat rushed to Beth's face. "I'm sorry."

The phantom pressed a gloved finger to Beth's lips. "Stop. Women spend too much time apologizing for what they want. You should be proud of your directness."

The phantom chugged down the rest of her beer. "So . . . you want to get out of here?"

Beth was tingling all over. "Yes."

The phantom offered Beth her arm and escorted her through the crowd. Once they emerged into the cool night air, the phantom said, "So . . . my place? It's close by."

Beth hesitated. Usually her rule was not to go home with anybody. In a private space with a stranger it was too easy to get yourself into a situation you couldn't get out of. But if she was going to live out this fantasy, then she couldn't exactly let the phantom fuck her up against the wall of a Laundromat or in the cramped backseat of a crappy compact car. No. She needed to be ravished on a bed, stretched out and luxuriating in the caresses of her dark phantom lover. "Okay."

On the living room couch in the dilapidated student shack, two women—one bald, one with long, dyed-black hair—were locked in a passionate embrace. They didn't come up for air to acknowledge Beth and her escort. "My roommate," the phantom whispered, "and a new friend, apparently."

Beth followed the phantom down the hall into a bedroom with a crimson-spreaded bed canopied by sheer purple curtains. The phantom flicked on a lamp that was covered by a dark paisley scarf and gave off a muted glow. "I'd like to light some candles, if that's okay with you."

"That would be perfect," Beth managed to say even though she could barely breathe.

The phantom lit six candles on the bedside table, turned off the lamp and stood face-to-face with Beth. "Will you take off your mask?" she whispered.

Beth pulled off the cat mask and tossed it aside, but when the phantom reached for her own mask, Beth whispered, "No. Leave it on."

"*Oh*," said the phantom. "I get it. This is some kind of fantasy you're playing out, right?"

"Right." Beth felt her face grow hot again. "Is that okay?"

"Hell, yeah. I love role-playing. Hey, I've got an idea. Just a sec."

The phantom riffled through a box near the bed, grabbed a cassette and popped it into the boombox. The lush sound of strings filled the room as the overture from *Phantom of the Opera* swelled from the speakers. Beth's heart swelled, too, as her phantom lifted her up and carried her to the bed.

It was hard to kiss without disturbing the mask, so the phantom mostly used her hands, peeling off Beth's unitard and stroking her skin with white-gloved fingers. Beth was so used to quick fucks in alleys that to be stretched out on a soft bed and stroked in a leisurely fashion seemed strange, though not as strange as the fact that these strokes were coming from a figure from her fantasies. As the phantom leaned over her, nuzzling her neck, her naked body was also stroked by the slick satin of the phantom's cape. Soon the phantom removed one glove and reached a part of Beth that, Beth was sure, also had to be as slick as satin. The phantom moved inside her in rhythm with the music, and by the time in the soundtrack when the chandelier falls, Beth felt pleasure lighting her up like a thousand shining crystals.

When the music stopped, Beth gasped. "That . . . that was great."

"Don't say 'was' just yet. That was only the first act. Are you ready for Act Two?" The phantom sprung from the bed, flipped over the tape and then settled down with her head between Beth's thighs.

At first Beth thought about pushing her away. Only one person had done that to her before, and it had been so special . . . something that they, for the longest time, thought that only they had figured out how to do. But that had been way back in high school.

Beth closed her eyes, and the waves of her drunkenness mixed with the waves of her pleasure. She couldn't push this woman away, not now. She fell deeper and deeper into the rhythm until she was falling, falling into a depth of pleasure she hadn't felt in so long . . . pleasure so deep that after she fell there, she fell even further, into sleep.

When the morning sun streamed through the window, Beth awoke in a panic, her mouth parched and her head muzzy with the aftereffects of the aptly named Dead Man's Punch. Where the hell was she, anyway? When she remembered, she leapt from the bed, horrified at the prospect that all she had to put on was her black kitty-cat costume. She struggled into her unitard and stepped into her shoes and prayed that nobody in the house was awake. Last night's phantom lay in the bed she had just left, her back to Beth. Beth tiptoed out of the room, making it a point not to peek at the phantom's face.

Still hungover, but freshly showered and somewhat recovered from her kitty-cat costumed Walk of Shame, Beth slid behind her desk in Women in Lit. She hadn't done her reading for this class or any other today, but really, what kind of nerd would stay home and study on Halloween night?

Beth watched her classmates file into the room; the dykey-looking chick whose hair was dyed magenta this week; the country girl who needed to get rid of those '80s mall bangs; the olive-skinned, hairy-legged dyke who could never keep her mouth shut in class. When the hairy dyke passed her, she dropped a folded sheet of notebook paper on Beth's desk. Figuring it must be some kind of mistake, Beth unfolded it and read:

I had a really good time last night.

—your Phantom

The room was getting smaller. The walls were closing in, the ceiling was lowering, and soon Beth knew she would be crushed against all these students whose faces were grotesque masks as they talked (about her?) and laughed (at her?). She couldn't stay here. She'd die if she stayed. There was no air in the room. With shaking hands, she stuffed her book and notebook into her backpack, then ran up the aisle and toward the door, bumping smack into Dr. Rivers, who was just entering the room.

"Beth, are you okay?" Dr. Rivers asked, steadying herself against the door frame.

Beth didn't answer. She just ran because to her ears, the question Dr. Rivers had asked her sounded far too much like, "Beth, are you gay?"

Liz

The old man carrying the bloody fetus sign elbowed Liz out of his way.

"Excuse me!" Liz called out to him. "If you're so pro-life, maybe you should try not to flatten people!"

The old man ignored her and yelled up at the podium, "You're killin' the babies, Sally!"

The speaker behind the podium, which had been set up in front of the courthouse steps, was Sally Marshall, the president of the National Women's Association. Dr. Marshall was doing a speaking tour in the Southern states, turning each engagement into a rally for those who were for her and those who were against her. Flyers advertising her speech had been posted all over campus, and the Students for Life group had defaced them with stickers reading, *Wanted for the Murder of Innocent Babies*. Dr. Rivers had urged her students to attend Sally Marshall's speech to show their feminist commitment.

But actually hearing the speech was no easy task, over the din of Mr. "You're-Killin'-the-Babies!" and his kind. Scanning the crowd, Liz saw that many of the anti-choice demonstrators had selected the bloody fetus motif for their signs, while a few others went for the more subtle *Thou Shalt Not Kill.* Liz wondered how these particular demonstrators felt about the war.

It was fascinating, too, to observe the differing fashions of the differing factions. The old pro-lifers tended to favor polyester clothing, with long, stringy hair for the women and barbershop-close clips for the men. College-age pro-lifers favored the preppy look . . . button-down shirts and chinos for the guys, pastel sweaters and slacks for the girls. The pro-choice folks, though, wore T-shirts with lefty slogans. The men were more likely to have the long, stringy hair and the women the barbershop-close clips. Both factions were looking at their opposites, Liz imagined, and thinking, *People like that are what's wrong with America.*

"Old Bloody Fetus got me there, too," a voice behind Liz said. "I'm pretty sure he's the same guy that knocked me flat at that other rally."

Liz turned around to see Audrey in a white blouse and super-short plaid skirt. A huge crucifix hung around her neck, and she wielded a sign reading, *Catholic Schoolgirls for Choice.*

"Wow," Liz said. "You're a walking blasphemy."

Audrey smiled. "I like to think so."

"So, um . . ." Liz struggled with the torturous shyness that swept over her in Audrey's presence. "Have you been to any more women's group meetings?" She kept meaning to go again, but she always seemed to have something going with Dan on those nights.

"Oh, Thalia's women's group kind of petered out." Audrey grinned. "Although maybe 'peter' isn't the word I should use. But hey, there's a party at my place tonight. It's for All Souls' Day, or so my silly-ass goth roommate says. You should come. We need to have a conversation sometime that's not in a politically charged setting."

"I might be able to make it."

"Do. And wear black or white and BYOB." Audrey stumbled when Mr. You're-Killin'-the-Babies bumped into her. "You know," she said to the old man, "what I don't get about your poster is . . . okay, well, of course it's disturbing to look at. But I would find a picture of any surgical procedure disturbing to look at. If you had a poster of an appendectomy instead of an abortion, I'd find it icky, too. And they're the same thing, aren't they? The surgical removal of something your body doesn't need."

Liz was afraid the old man might hit her, but Audrey flounced away before he had the chance. All he could do was yell something about praying for her, but his yell was absorbed by all the other yells of all the other protesters. Meanwhile, Sally Marshall continued to stand behind the podium, speaking passionately but inaudibly. Liz hoped that Dr. Rivers wouldn't ask her about the content of Marshall's speech. The woman could be up there talking about needlepoint, for all Liz could tell.

All day Liz had felt like she should get in touch with Dan to see if he wanted to come with her to the party. But something had stopped her. It wouldn't have been hard to find him. He was probably drinking pitchers down at Mario's, or else he was at Stu and Todd's doing bong hits and watching videos of old *Star Trek* episodes. She told herself that she was too lazy to walk all the way to Stu and Todd's and she couldn't call them because their phone had been disconnected again, but she knew that wasn't the real reason. The truth was that she wanted to go to this party alone, a fact that surprised and puzzled her.

Usually she relied on Dan to be the dominant one in social situations. He'd get the conversation up and running, and she'd chime in occasionally with a witty one-liner. But for some reason she couldn't quite figure out, she wanted Audrey to see her without Dan, to see the person she was on her own, even if that person was shy and awkward.

She could hear the party before she could see it. From almost a block away, the dance music and laughter reached her ears. Liz felt all her insecurities wash over her and thought of turning back and heading toward the Sagebrush, toward the comfort of the familiar. *No*, she told herself. *You said you would go to this party, and you will go.* She unscrewed the cap of the forty of Schlitz Malt Liquor she was carrying and chugged down a few ounces. Feeling braver, she screwed the cap back on and picked up her pace toward the ramshackle green-and-yellow Victorian house from which the sound of the Cure's "Kiss Me Kiss Me Kiss Me" was now discernable. She smiled, thinking of what Audrey said about her goth roommate.

The porch was packed with pasty-skinned, black-clad guys smoking cigarettes and passing around a bottle of Chianti, which they were pouring into paper cups. Liz opened the screen door to a room of uncompromising whiteness. White sheets had been tacked to the walls and ceiling and draped over the furniture. White packing peanuts covered the floor like snow. Bare white lightbulbs glowed overhead, and white-clad guests gathered in clumps, drinking and laughing. Audrey was nowhere in sight, and for a moment Liz wished she hadn't come . . . or at least, that she hadn't come alone.

Just as she was about to slip out to the Sagebrush, a tall figure with red hair and a white evening gown moved toward her, almost floating over the packing peanuts on the floor, and Liz was reminded of Glinda the Good Witch from *The Wizard of Oz.*

"Well, aren't you adorable with your little pink butch cut, clutching that big bottle of beer in your tiny little hand!" This version of Glinda, Liz realized, was a guy, albeit a very skinny one with delicate wrists and hands. His perfectly applied makeup was heavier than that of any biological woman, short of Mary Kay herself, and a telltale Adam's apple bulged above his glittering rhinestone necklace.

The white queen extended a hand. "I'm Margo." On impulse, Liz kissed the hand instead of shaking it. "I'm Liz. Audrey invited me."

"Oh, she'll be tickled you're here. She was just saying this soiree was low on lesbians." Before Liz could correct the implication, Margo swept her arm outward to encompass the room. "So this is the white room . . . Heaven, we're calling it. If you want to find Audrey, you'll see her in Hell." Margo tittered. "That joke should be getting old by now, but I still like it. Audrey said that Heaven and Hell were too Judeo-Christian . . . that we ought to call the different rooms Yin and Yang or something. But yin and yang are like stalagtites and stalagmites to me . . . I can never remember which is which."

"Well, the Heaven/Hell thing does fit right in with All Souls' Day," Liz said. A potent bit of Catholic imagery flashed in her mind. "And besides, that makes you the Queen of Heaven."

Liz drank some more Schlitz and wandered through Heaven. She spotted Thalia, in a white T-shirt and white painter's pants, having an intense conversation with a guy in a white sarong-like garment that made him look like a Hare Krishna who'd had a run-in with some Clorox.

Liz herself was wearing a black turtleneck with black pants and a black tuxedo jacket, so being in the white room was starting to make her feel like the proverbial fly in the buttermilk. She followed the sound of the Cure to the room at the end of the hall. The walls were painted black, and black cloth hung over the window. The one place to sit in the room, a double bed, was covered with a black bedspread. A black light provided just enough illumination to keep Liz from bumping into other partygoers.

"Liz!" Audrey was sitting on the foot of the bed between two guys, one all gothed out with black eyeliner and black hair in Robert Smith-style spikes. The other, an older, slender guy with a five o'clock shadow and a black turtleneck identical to Liz's, was smoking a thin, beautifully rolled joint.

"Hey," Liz said. Standing over Audrey, she could see straight down the top of her low-cut black dress—a fact that made her turn her attentions to peeling the label off her bottle of Schlitz.

"That's a sign of sexual frustration, you know," Goth boy said. "Peeling the label."

"It's also one of the parlor games in *Who's Afraid of Virginia Woolf?*" the five o'clock shadow guy said. "That should be our next theme party, Audrey. An Edward Albee evening. We can all get drunk and hurl insults at each other."

"And how would that be different from our usual evenings?" Audrey said, then looked up at Liz. "Liz, these are two of my housemates and sparring partners. Gideon the Goth here is the maniac who painted this room black. And Derek is a fellow grad student in the theater department."

Gideon only nodded at Liz, but Derek grinned and proffered his joint. "Would you care to help me out with this doobie, Liz? Audrey's too clean-living to be any fun, and Gideon's afraid that if he takes a toke, somebody will mistake him for a hippie."

"Well, lucky for you, I'm neither clean-living nor image-conscious." Liz took the joint between her thumb and forefinger and inhaled gratefully. Between her forty of malt liquor and the free weed, she no longer feared inadequate social lubrication.

"You probably already met our other roomie," Audrey said. "She's the official greeter."

"Margo?" Liz wondered if Margo was Margo all the time or if he had just donned drag for this occasion.

"That's her," Audrey said. "She can work a room like nobody's business. You know, maybe the white/black thing isn't about heaven or hell so much as personality types."

"The extroverts and the introverts?" Gideon said.

"Exactly," Liz said. "Listen to all that racket coming from the white room, and in here we're quiet as little mice." She thought about the mingling folks in the white room. Thalia was an extrovert if ever Liz saw one. Here, though, people were huddled in small groups or talking one-on-one. But what about Audrey? She of the bold opinions and the pantyless protesting. "But you're not an introvert, Audrey."

"Sure I am. I can be loud sometimes, but don't let that fool you. I mean, look at me. Here I am at a party with half the neighborhood here, and who do I sit and talk to? The two people I talk to every damn day and night." Audrey smiled. "Well, and one more person I've been wanting to know better, so I guess I'm not totally helpless."

Liz busied herself with drawing on the joint to hide her self-consciousness.

"Liz should come to Tea and Sympathy sometime," Derek said.

"Definitely," Audrey said. "Every Wednesday at four we have tea for whoever wants to come. It's always a small gathering . . . much more my scene than this sort of thing, which was Margo and Gideon's idea. But now Gideon's too depressed to enjoy it."

"Boyfriend trouble," Gideon explained, lighting a cigarette.

"I've had to physically restrain him to keep him from playing 'Tainted Love' all night," Derek said.

A white-clad, mustachioed man flounced into the room carrying a big black camera. "Hide the pot, people! It's picture time!"

"Oh, no, it's the paparazzi." Gideon groaned.

"I'm not the paparazzi; I am an artiste. Now put out that doobie, Derek. We don't want anything too incriminating."

Derek stubbed out the joint in an ashtray. "I swear, Shaun, one day I'm going to pull a Sean Penn on you and smash that camera of yours."

"Well, if you were as cute as Sean Penn, I just might let you." Shaun adjusted his camera. "Now, let me see if the flash will work in this black hole of Calcutta. Scrunch together, people."

Derek pulled Liz down so she was sitting on the bed squeezed between him and Audrey. Liz felt Audrey's thigh pressed against hers, and as the camera flashed, Audrey pressed her lips against Liz's cheek. "I'm glad you came tonight," Audrey whispered.

And Liz, whether it was from the flash, the weed, the kiss or some combination thereof, saw purple and orange and green lights dancing toward her out of the blackness.

Elisa

Jo leaned forward, propelling the bowling ball from her hand down the center of the alley. "Strike!" she yelled, just one second before the ball knocked down all ten pins. Jo turned to smile at Elisa. "See if you can beat that, missy."

"You know I can't," Elisa said. "But I'll take a turn just to give your arm a rest."

Elisa could never figure out why Jo's competitiveness came out when the two of them played a game together. Whether it was bowling, pool, badminton or anything else that required motor skills, it was always a sure bet that Jo would come out the winner, even if she didn't put forth any effort.

But Jo always put forth effort. She played every game, whether it was bowling at the student center or badminton at a backyard barbecue, like it was an Olympic event. And when Elisa played especially badly, rolling the ball straight into the gutter or missing the birdie entirely, Jo would chide her, saying, "Put some effort into it, why don't you? It's not that you're bad; it's just that you don't try hard enough."

Jo probably had a point. Elisa didn't put much effort into games. Why should she try so hard at play that it turned into work? She put so much effort into her schoolwork she didn't have much competitive energy left for anything else. She guessed that's how Jo was about sports—she used up so much of her energy on softball there wasn't much left for schoolwork. And when Elisa and Jo got their grade cards at the end of every term, Elisa chided Jo the same way Jo chided her about games: *It's not that you're bad; it's just that you don't try hard enough.*

"Are you gonna go? I ain't getting any younger back here," Jo hollered.

"Yeah . . . sorry." Elisa hurled the ball without paying any attention to what foot she led with or any of the other details Jo had lectured her about. But the ball did manage to stay out of the gutter. It even knocked down a couple of pins.

"Nice try," Jo said. "You should've led with your other foot, though."

Elisa poked Jo in the ribs. "Stop coaching."

"Sorry, lady. It's just that I can see how you ought to be doing it."

"And you can't resist explaining it to me. I know." Elisa did know. She had tried to show Jo how to fix her English papers—how to rearrange her ideas and develop them more. But it had only ended in frustration.

Another strike for Jo, who pumped her fist in victory. "I'm gonna get me another Pepsi. You want another Diet?"

"Sure." Elisa watched Jo lumber happily to the snack bar. She wondered what Dr. Rivers would think of this place, with its cheap, molded plastic chairs; waxy cups of watered-down soda; and rented shoes sprayed with an alleged "disinfectant." Dr. Rivers would probably feel as out of place here as Elisa had at that sushi restaurant.

The strange thing was that Elisa didn't feel like she belonged here either. Or at least she didn't want to belong. She didn't want to be like her parents and the other folks back in Odessa, who celebrated the end of a mind-numbing week with a Friday evening of frozen pizza and tepid beer at the bowling alley. Even the vocabulary of bowling sounded low-class: Alley. Gutter.

When Elisa had told Dr. Rivers about being a teenaged lesbian in a small Appalachian town, Dr. Rivers had looked as though she might cry. "I can't imagine coming out under those circumstances," she had said. "Now, granted, at least I had the advantage of coming out in a cosmopolitan environment where, except for my undergraduate students, I didn't even know anyone with less than a master's degree. Except for my husband, who, understandably, was a little upset, everyone I told was supportive. The more educated circles you move in, the more you can insulate yourself from prejudice and narrow-mindedness."

Elisa looked around the bowling alley. As soon as she and Jo had walked in she'd felt judgmental eyes on her, from the guy at the shoe rental booth to the straight couple in the next lane, everybody's look said, *We know what you are.* If she moved in the same circles as Dr. Rivers, would she be free of such stares?

"Are you okay, lady? You're awfully quiet tonight."

Elisa wasn't sure if she was okay. With Dr. Rivers' help, she knew she was in the process of changing into the woman she wanted to become, but right now she was in an early, awkward stage of change—like a tadpole that had grown legs but wasn't yet enough of a frog to hop out of the pond. "I'm fine," she said. "Just tired."

Beth

Beth hadn't left her room for two days. She had told Quimby she thought she had the flu, and Quimby had been so sweet, making canned chicken noodle soup in the hot pot and fetching orange juice from the cafeteria, that Beth felt even worse for lying. She didn't touch the soup or juice and declined Quimby's offer to drive her to the student clinic.

Beth knew she was going to have to do something. There were only so many sorority meetings you could miss before your sisters started checking up on you, so many classes you could miss before you flunked out entirely.

With Quimby safely gone to her afternoon classes, Beth made herself sit up. She caught a brief, horrifying glimpse of herself in the mirror, her hair matted and her eyes puffy from two days of nonstop crying. She was tempted to flop back down and pull the covers over her head, but instead she steeled herself and picked up the phone.

"Epsilon house."

Beth cleared her throat. "Is Mike Turner there, please?" Her voice was nasal from crying and scratchy from disuse.

"Hello?"

"It's Beth."

"You don't sound like yourself. Are you okay?"

She swallowed hard to suppress a sob. "Listen, Mike. I, uh . . . I need to see you."

"It's Beer Bust over at the Half Time tonight. You wanna go there?"

"No, listen. I need to talk to you alone."

"Oh." She could hear the fear in his voice. "Okay, well, then why don't I pick you up around seven? We can go for a drive or something."

"Okay." She couldn't talk anymore; her throat had closed, and her eyes burned with tears.

Beth sat in the passenger seat of Mike's BMW. She had showered and brushed her hair but couldn't do a damn thing about her swollen eyes, so she was wearing sunglasses even though it was dusk.

"I thought we might go to the park," Mike said.

The park was on a lake in Cherokee Hills, Knoxville's most expensive neighborhood—the neighborhood where Beth had grown up until her parents decided to build a house in the country. The park was full of happy, prosperous people—slim, muscled joggers, laughing children, a young couple throwing a tennis ball to a perpetually delighted golden retriever. Mike put the car in park, then turned to Beth and said, "Okay, what's wrong? Nobody at the place roughed you up the other night, did they? You look like a battered wife in those sunglasses."

"My eyes are just puffy from crying." She took off the glasses and let him see. "I . . . uh . . . the other night I met somebody at the Merry-Go-Round."

"I kinda figured since you bailed on me."

"Yeah. Sorry about that, but you know how drunk I was."

"I know all too well."

"There was this . . . this woman dressed like the Phantom of the Opera."

"I saw her."

"Yeah, well, I went home with her. She kept the mask and costume on."

Mike grinned. "Superfreak."

Beth couldn't return his smile. "Yeah, I am. So in the morning I went home with no idea who this woman was . . . I didn't know her name, and I hadn't seen her face." She took a deep breath, trying to prepare herself for the next part of the story. "But later I'm sitting in women's studies, and this woman drops a note on my desk that she signed, 'your Phantom.' And it's this loud, hairy dyke who's always running her mouth in class. And so . . . she knows who I am."

Mike gaped. "Holy shit! Holy shit, Beth. This is bad."

"I know." She did know, but hearing him say it made the tears start again. "I don't know what I'm gonna do, Mike. I've not been back to class, but I can't just quit going altogether, or I'll flunk. I'm hanging on the edge of a C in that class anyhow."

"Okay, let me think." He stared out at the lake for what felt like an hour, then said, "Here's what you do. You go to that class, but you get there five to ten minutes late and leave five to ten minutes early. It'll probably piss off your professor a little bit, but at least that way you'll be showing up, and you can get in and out without your friend the Phantom getting the chance to talk to you. And besides, the class is almost over; you won't have to worry about her for long."

"But what if she follows me out of class and tries to talk to me?"

"Then you cut her dead." Mike's tone was cool and even. "You say she's real dykey-looking?"

"Oh, yeah. She wears camouflage pants and is covered in hair everywhere but her head."

He smiled. "Then it's easy. If she comes up and talks to you, act like she's crazy, like you have no idea what she's talking about or why she's talking to you. I mean, really, among people who matter, who's going to take the word of someone like her over you?"

Beth wiped her eyes. She had known Mike would be able to help her. "You're right. You know what sucks, though? I had a really good time with her."

"Well, you play, you pay. That's how life works."

"Yeah. Sucks, though." She looked through the windshield at the happy people in the park and felt that there was more than just a layer of glass separating her from them. She watched the young couple, the handsome guy in a Jimmy Buffett T-shirt and the blond girl with her swinging ponytail as they held hands and laughed, their golden retriever frolicking at their heels. Beth felt her tears start again—big, hot and angry. "You know, Mike," she said, "I look at that couple laughing with their big, stupid dog, and I think, why can't you and I be like that? Everything would be so . . . easy."

"Yeah, well, you and I can't be like that couple for the same reason that little Pomeranian over there can't be a golden retriever. He's a different breed." Mike's blue eyes were intense and serious. "But I'll tell you one advantage we have that little pipsqueak of a dog doesn't. As tiny as he is, nobody will ever mistake him for a big dog. But with us . . ." He reached out and took Beth's hand. "Our difference is all on the inside. As long as we're careful, nobody will see it."

Liz

"Have you ever been diagnosed with a sexually transmitted disease?" the elderly black nurse asked in a tone that suggested she had asked this question a hundred times a day for the past decade.

Liz sat on the edge of the examining table, rattling the paper under her as she shifted. "No, ma'am."

"How many sexual partners have you had?" Her inflection didn't rise at the end of the question; she rattled off the syllables like the nuns in high school saying their Hail Marys.

"Just one," Liz said.

The nurse cocked an incredulous eyebrow but marked her chart just the same.

Why was it so hard to believe that Liz had only been with one person? Maybe her dyed hair and funky clothes signified promiscuity to some people. But the truth was that back in high school, her bohemian looks and outlook had marked her as too much of a weirdo to be dateable, let alone fuckable. She had come to college a virgin and met Dan who, despite his claim of having had several girlfriends in high school, was also a virgin.

That's why it was so perfect that she was going to surprise him by getting on the pill. They didn't need condoms because neither of them had a prior sexual history. Plus, she thought that condoms were probably the reason her and Dan's sex life was currently less than perfect. Dan hated condoms and often lost all sexual interest when confronted with one. He said they destroyed sensation, and as a result, in their two years of dating, Dan and Liz had only attempted actual sexual intercourse four times. Each time was abbreviated and marked by pain for her and, it always seemed to her, boredom for Dan, who claimed to feel nothing through the latex. But now, with the pill, they could dispense with the latex altogether and be as close as a man and woman could be to each other. Liz had heard a lot of girls, her roommate included, go on and on about the pleasures of condomless sex with their boyfriends. She wanted to feel what other girls felt.

"If you'll just wait on the table, the doctor will be in to examine you shortly."

But of course, it wasn't shortly at all, unless time was being measured geologically. Instead Liz had at least half an hour to freeze in her flimsy examination gown and feel the paper on the table sticking to her bare behind. She thought back to the sex ed class she'd had her senior year at Saint Boniface, taught by a red-faced priest who fervently believed that taking the pill was the equivalent of murdering a whole day-care center full of babies. Her mom's views on birth control were decided more from practicality than religion, but still, Liz wasn't sure that her mom would approve of her starting the pill. At least not in order to have sex with Dan, whom, for all her mother's politeness, it was still quite obvious she hated.

Liz remembered the look on her mother's face the first time she brought Dan home for a visit. At dinner, Dan had pushed around the Campbell's soup-based casserole on his plate, his thin upper lip curled in disdain. Liz had seen her mother look at Dan and felt she was reading her mother's thoughts: *This boy is a snob.* Her mother detested snobs, and

Liz wished she could make her mom understand that he wasn't one. He was just sophisticated.

The exam room door swung open, and in stepped a squat, balding man in a lab coat and a Mickey Mouse necktie—an accessory that might have put his patients at ease had he been a pediatrician. He was followed by the same bored nurse. "All right, miss, if you'll lie back on the table now."

Liz tried not to be an uptight English major, but she hated it when people treated dependent clauses as full sentences.

After Liz had lain as instructed, the doctor said, "If you'll let me examine your breasts."

She was tempted to say, "Then what? You'll give me a quarter?" She suppressed a giggle as he squeezed first one breast, then the other, as though they were produce he was testing for ripeness.

"And now if you'll put your feet in the stirrups."

Yippee-ki-ay, cowgirl, Liz thought, as she let the bored nurse guide her bare feet into position.

"And if you'll let me insert this speculum."

This speculum, Liz thought, which you've been keeping in the freezer for that special tongue-on-a-frozen-flagpole feeling. The doctor's finger felt as though it had spent some time in the deep freeze as well . . . it had all the warmth of a Popsicle lubed with K-Y. Before she had a chance to rejoice that the chilly digit had abandoned her nether regions, it penetrated another orifice, one that was much less accustomed to visitors.

"If you'll let me put my finger in your anus."

"You just did," Liz snapped.

"Ah, yes. So I did."

What would it be like, Liz wondered, to put your finger up so many people's butts everyday that you didn't even notice you were doing it? This dude was probably sleepwalking through hundreds of birth-control-seeking girls' gynecological exams like the guy in a slaughterhouse whose job is to stun every cow that comes through the line.

"If you'll go ahead and get dressed, the nurse will get you your pill packets."

At last the man had finally uttered a complete sentence.

• • •

Staggering back from the Sagebrush, her stomach sloshing with beer, Liz felt some of the K-Y from the morning's ordeal squish into her panties. She needed to tell Dan her secret. She took his hand.

"Too many pitchers?" he said. "Need help walking?"

"No, I just felt like holding hands."

"Well, all right." He sounded puzzled, but he didn't let go.

When they approached the courtyard of her dorm, Liz said, "You want to sit on the bench for a minute?"

"Sure. I was going to sit here and smoke a cigarette anyway."

They sat on the bench, Liz on the seat, Dan perched on the back. She watched his unvarying cigarette ritual: tapping one halfway out of the pack, then catching it between his lips, flicking his silver Zippo and inhaling with a look of real pleasure. Once the cigarette pack and Zippo were back in his jacket pocket, Liz swallowed hard and said, "I . . . uh . . . have a surprise for you." As soon as she said it, she felt stupid. How could she have opened an adult conversation so childishly?

"Really? Do tell."

Liz found herself staring at the bricks of the courtyard instead of looking at Dan. "Well, uh, I know you don't like condoms, and since I've not been using anything else, it's kind of put a damper on our sex life. But today I went to the doctor and got on the pill, so we won't have to make any more drunken late-night runs to the convenience store." She took a deep breath since all her words had tumbled out together. "No more latex. Just you and me with nothing between us."

Dan stared into the distance a long time and then said, without looking at her, "Actually, Liz, I haven't been feeling very sexual lately."

She felt like she'd swallowed a rock, which was somehow expanding in her throat. "What . . . what do you mean?"

"Just what I said." His tone wasn't angry; it was as distant as the moon in the sky above them. "The last time we had sex, I didn't feel much of anything. I had all the appropriate biological responses, of course, but on a deeper level, it was devoid of meaning."

Liz had never cried in front of him before, but she was in danger of starting now. "Are . . . are you breaking up with me?"

He looked in her direction and favored her with a little smile. "Of course not. I simply don't feel like being sexual with you—or with anyone else—at this point in time. This feeling will probably change in the foreseeable future, and I'll let you know when it does. In the meantime, however, there's no need to start pharmaceutically altering your hormones."

"Oh," Liz said because she didn't think she could pronounce more than a syllable without sobbing.

Dan stood and dropped his cigarette butt in the ashtray beside the bench. "Good night, Liz." He gave a little mock bow and then walked away.

Saving her sobs until he was too far away to hear them, Liz stared at Dan's cigarette butt in the tray as it smoldered to ashes.

Elisa

"Elisa, may I see you for a moment?" Dr. Rivers asked over the shuffling and rustling of the students exiting class.

Dr. Rivers was wearing a lavender sweater that brought out the blue in her eyes. Elisa had found herself noticing a lot of physical details about Dr. Rivers lately—the colors she wore, the angles of her cheekbones, her elegant hands. Dr. Rivers was pretty. Elisa hadn't noticed this fact when Dr. Rivers was just her teacher, but now that they were friends, she could see it.

It was strange. Elisa had never been so physically aware of another feminine woman before—drawn to her softness and prettiness. Jo was handsome, but she'd laugh her head off if you called her pretty. Elisa supposed that her heightened awareness around Dr. Rivers was some kind of heroine-worshipping schoolgirl crush. When she looked at her teacher, she didn't feel sexual tension; she felt like a gawky little girl looking at a prima ballerina and thinking, *That's what I want to be.*

Elisa approached the podium and waited for what seemed like hours while Thalia, bless her heart, babbled on in great detail about her final paper and the silenced lesbian voice and a mishmash of other ideas that caused Dr. Rivers to nod politely.

When Thalia finally left with the assurance that her paper sounded very interesting indeed, Dr. Rivers said, "I'll be with you in a moment, Elisa," and then busily shuffled some papers until the last of the other students had left the classroom. When they were alone, she looked up from the papers and smiled. "Listen, I've decided to be naughty today and skip my office hours to do a bit of shopping. Care to join me?"

Elisa loved to shop. She could spend all day at the mall, looking for just the right shoes to go with a top. As opposed to Jo, who, if she needed shoes or a shirt, would proceed directly to one store and be in and out so fast it seemed like she was grabbing items for a scavenger hunt. It would be fabulous to shop with someone as tasteful and sophisticated as Dr. Rivers, but shopping required money. "I'd love to if I wasn't so broke."

"You don't have to buy anything," Dr. Rivers said, smiling. "I just wondered if you'd like to keep me company."

"Sure, okay." A warm glow washed over Elisa—the thrill of knowing that Dr. Rivers was choosing her for company.

In her car in the parking garage, Dr. Rivers said, "The first thing I've got to do is get rid of this sweater. It felt good this morning, but now it's far too warm." She pulled her sweater over her head and sat in the driver's seat in a purple lacy bra. Elisa felt herself coloring, but Dr. Rivers didn't seem to notice. She just reached into her backseat for a knit top that lay on top of a pile of books and other garments. "My car is my closet," she said, pulling the shirt over her head.

Elisa felt much more comfortable once Dr. Rivers was dressed again. It obviously meant nothing to someone of her sophistication to strip down to her bra in front of a student, but for Elisa, it was too much information to know what color underwear your teacher preferred.

"Well," Dr. Rivers said, turning the key in the ignition. "Shall we shop?"

Dr. Rivers didn't drive to the mall at all but to a tiny shop called La Dolce Vita. "This is the only store in Knoxville where I'd buy a scrap of clothing," she said. "I usually try to do my shopping in a real city, but I'm presenting at a conference this weekend, and I've got to have something to put on my back."

One window of La Dolce Vita displayed a faceless mannequin in a tailored but feminine pink-and-black suit holding a sign that said "Day." In the other window, another mannequin was wearing a strapless cocktail dress, also black and pink, and holding a sign that said "Evening."

When they walked in, a middle-aged lady with bobbed black hair looked up from the sweaters she was arranging and said, "Hello, Dr. Rivers. Looking for something special today?"

"I am, as a matter of fact, Sondra," Dr. Rivers said. "I'm presenting at a conference this weekend, and all the suits in my closet are positively threadbare."

"Well, we have some lovely fall suits over here." Sondra led Dr. Rivers to a rack of suits in all colors, from conservative charcoal and tan to fire engine red and canary yellow.

Elisa did not follow them. Instead, she wandered around the place, trying to take in everything: the jewel-toned cashmere sweaters arranged like a rainbow on a table, the dozens of dresses by designers whose names she knew only from magazines.

"What do you think of this suit?" Dr. Rivers called, and Elisa scurried to be near her.

Dr. Rivers was holding up a tailored suit jacket and matching skirt in a houndstooth pattern. "It's real nice," Elisa said, feeling the saleslady's eyes on her.

"Sondra, this is my friend Elisa," Dr. Rivers said.

As Elisa said hello, she felt herself beaming because Dr. Rivers had introduced her not as her student or advisee, but as her friend.

"I think maybe a red blouse with this," Dr. Rivers said, selecting a Liz Claiborne top from another rack.

While Dr. Rivers tried on the suit in the dressing room, Elisa browsed through the selection of blouses and dresses, lightly touching the rich fabric and shocking herself by peeking at the items' price tags. As she wandered around the boutique, she felt Sondra looking at her with a gaze that felt judgmental somehow.

"Come tell me what you think," Dr. Rivers called.

The suit fit Dr. Rivers as if it had been made for her. "It's beautiful," Elisa said, though she couldn't help noticing that the suit didn't go with those ugly sandals Dr. Rivers wore all the time.

"I see you staring at my Birkenstocks, and no, I'm not going to wear them to the conference. I'll squeeze my feet into some torturous dress shoes for the occasion."

When Dr. Rivers emerged from the dressing room in her old clothes, she touched Elisa on the shoulder. "Is there anything here you would like?"

Elisa laughed. "Well, I'd like all of it, but I can't afford any of it."

Dr. Rivers smiled. "Let me buy you something, then."

Elisa was overwhelmed and a little embarrassed by Dr. Rivers' generosity. "Oh, I could never let you do that!"

"Of course you could. Between my salary and my inheritance, I have plenty of money. And I know that as a college student, you don't have the money to buy yourself pretty things—"

"But—"

Dr. Rivers put her index finger to Elisa's lips to shush her. "Elisa, I'm afraid that as your advisor, I must insist. It's my professional responsibility. You see, Elisa, you have a brilliant mind, but your appearance doesn't reflect it. If you want a future in academia, you need to look like a woman to be taken seriously, not like a girl working the counter at a fast-food restaurant."

Elisa couldn't bring herself to tell Dr. Rivers that she had spent her summer being that girl. "I won't take charity."

"It's not charity; it's a gift. But if you'd prefer, perhaps you could give me some of your time in exchange for some of my money . . . helping me out in the office or maybe around the house."

This seemed fair to Elisa, especially when she thought about the jumbled piles of papers and books cluttering Dr. Rivers' office. The woman could obviously use some help. "Okay."

"Good. Now, do you know what I think would look fantastic on you?" She pulled out a royal blue suit with a collarless, gold-buttoned jacket. "It's very professional, but very feminine."

Elisa was in love with the suit as soon as she tried it on, and she made herself not look at the price tag so she wouldn't know how much

Dr. Rivers was spending on her. She would probably have to do years' worth of office work and housework to pay her back, like one of those indentured servants she read about in World Civ.

In the car, Dr. Rivers said, "If you don't mind, I'm going to stop at my hair salon before we head back to campus. I've got to get rid of these split ends. And I was thinking you might like a new hairstyle to go with your new suit."

Elisa felt the pinch of nervousness. Jo liked her hair the way it was, and except for the fact that styling and moussing it every morning was a pain, so did she. "I don't know. I've been wearing my hair like this since ninth grade."

"Which is exactly why you need a new style," Dr. Rivers said.

The salon was a far cry from the Kountry Kurl beauty shop where Elisa got her hair done in Odessa. Salon Bella was a luxurious place, all chrome and glass and black leather sofas in the waiting area. Elisa was paired with a hair stylist who was, incongruously, bald, with a single gold hoop in one ear.

When she sat down in the styling chair, the stylist ran his hands through her tresses while clucking, "Girl, this is what I call some Southern fried hair! Let's lean you back in the sink and wash some of the goop out." She lay back and let his nimble fingers massage her scalp. "Now . . ." he said. "Your friend told me you wanted something sleek and modern."

"Um, yeah," Elisa said.

By the time the stylist had finished snipping, stripping and conditioning, Elisa's hair was in a neat, straight, just-above-the-shoulders blunt cut, with a fringe of bangs across her forehead.

Dr. Rivers, whose hair looked the same as it had before, gave her a wide smile. "Fabulous!" she exclaimed. "Do you like it?"

Elisa looked down at the mass of curled, highlighted hair on the floor, then ran a hand over her straight bob. "I feel so different. Good, but different."

That evening, while Jo was at softball practice, Elisa tried on her new suit and stood in front of the mirror. She did look like a person to be taken seriously, a person who mattered.

The door swung open, and Jo looked at her in apparent confusion.

"Hi, honey." Elisa was nervous about how Jo was going to take this sudden change.

"Lady?"

"Dr. Rivers took me shopping today . . . and to a hair salon."

"I can see that," Jo said, approaching Elisa and stroking her newly sleek hair. "For a minute there, I thought I'd walked into the wrong room or something."

Elisa couldn't wait any longer to ask. "Do you like it?"

"Like it? Well, shoot, lady, you look beautiful. You're always beautiful. This is just a different kind of beautiful . . . like you're a lawyer on a TV show or something. I like it, I guess, but it's gonna take a little getting used to." She took both of Elisa's hands in hers and grinned sheepishly. "For a minute there, I didn't even know it was you."

Beth

"Wait!"

Shit. She had known it was going to happen sometime—that when she walked out of Women in Lit class early, Thalia was going to get up and follow her. What should she do? Stop, or walk faster? Up ahead in the hall, she saw Chad talking to another frat brother. She couldn't risk Thalia yelling at her again—couldn't handle Chad and his friend teasing her about some dyke chasing her down the hall of the humanities building. She stopped and turned to face her tormentor. "What?"

"Listen." Thalia shoved her hands into the pockets of her army pants, which, Beth noticed, were accessorized by a wallet with a chain. "I know I didn't give you any diseases or anything, so why are you avoiding me?"

Beth looked around frantically to make sure nobody had heard. "I . . . I can't talk to you here."

Thalia rolled her eyes. "Okay, so where can you talk to me? Why don't we go back to my house?"

"I can't. I've got another class."

"So come over after you're done with class."

Beth saw one of the Amys in her sorority colors coming down the hall. "Okay. After class. I've got to go."

After she turned to leave, Thalia called, "You are being honest with me, right? You will be there?"

Beth nodded, but she didn't stop walking. She didn't have another class right now. She just couldn't take the chance of anybody she knew seeing her walking with somebody who looked like Thalia.

By the time Beth got back to her room, she was shaking. She opened the dresser drawer that she and Quimby jokingly called the mini-bar, found an airplane bottle of Smirnoff and drank it straight down. The vodka warmed her empty stomach. Okay, so what the hell was she going to do? Obviously, hiding here was the easiest choice in the short-term, but avoiding Thalia would just make her more confrontational, more likely to cause a scene. So she would go talk to her. Once she got into the student slums, she wouldn't see anybody she knew. She would go to Thalia's and stay five minutes, during which time she would explain that nothing, not even a conversation, was ever going to happen between them again.

It was strange that she remembered the way to Thalia's house, as drunk as she'd been the night she went home with her. But it wasn't the blind stagger from the Merry-Go-Round that made her remember the route; it was the Walk of Shame from Thalia's house the morning after, hung over in her bedraggled kitty cat costume, terrified against all logic that someone somehow, upon seeing her, would know what she had done.

Thalia opened the door. "You came. I'm surprised."

From the couch where she was sitting with a young man in a Grateful Dead T-shirt who looked strikingly like Mick Jagger, Thalia's roommate called, "Thalia says that to her girlfriends all the time."

Beth was gripped by the urge to run, but Thalia said, "Come on in," right after she shot a joking "fuck off" to her roommate. Beth looked around the apartment—the picture of the ugly woman with one eyebrow like Bert on *Sesame Street*, the nose- and lip-ringed girl on the couch who was now straddling the Mick Jagger look-alike. What kind of place was this?

As she followed Thalia down the hall she said, "Your roommate. When I was here before, wasn't she—"

"Making out with a woman?" Thalia said. "Probably so. Our Chloe is a very adaptable girl. She's willing to work with all kinds of equipment."

Beth had heard, vaguely, of people who were bisexual, and in a way, she envied them. If it was just as satisfying to be with the opposite sex as with the same sex, then you could just choose the opposite sex—no worries, no fear.

Beth's stomach clenched when she saw Thalia's bedroom again. It was the last place she wanted to be, really, but given what was happening on the couch, they couldn't exactly talk in the living room.

Thalia sat down on the bed, her bare feet folded under her. "I thought I might smoke a joint. Will you join me?"

Despite having grown up with Nancy Reagan's admonition to just say no, Beth had said yes to pot a few times, but only at parties when she was drunk already. The effects of the pot, if any, had been impossible to detect through the buzz of the alcohol. Now, though, her nervousness had eaten away the effects of the tiny bottle of vodka she'd drunk, and she was willing to ingest anything that might dull the sharp edges of her panic. "Yeah, I guess so."

"Cool." Thalia reached into her nightstand and retrieved a joint and a lighter. She patted a spot on the bed next to her. "Come here."

Hot panic bubbled up in Beth's throat. "Uh . . ."

"Oh, for God's sake, I'm not going to rape you or anything. I'm a good dyke. I won't touch you unless you want me to."

"I—" Beth was surprised to hear her voice break. "I don't want you to."

"Fine. But at least sit close enough that I can pass you this doobie."

Beth sat on the very edge of the bed, her feet touching the floor. She took the joint, sucked on it, took in too much smoke and coughed out clouds of it in short, violent barks.

"Christ, are you okay? I'd pat you on the back if I were allowed to touch you."

"I'm okay," Beth managed to sputter, handing the joint back to Thalia. When Thalia passed it back the next hit was smoother. By the third hit, a pleasant haze was creeping up her neck and into her brain.

"Okay," Thalia said, exhaling the sweet-smelling smoke. "So did I do something to piss you off, or are you such a closet case you're avoiding me because I fucked you?"

How could she answer that question? "Um . . . is there another choice?"

"You tell me."

With the fog filling her brain, it was hard to find the words she wanted. "You didn't do anything to piss me off. It's just that I'm . . . not like you."

Thalia blew out so much smoke she resembled a dragon. "Not like me how? I mean, okay, you're all blond and femmey, and I'm all swarthy and butch, so if that's what you mean, then I can accept it. But if you're trying to say I'm a dyke and you're not, then that's bullshit. Your little sorority girlfriends can fake orgasms all the time with their boyfriends, but you can't fool another woman. I know you liked what I did to you, and that makes you as big a dyke as I am."

"I did . . . like it. Listen, I'm not saying this the way I want to say it. When I say I'm not like you, I mean, like, what do your parents do for a living?"

"They run a deli downtown, but I don't see what that has to do with me being a dyke."

"It has a lot to do with it. They run a deli. So what? They don't have anything to lose from you being the way you are because nobody cares what you do. My dad is a partner in the biggest law firm in town, and my brothers work there, too. My mom is the vice president of the oldest women's club in town."

"Your point being?"

"My point is that they . . . we . . . my whole family have everything to lose. We can't afford any scandal to drag the family name through the mud. And so I'm a good girl. I'm in the same sorority my mom was in, and I let myself be seen at parties with a guy from the same frat Dad was in. I can't put myself in a position where my family could lose everything because of me."

Thalia scooted in so close that Beth could feel her breath on her cheek. "But don't you have a lot to lose by running and hiding all the time? Being gay doesn't mean you have to live like you're in the witness protection program."

Beth wondered how it would feel to be Thalia, a nobody from a family of nobodies with nothing to lose. If she were in Thalia's cheap, scuffed shoes, she could openly date all the women she wanted with no need for a pretend boyfriend. Her whole life would be built around doing what she wanted to do. It was hard to imagine such a life. In a way it seemed selfish . . . to spend your days saying and doing exactly what you wanted. Beth couldn't do that to her family. She owed them too much for her good fortune; the least she could do was put aside her personal pleasure—or at least, be discreet about it—to make them happy.

"Beth?"

Beth noticed Thalia's hand was on her forearm and wondered how long it had been there. She moved away before she said, "What?"

"I was asking you if you've ever been in love."

Thalia's tone was so gentle that Beth found herself saying, "Yeah. There was a girl in high school, but that was a long time ago."

Thalia let out a pot smoker's giggle. "It can't have been that long ago. You're just, like, twenty or something. So what was her name?"

"No names." Beth's answer was automatic.

"Sorry. I forgot for a second that asking you questions about being a dyke is like asking somebody questions about being in the CIA. Okay, so we'll call her Mademoiselle X. What was she like? Was she lipsticky? Or was she a devastating neobutch like yours truly?"

Beth looked at Thalia's cocked eyebrow and let herself smile. She should have left fifteen minutes ago, but smoking the joint had rooted her to this spot on the bed . . . Well, that and the fact that although she hated to admit it, she really did like looking at Thalia. "She wasn't lipsticky. She was the daughter of my dad's best friend, and she was the placekicker for the West View High School football team. She'd come over to the house when her parents were visiting mine, and things between us started, you know, happening." Beth thought of how different it had been with Gina than with her high school boyfriend . . . just being touched for the pleasure of touch instead of playing that teenaged boy game where one part of you got touched only as sort of a test to see if he had permission to touch you somewhere more personal. But then something must have happened between Gina's parents and hers because they stopped coming over, and Gina stopped returning her calls. Eventually, Beth's dad had mentioned that Gina's dad had gotten a job in another city. "But then she moved away my junior year, and I never heard from her again."

"That sucks," Thalia said. "Sounds like her parents must've caught a clue about what was going on between y'all."

"No." Beth jumped up from the bed. "Nobody knew. *Nobody.*"

"Okay, okay." Thalia was up now, too, her hands on Beth's shoulders. "Bless your heart, Beth. You're afraid all the time, aren't you?"

The tears Beth had been holding back poured out now, accompanied by big, racking sobs that made her whole body shake. She felt Thalia's arms around her shoulders and back, holding her steady. When Thalia's lips touched hers, she realized this was the first time since Gina that she had kissed a girl in full daylight. She pressed her lips against Thalia's, tasting her own tears.

No, she told herself. She couldn't let herself sink into emotional quicksand with this loud dyke who could never understand why things had to be the way they were. She broke the kiss. "I can't do this."

"Can't do what?"

"This . . . any of it." She rubbed her fingers under her eyes to minimize the mascara damage. "Look. We had a great night together, but it's over, and there's never going to be another one. So don't follow me out of class, and don't try to talk to me. If you hadn't been wearing that damn mask, nothing would have happened between us!"

She flung open the bedroom door and ran down the hall, ignoring the couple making out on the couch and trying to ignore Thalia, who yelled, "Maybe you're the one who needs to take off the mask!"

Liz

"Sugar or lemon?" Margo, Audrey's drag queen roommate, was playing the role of hostess, right down to wearing a set of brown paisley "hostess pajamas," which would have been in fashion during Liz's infancy.

"Lemon, please," Liz said, trying to sound light and pleasant despite her real feelings. She wouldn't even be here if Audrey hadn't spotted her walking across campus and yelled, "Hey! You're on your way to tea at my house, right?"

She had actually been on her way to her room for a nap. She had been napping a lot lately and sleeping late in the mornings, too, barely hauling herself out of bed in time for class. It was pathetic, she knew, to be so depressed over a little thing like Dan's sexual rejection of her. After all, it wasn't like a real breakup or anything; she and Dan still ate together in the cafeteria and drank together at the Sagebrush. But somehow only one glance at that only once-used pink compact of pills would set her off on a crying jag, and the only way to stop the tears was to fall asleep.

She wasn't asleep now, but the social environment in which she found herself had all the surrealistic qualities of a dream. In addition to the drag queen hostess, there were Gideon and his goth friends, smoking and moping, and Derek and his theater fag friends who were composing lewd parodies of Andrew Lloyd Webber songs. Then there was Audrey and her dykey friends—Thalia and her housemates, as well as a woman with a green Mohawk and a nose ring who may or may not have been there as somebody's date. The scene grew even stranger as Liz noticed a gray tabby cat carrying a tiny, identically tabby kitten in her mouth.

"Oh!" one of the theater fags crowed. "Sappho had her kittens!"

"Yep, Sapph's the only heterosexual we allow around these parts," Audrey said, setting down a plate of cookies. "But I have to say her status as a breeder does make her name seem less appropriate."

"Yeah, well, a little trip to the vet will take care of the breeding problem," Margo said. "If only more humans would follow suit." She stooped down to the towel-lined cardboard box where three more striped kittens stumbled over each other. "I love a little pussy . . . oh, yes, I do."

"What . . . nobody's gonna take that bait?" Audrey said.

Gideon peered through his fringe of black bangs. "Too easy . . . like shooting fish in a barrel."

"Fish, pussy . . ." one of the theater fags began.

"Hold on. You don't get into the fish thing if you expect to sit in my house and drink my tea," Audrey said. "You treat your sisters with respect."

"My apologies, Miss Steinem," the offending theater fag said.

"That's *Ms.* Steinem to you," Audrey said, to the hoots and applause of the women in the room, including Margo.

Liz didn't applaud, but she looked at Audrey with envy. Where did all that self-confidence come from?

When the tea drinkers started to scatter to various locations—to the women's house to scramble some tofu for supper, to rehearse a show at either the Merry-Go-Round or to the student theater, Liz got up to leave, too. But Audrey pulled her aside. "Listen," she said, "if you don't have anything else to do, why don't you stay and have dinner with me? My roomies are leaving, and I don't want to eat all by my lonesome."

Liz felt a ripple of excitement and something else—fear? The fear outweighed the excitement enough that she had an excuse on her lips, but really, what did she have waiting for her back on campus? A gruesome meal in the cafeteria, eaten in the company of whoever happened to show up at the same time she did, or a package of sodium-laden Ramen noodles eaten in solitude straight out of the hot pot in her dorm room. "Um . . . okay. I guess so. If it's no trouble."

"If it were trouble I wouldn't have asked you," Audrey said. "I'm delighted to have the company. Some people can't stand to sleep alone, but I can't stand to eat alone."

Liz smiled. "I guess, given the choice, your way is better. I mean, I've never regretted eating with someone. Sleeping, however . . ."

"A good point. Come in the kitchen with me while I make the corn bread."

"I've not had decent corn bread in ages. The stuff they call corn bread in the cafeteria is like eating a yellow bath sponge."

Audrey took some buttermilk and a bag of cornmeal out of the fridge. "I'm against most things institutional, but especially food." She shut the fridge door with a graceful sway of her hip. She set the milk and meal on the counter, then nodded back toward the fridge. "There's beer in there if you want one."

Want was an inadequate word to describe the intensity of Liz's desire for a beer. Her throat was dry from the same nervousness that made it difficult to think of what to say next; she needed both the physical and the social lubrication. "Thanks. Can I get you one?"

"Not yet. Maybe with dinner."

Liz opened the fridge to find a pristine six-pack of Becks nestled beside an eggplant, a pineapple and a box of tofu. "Wow . . . good beer, too."

"Yeah, I'm not a big drinker, so I tend to go for quality over quantity." She oiled a cast iron skillet and slipped it into the oven.

"Well, that definitely puts you in the minority among my friends. Of course, I'm used to hanging out at guys' houses where the fridge is full of Carling's Black Label and nothing else."

"Yeah." Audrey laughed. "Two cases of Black Lab, crusty bottles of ketchup and mustard and no other food items whatsoever."

Liz grinned. "You know my friends, then."

"Let's just say I know Straight Guy Refrigerator Syndrome." She stirred the corn bread batter. "There's a bottle opener on the fridge."

The magnetic bottle opener was holding down a flyer for the Take Back the Night march. A photo taped to the wall showed a willowy young blond man leaning to kiss a tall, shaven-headed black man on the cheek. "This blond guy looks familiar."

Audrey grinned. "That's Margo. Andrew's his mundane name. I don't guess you've ever seen him out of drag, have you?"

"No. I guess I've only seen him on special occasions."

"And he applies the term *special occasions* quite loosely . . . any excuse to put on a dress. That's his boyfriend, Angelo, with him. He lives in Nashville."

"They're a cute couple." Liz immediately worried that this was a condescending thing to say. "So do you have a . . . a . . ."

Audrey poured the batter into the sizzling pan. "Please tell me you're not about to say boyfriend."

"No, I wasn't."

Audrey slid the pan into the oven. "You're very sweet, you know that? So worried about saying the wrong thing. No, I don't have a girlfriend or life partner or whatever we're supposed to call them this week. I had a two-year relationship before I moved here, but a lot of it was sheer torture. She was one of those sensitive types, you know. I loved her, but God . . . she spent all her time crying, and I spent all my time apologizing and feeling like a total bitch. So anyway, if you know any cute dykes . . ."

"You're the only one I know." Liz realized once it was too late that she had implied Audrey's cuteness in that statement.

"Hmm . . . are you suggesting I date myself? Not that I'm above that sort of thing. I do it fairly often, as a matter of fact. Oh, my God, Liz, are you blushing?"

Dinner was homey and delicious: cumin-laced black beans and rice with grated cheddar cheese on top and corn bread on the side. When they had finished and retired to the couch, Liz said, "Thank you for asking me to stay. I appreciate the home-cooked food and the beer that actually requires a bottle opener."

"And I appreciate the company and the conversation," Audrey said, "so think nothing of it."

"I only wish my conversation was as good as your food."

"It's better. And I'm glad you stayed. You looked a little sad to me today. It made me want to feed you. Misguided maternal instincts, I guess."

Liz was both touched and stunned. She had been in a huge funk for the past week, and Audrey, someone she didn't even know well, had been the first person to notice it.

"I'm sorry," Audrey said. "I have a tendency to blurt out whatever's on my mind."

"It's okay. I'm just surprised you noticed because nobody else has. My sadness, I mean."

"Well, I don't think I'm extraordinarily sensitive, so the people you normally surround yourself with must be extraordinarily oblivious."

Liz thought of Dan and Todd and Stu and the gurgling of the bong that accompanied the *Star Trek* theme song. "Maybe."

Audrey shrugged. "Well, if you want to talk about what's bothering you, feel free. If you don't, that's cool, too."

Liz wasn't sure she wanted to talk, and even if she did, what would she say? Finally she settled on, "It's just boyfriend stuff. Not that he'd want me to call him that . . . he hates words like *boyfriend* and *girlfriend*—he calls me his old lady most of the time."

"Which makes you sound like his mother. I wonder what Dr. Freud would have made of that."

Liz felt bad for laughing, but she laughed anyway, and when Audrey offered her a second beer, she accepted. Soon she was telling Audrey about the gynecologist who couldn't complete a sentence, the bored nurse and the unannounced anal penetration.

Audrey, who was also on her second beer, laughed right up until the moment Liz told her about Dan announcing his lack of sexual feelings. Then her face became serious, and she said, "Hmm."

"Hmm what?"

"I was just thinking, this guy's got some major intimacy issues, don't you think? I mean, he can fall into bed with you occasionally in a drunken, unplanned way, but once you make an acknowledgment that the two of you have an ongoing relationship, he runs like a scalded dog. Intimacy issues." Audrey rolled her eyes. "Not that announcing that some straight white guy has intimacy issues is some kind of genius statement. Straight white boys have intimacy issues like cats have hairballs."

"Don't you think you're stereotyping a little bit?"

"Oh, probably. In this case, I think I'm right, though. Unless . . ."

"Unless what?"

"Unless your guy isn't even straight. Maybe he's gay and just hasn't figured it out yet."

Liz flipped through the Rolodex of her brain for indications that Dan might play for the other team. He did speak French and like frou-frou food, but he abhorred fashion, drank Black Label out of the can and peed in the bushes on the way home from barhopping. "I don't think so."

Audrey grinned. "He's probably not. See, this is why I shouldn't drink. You get a beer and a half into me, and I think everybody's gay. Three beers, and I'd make a pass at Phyllis Schlafly."

"Now, that's what I call a low-alcohol tolerance."

"Well, it might actually take four beers for me to go after ol' Phyllis, but I'd be doing it as a public service. Some fine lesbian lovin' would set that old biddy *free*." Audrey took another swig of beer. "But we were psychoanalyzing you, not me. So . . . do you love this guy, Liz?"

Liz felt her eyes start to mist. "Yeah, I do."

"And does he love you?"

Now the mist was a stream. "I don't know. I mean, I think he does, but he's never said. He's not the kind of person who says things like that, you know?"

Audrey slammed her beer bottle on the table. "See, that's the kind of thing that drives me crazy! All the things people don't say to each other. If you don't let yourself feel—and tell other people how you feel—then what's the point of even being here? All we've got in this world is each other."

Liz was surprised by Audrey's sudden passion, but she was even more surprised when Audrey took the beer bottle out of her hand, set it on the table and then took both of Liz's hands in hers. Audrey's skin was cool, and Liz hoped her hands weren't sweaty.

"Listen, Liz." Audrey was looking right into Liz's eyes. "I'm going to say something to you that somebody needs to say, and I know your uptight pseudo-boyfriend isn't going to be the one to say it. You, Liz, are a fucking beautiful, brilliant woman. You don't know this about yourself yet, and you hide in your booze and your pot and your self-deprecation—but you are beautiful and brilliant, and you should never let anybody treat you like you're less than that."

Liz looked away, her face burning. She was trying to come up with a joke, a flippant comeback, but before she could find any words, Audrey took Liz's face in her hands. And then Audrey's face was coming closer to hers, and Audrey's full, slightly parted lips were pressing against hers, and no matter how much Liz wanted to tell herself that this kiss meant nothing, it was like that split second on a roller coaster when you crest the top of a hill, and then the whole world drops out from under you.

Elisa

"So now you know my secret," Dr. Rivers said. "I like fairies."

"You sure do." Elisa gazed in wonder at Dr. Rivers' living room. Fairy figurines of porcelain and glass and cloth were suspended from the ceiling, dangling at different levels as though caught in mid-flutter. The walls were painted with murals of fairies that appeared to have been lifted from the pages of a Victorian children's book. Elisa was enchanted. "This is the prettiest room I've ever seen."

Dr. Rivers smiled. "I'm glad you like it. I know, given my area of expertise, that I should probably collect images of Amazons or fertility goddesses or some such." She fingered a fairy dangling over her head. "But these comfort me."

"My mamaw collects angels." Mamaw's Christmas tree was always so cluttered with angel ornaments that no greenery showed through.

"Angels are different, though, aren't they? All ethereal and imbued with religious significance. Fairies suit me better . . . they're connected

to the earth, but they have wings to transcend it. That's the image I like
. . . to be a woman with wings." She sat on the purple sofa. "Please sit,
Elisa."

Elisa settled into a rose-colored armchair. "When I was little, my
momma took me to see *Peter Pan*. I made everybody call me Tink for
months after that."

"Well, 'Tink' suits you, I think. I may start calling you that myself.
Where did you see the play?"

"What play?" Elisa hadn't seen a play other than a church Christmas
pageant or high school play until she came to William Blount.

"*Peter Pan*."

"Oh, I didn't see a play of it. I saw the cartoon—the Disney
version."

"Too bad," Dr. Rivers said with what, to Elisa's sensitive ears, sounded
like disappointment. "I never liked what Disney did to Tinkerbell,
turning her into a Marilyn Monroe type with tiny wings that couldn't
possibly lift that voluptuous body off the ground. Plus, he made her
much more petty and vindictive than Barrie's Tinkerbell. Typical Disney
misogyny. Did you know that in the play, Tinkerbell is just a point of
light?"

"Really? That sounds like something George Bush would say."

Dr. Rivers laughed. "You really are clever, you know that?" She stood
up. "So, clever girl, are you sure you want to spend the day doing work
that is intellectually beneath you?"

"Of course I'm sure. Like I said, if I can't pay you back in money, the
least I can do is pay you back in time."

"And as *I* said, you don't have to pay someone back when she gives
you a gift."

"But you can let me give you the gift of my time."

"Fair enough, Tink. Let's get started, then, shall we?" She motioned
for Elisa to follow her. "Now when you see my study, I am absolutely
confident that you will not say it's the prettiest room you've ever seen.
The messiest, perhaps."

Dr. Rivers' office wasn't the messiest room Elisa had ever seen. That
honor would have to go to the living room of Jo's parents' trailer the
night after they'd had a particularly wild party. This was a different kind

of mess: piles of paper on and around the desk, books strewn on the floor instead of shelved. The clutter here struck Elisa as evidence of a busy mind at work, and while it was a mess, it was a beautiful mess.

"You're not speaking. Are you in shock?"

"No, I've seen worse," Elisa said, thinking of the spilled beer and puke she had once helped Jo clean up. "Should I start by shelving the books?" The walls of the study were lined by nearly full bookcases.

"Yes. The ones on the shelves are alphabetized by author, so you see, I have my moments of organization. But then I have my moments of inspiration where I snatch the book I need off the shelf and throw it down once I've gotten what I need. It's like tearing off the meat and throwing the bones to the dogs on the floor."

"Well, I'll be happy to pick up the bones . . . and alphabetize them."

Dr. Rivers patted Elisa's shoulder. "Tink, if you're not careful, you may find yourself becoming absolutely indispensable."

Elisa looked down at the books on the floor, smiling.

"Feel free to peruse any titles that look intriguing." Dr. Rivers was on her way out of the room. "That's always my trouble. I'll intend to shelve books and end up reading all afternoon instead."

Elisa could understand the temptation. Every book she picked up, she wanted to read. Some titles were intriguing because of their strangeness (*Gyn/Ecology*, *The Female Eunuch*), while others sounded downright sexy (*Language and the Lesbian Body*). Shelving Dr. Rivers' books was strangely intimate, making Elisa recall her teenaged babysitting years when she had snooped in the adults' bedrooms after the kids were asleep.

"Dr. Rivers?" The books shelved, Elisa was ready to move on to her next task.

"In the kitchen!"

Dr. Rivers was standing barefoot in the bright kitchen, which was heavy with the scent of pastry. "Here, I want you to try one of these. I'm taking them to a party tonight." She picked up one of the tiny pastry pockets from the baking sheet on the stove, moved closer to Elisa and held the pastry to her lips.

Elisa felt a little like a dog, but she took the pastry and chewed.

"It's puff pastry with roasted red peppers and gorgonzola," Dr. Rivers said.

"Delicious," Elisa said, even though the cheese tasted like it had gone bad.

"I thought so, too, but I wanted to get a second opinion. Are you finished in the study?"

"Sure am."

"You are an absolute goddess, Elisa. Are you up for a bit more shelving?"

"Sure."

"Follow me upstairs, then."

Elisa followed her up the spiral staircase, past the framed fairy prints in the hallway and into another bookshelf-lined room that, to Elisa's surprise, also contained a queen-sized bed covered in jewel-toned throw pillows. More fairy figurines dangled from the ceiling.

"As you can see," Dr. Rivers said, "I'm just as lazy about shelving my leisure-time reading as I am with my academic titles."

Elisa looked down at the piles of books on the floor. "I'll take care of them. Should I alphabetize them, too?"

"Please. And again, feel free to peruse any titles that interest you. Or take some home if you like."

"Thank you." All college professors should be as generous with their knowledge as Dr. Rivers, Elisa thought, but surprisingly few of them were. They flaunted and hoarded their knowledge and dispensed crumbs of it during class time, but only grudgingly.

"Well, if you'll excuse me, I think I'll pop into the shower. I have to get ready for this wretched party." Dr. Rivers disappeared behind the door of the adjoining bathroom, and Elisa grabbed an armload of books to shelve. It was immediately apparent, however, that these were not books Dr. Rivers had collected for scholarly purposes. She was okay with the first book she saw, titled *Delta of Venus* and labeled "erotica"—the garter-belted flapper on the cover gave it an old-fashioned, almost innocent air. The second book, *Herotica*, the cover of which showed a line drawing of a flower that looked a lot more like something in the animal rather than the vegetable kingdom, made her feel a twinge of excitement and anxiety.

But the third book, Susie Bright's *Lesbian Sex World*, proved to be too much for her. She dropped it on the floor like it was too hot to handle.

What could Dr. Rivers mean by asking her to shelve her naughty books? Handling these personal items felt as intimate as pawing through the professor's panty drawer. To make it even worse, she could hear water running in the room next door. Dr. Rivers was naked, not twenty feet away from her, with only a thin door between them.

She wondered if this scenario—Elisa in the bedroom with the sexy books, Dr. Rivers close by in the shower—could be an attempt at seduction. But as soon as she thought it, she laughed it away. What would Dr. Rivers want with an ignorant little hillbilly like her? Dr. Rivers could surely have her pick of beautiful, sophisticated lesbians. It was the worst kind of vanity for such a thought to have even entered Elisa's mind, and yet she had to admit that the thought that Dr. Rivers could want her was an intriguing fantasy. It was like when she used to see those Walt Disney movies with Jodie Foster when she was a kid and would imagine that Jodie wanted to be her best friend.

"Have you seen anything of interest?"

Elisa looked up to see Dr. Rivers in a sapphire silk bathrobe embroidered with peacock feathers. Her cheeks were rosy from the shower's heat, and her long hair was a riot of wet, shiny curls. "Um . . . what?"

"Have you seen any books that interest you?"

"Um . . . well, I really wasn't paying that much attention to what the books were about. I was just, you know, looking at the authors' names so I could alphabetize them . . ."

"You're too good of a girl to be a good liar," Dr. Rivers said, smiling. "Of course you're interested in the books. You're a beautiful, sensual twenty-year-old lesbian. How could you not be?" She took a step closer to Elisa. "I wanted you to see them in hopes that some of these titles might help you recover from your Bible Belt upbringing. No one so young should be sexually repressed."

"I'm not. Jo and I are very happy . . . in bed." She wished she had found a more elegant way of expressing herself. Ending with the phrase "in bed" made her think of the teenaged game in which you mentally sang the phrase "in bed" after every line of a hymn in church.

"I'm glad you're happy. Still, twenty does seem awfully young to be tying yourself down to one person." She smiled again. "Oh, there was something I wanted to show you." Dr. Rivers loosened the tie on her robe and pulled it down to reveal one golden shoulder. "Now that you know my secret, I guess it's safe for me to show you this."

For a second, Elisa couldn't process what was happening, but then she saw what she was supposed to see. Below Dr. Rivers' collarbone on the left side was a delicate tattoo of a fairy in profile, her light blue wings as diaphanous as a dragonfly's. "It's beautiful," she said.

"You can bet I won't be showing this to the old boys at the cocktail party tonight," Dr. Rivers said. "I got it to mark my fortieth birthday. That's been a couple of years, but it's funny . . . the skin here is still more tender than the rest of my skin." She took Elisa's hand and lightly brushed Elisa's index finger against the fairy tattoo.

Elisa had to remember to breathe. Dr. Rivers was so close to her that they didn't feel like teacher and student or mentor and mentee, but only woman and woman. It would be so easy for Elisa to lean forward, her lips parted . . . But she had to remember to think. Jo would be waiting for her to come home at five thirty, and they had planned to go to Mario's for pizza and then to the movie that was showing at the student center. After the movie, though they hadn't discussed it as part of their plan, Elisa knew they would go back to the room and make love. And she knew it would be good because it always was. "I think you'd better take me home," she said.

Beth

Her mother had helped organize the Festival of Trees for as long as Beth could remember. Held at the civic center downtown, the festival displayed dozens of huge Christmas trees, each of which had been donated and decorated by a corporate sponsor. Thousands of people came to look at the trees, and all proceeds from the price of admission went to the Children's Hospital of East Tennessee. The festival was one of Knoxville's premiere charity events, and Beth's mom's position on its board was a glittering star in her social tiara.

Beth hadn't really wanted to help her mother at the festival, but her mother had refused to hear any of her excuses. "It'll be *fun*," her mother had said in a tone that made it clear that this fun was mandatory. "Besides, you know how I love showing off my little girl to my friends."

So here Beth was, dressed in a jolly red sweater, standing at the entrance to the Festival of Trees, handing out programs and trying to follow her mother's strict orders to smile. Sometimes it was easy to smile

. . . when a mother stood in the doorway with a preschool-aged girl who had obviously caught sight of the lights and colors ahead and whose little pink mouth was an "O" of excitement.

Beth remembered coming to the festival when she was about that size, remembered her wonder at the tiny lights and the trees so tall they scraped the ceiling. Her mother had always been busy running the event, so her daddy would take her on the tour, letting her look at each tree for as long as she wanted, her tiny hand engulfed in his enormous one. Afterward he always took her across the street to the now-defunct Harry's Diner for hot chocolate, and as a result, she had always thought of the hot chocolate at Harry's as the first taste of Christmas.

Beth wouldn't mind trading places with that preschooler—to let the little girl try playing the grown-up college student so Beth could go back to a time when she was expected to do nothing but wallow in the pleasures of her senses: to stare at Christmas lights and slurp hot chocolate and huddle beneath her daddy's coat when the wind got too cold. Back then, it was even okay to hold hands with another girl, to hug and kiss her. People said it was sweet, what little girls did. There had been no decisions to make, no price to pay for pleasure, no fears that couldn't be laid to rest by Daddy looking under the bed and announcing he didn't see a single monster.

"Excuse me, may I have a program?"

Beth snapped out of her daydream to see an irritable society matron, her hair colored and coiffed, her thin, nervous lips painted with the same shade of Clinique lipstick that Beth's mother used. "Oh, I'm sorry. Enjoy the festival." Beth handed the lady a program and smiled as instructed.

But she didn't feel like smiling. If the wide-eyed little girl had been her ghost of Christmas past, then the nervous, irritable lady was her ghost of Christmas future. That's what she'd look like, twenty-five years down the road, Beth thought, her face pinched but carefully made up, her middle-aged body tortured into slimness by starvation and hours on the exercise bike. Well preserved, people would call her. And she'd live in one of those big-ass houses in Cherokee Hills and trot out to the same social events every year. There'd be a husband, too—maybe Mike—who'd be fit from hours at the health club and perpetually exhausted from long days at work. And kids—maybe there would be kids, if the two of them could bring themselves to perform the act that could result in them.

And there was the reason she could never quite be that society matron. Because even if that society matron was repelled by her husband's touch (as Beth's mother seemed to be by Beth's daddy's), it wasn't because she preferred the touch of women. But maybe, Beth thought, once her youthful hormones had time to settle down . . . maybe then her hunger for women would fade. Maybe Mike's desire for men would die down, too. Maybe, if they married, their lie would become the truth, and Beth would feel the way she hadn't felt since she was a little girl. Safe.

Beth kept smiling and handing out programs, not even looking at the owners of the hands into which she pressed them. Not until a familiar voice said, "Hey."

Thalia was wearing a ratty black sweatshirt and fatigues, standing next to an older woman with ink-black hair and wearing what appeared to be a mink coat. Beth couldn't find any words, and her hand was shaking too badly to pass her a program.

"My mom's dragged me to this thing every year since I was a kid," Thalia said. "I do kinda like the trees, though."

Beth felt a hand on her shoulder and turned her head to see her mother's face. "I just wanted to see how you were getting along," her mother said, smiling her dazzling socialite smile. "Oh, is this someone you know from school?" She directed a rather judgmental glance toward Thalia. "Aren't you going to introduce me?"

Beth looked at her mother's face, then the thousands of tiny Christmas lights that swam and swirled before her eyes. The programs fell to the floor, and so did she, muttering before she lost consciousness, "The ghost of Christmas present."

Part II:

Spring Semester

Liz

Winter break had been weird. Back when Liz had been a freshman, visits home had been comforting, with home-cooked meals, long soaks in the bathtub and a soothing feeling of the familiar. Now that she had made a life for herself in college, though, a visit home felt more like a visit and less like home, a fact that made family events, from trimming the tree to Christmas dinner, tinged with sadness.

She was sure her parents shared some of her feelings. It had to be obvious to them, too, that things had changed. As a teenager, she had told her mother everything, not that there had been much to tell. Now, though, her mother's questions about Liz's life yielded mostly evasive answers about the academic aspects of school: Women in Lit had been a great class—totally eye-opening—and it was a good thing she'd had it this semester, too, since the A she earned in it would keep the C she'd scraped out in Rocks for Jocks from hurting her GPA too badly.

Liz was acutely aware of everything she wasn't telling her parents, but what was she supposed to do? Should she be sitting at the Christmas dinner table, right across from her visiting grandma, and saying, "Yeah, well, this semester I studied just enough so I could keep up my GPA while still drinking and smoking lots of pot. And I'm totally in love with Dan, but he never talks about his feelings for me, and when I told him I'd gotten on the pill, he refused to have sex with me anymore. Oh, and did I mention that just before finals this girl kissed me right on the lips, and I'm freaking out because I think I kinda liked it? Damn, I'd kill for a joint right now. How 'bout you, Grandma?"

But now that the New Year had come (during a depressing evening spent watching Dick Clark's *New Year's Rockin' Eve* alone in her childhood room) and she was back on campus, she could return to being her full-fledged self. And that self was a total, unadulterated mess. But at least she didn't have to hide it here.

She was sitting on a bench in the courtyard in front of the dorm, chilly despite the black leather jacket she had gotten for Christmas. She knew that Dan would be here before long, not because they had arranged to meet, but because this courtyard was the traditional gathering place for the "what-do-you-want-to-do-I-don't-know-what-do-you-want-to-do?" preliminaries to an evening out.

She hadn't talked to Dan since she had left for winter break. He had her phone number at her parents' house, but he never used it, and she had his phone number at his parents' house, but she didn't use it either because being the one who called first would make her seem needy. She had only talked to Dan once since the kiss with Audrey had happened, and of course she hadn't talked to him about the kiss at all. It wasn't important enough to talk about. A kiss was probably just like a handshake to Audrey, and if it had felt like more at the time to Liz, it was probably because of the two beers and her state of sexual frustration.

When it came to making herself less of a mess, Liz's plan was twofold. First, she would avoid Audrey for a while—no tea at the theater house, no protests, no visits to the theater department. Just in case the kiss had meant something to Audrey, it would be best to give her a wide berth so as not to give her the wrong idea.

The second part of Liz's plan was to make herself irresistible to Dan. She wasn't sure how to do this short of dipping herself in beer and then rolling in marijuana, but she had had quite enough of this enforced celibacy and more than enough of Dan's arm's-length style of dating while claiming not to be dating. She loved Dan, goddamn it, and he loved her, she was sure of it, and even if he didn't, she was going to make him love her. She had been listening to a lot of Janis Joplin lately and had embraced Janis's identity as a chick who loves her old man with painful intensity, who gives herself over entirely to love. Of course, she had also once read that Janis liked to get it on with chicks sometimes, but she decided not to think about that little complicating factor.

Liz watched her breath as she exhaled the cold evening air, thinking of how when she was little she used to hold a stick between her fingers on cold days and pretend she was smoking. Then she saw him, hands in pockets, hunched in the cold like Bob Dylan on the cover of his second album. The first thing she noticed was that he had shaved the goatee he'd had ever since they met. His face looked naked without it, as if he were exposing parts that shouldn't be seen in public.

"Hey," he said.

"Hey. At the risk of stating the obvious, you shaved your beard."

"Yeah. My chin's cold now."

"You know," Liz said, hoping to sound sexy, "your chin is the only part of your body I hadn't seen until now."

"Hmm," Dan said. "You haven't seen my intestines."

So much for sexy. "Okay, it's the only external part of your body I haven't seen."

"Well, now you've seen it, so the suspense is over. I was heading up to Todd and Stu's. You want to come with?"

It was just like they hadn't been apart at all. No "I missed you" or "how was your break," just the usual casual invitation to tag along. "Sure, I'll come." She rose from the bench. "You know, if we walked in the cold with our arms linked, we'd look just like the cover of *The Free-Wheelin' Bob Dylan*."

"Cool." He gave her his arm, so this gambit obviously worked better than the comment about his chin.

Stu and Todd's apartment was heated by a space heater they moved from room to room depending on whether it was time to sit or sleep. Now they huddled around its meager heat in the living room like Depression-era hoboes in front of a campfire. "Hey," Todd said when Liz and Dan walked in. "Have a bong hit—the smoke in your lungs'll warm you up."

"Not as much as this will," Stu said, holding up a big bottle of Maker's Mark. "I bet you can really put some bourbon away, Liz, being from Kentucky and all."

"Hey, that's the same brand my mama used to put in my baby bottle," Liz said, though in truth, she'd take gin over bourbon anyday.

Stu put a Doors album on the stereo. He was one of those guys who thought Jim Morrison was a poetic genius. Dan did a shot of Maker's.

"I'm gonna get a Coke mixer for mine," Todd said. "You want one, too, Liz?"

Liz would've preferred a bourbon and Coke to a straight shot, but if she asked for a mixer Dan would think she was being girly. "No, thanks. I'll just do a couple of shots."

"Now there's a real woman for you!" Stu said.

"Well, I'd never have an old lady who drank daiquiris and shit," Dan said, casting an approving glance at Liz. "I always say my idea of a mixer is ice."

Happy to have gained Dan's praise, Liz tossed back a shot. It was surprisingly smooth and left a nice, warm glow. Maybe bourbon wasn't so bad after all.

"Hey, watch this," Stu said. He sucked in a bong hit, threw back a shot of Maker's, then exhaled a tremendous cloud of smoke. He closed his eyes in apparent ecstasy. "I am the Lizard King," he said.

Liz stifled a snicker. The Lizard King, she knew because Stu had once told her, was what people in the know called Jim Morrison. Stu was no Lizard King. He was about two heads shorter than Morrison, with a greasy complexion and no hope of filling out a pair of leather pants. Even though Liz found Jim Morrison's drug-addled pseudo-Beat poetry annoying, she had to admit that Jim had been (unlike Stu) a sexy-looking guy. She always figured that if she time-traveled and happened to meet Morrison, she'd probably try to fuck him in part because he was cute and in part because sex would probably be the easiest way to make him shut up for a few minutes.

She did another shot. "If you could travel back in time and meet any famous person, who would it be?"

"Easy," Stu said, nodding toward the stereo.

"We all kinda knew yours," Liz said. "How about you, Todd?"

"Hmm . . . probably King Arthur. Remember *Excalibur*? I fucking love that movie."

"King Arthur's not real, man," Stu said.

Todd stopped in mid-bong hit. "What, and time travel is? If I want to meet King Arthur, I can fucking meet King Arthur."

"Fair enough," Liz said. She leaned into Dan just enough to touch him. "How about you, old man?"

Dan accepted the bong from Todd. "Voltaire, maybe. Or Aristotle, if I didn't fear for the safety of my anus. Of course, I'm probably not his type. And you, Liz?"

"I don't know . . . John Lennon, maybe. Or Dorothy Parker, but I'd be terrified she'd take a dislike to me and rip me to shreds."

"You're witty enough to hold your own," Dan said.

"Now that she's dead maybe"—Liz laughed—"but not if we're talking time travel." She was glowing from the bourbon and from Dan's compliment. He seemed more focused on her than he had been before winter break. Maybe he had missed her. Maybe he had started to want her again.

The bourbon flowed. By the time they had almost reached the bottom of the bottle, they had all ended up in Todd's room because he wanted to show them some game on his computer.

Liz and Dan were sitting on Todd's bed, though given the amount of bourbon they'd consumed, they weren't really sitting up under their own power, but propped against the wall. Dan listed and leaned against her, his cheek resting on the top of her head. In half an hour or so, after the bottle was empty, Liz decided, she'd ask Dan if he wanted to walk back to campus. Between the alcohol and their lengthy absence from each other, she liked her chances of him asking her to his room.

"Liz?" Dan murmured into her hair.

"Mmm?" She was practically purring.

"If you'll excuse me, I think I have to vomit." He lurched forward and half-ran to the bathroom next door. It was impossible to ignore the sounds of his retching.

"Pleasant," Todd remarked, not looking away from the computer screen.

Dan emerged, pale-faced and sweaty.

"Are you okay?" Liz asked.

"Fine, fine. I just need to lie down for a second."

Liz rose from the bed just in time for Dan to fall upon it. Almost immediately, he was snoring.

"Well, I guess I'm sleeping on the couch tonight," Todd said.

And I guess I'm sleeping alone, Liz thought.

"Hey, Liz, do you need me to drive you home?" Stu wore a gleeful look that said, "Dan's unconscious; here's my chance."

"No, thanks, man. I've got my pepper spray. I'll just walk." It had only taken Liz a second to weigh her options: walking the streets of Knoxville drunk after midnight or riding in the car alone with a drunk and sexually desperate Stu. She liked her chances better on the street.

Elisa

Elisa and Jo cuddled under the covers. After two hours of lovemaking to make up for the sneaking kisses that had been their only sustenance over winter break, they were finally ready to talk.

"So at Christmas," Elisa said, "Uncle Ronnie gave Momma this animated elf doll that sings 'Grandma Got Run Over by a Reindeer.' The thing was sound-activated, and with the house full of people, it never shut up. 'Grandma Got Run Over by a Reindeer' was the soundtrack to our Christmas dinner . . . if you don't count the sounds of Uncle Ronnie belching."

Jo laughed. "Hey now, your redneck Christmas is downright elegant compared to our white-trash Christmas. Soup beans and Kraft Macaroni Dinner on the table right next to the turkey, and the second dinner was over, all the boys ran outside to shoot guns and go four-wheelin'."

"I bet you went with them."

Jo grinned. "Hell, yeah, I did. What was I supposed to do? Stay inside with the grannies and talk about female complaints? Besides, my uncle gave my momma one of them singing elves, too. I had to get out of there."

It felt so good to lie in each other's arms and laugh about familiar things that Elisa almost forgot her anxiety about Dr. Rivers. But almost forget was the best she could do since tomorrow morning was the first meeting of Dr. Rivers' Women in Modernism class.

Elisa hadn't told Jo about what happened the last time she was at Dr. Rivers' house—about the sexy books or the peacock robe or the tattoo. She hadn't said a word about any of it even though an hour never passed without her replaying the events in her head. Dr. Rivers had been silent on the drive home until she pulled up in front of the dorm and said, "Elisa, if you're going to turn into the woman you want to become, you're going to have to shed some of that Bible Belt provincialism."

Elisa had said "yes, ma'am" automatically, but she didn't really know what Dr. Rivers—or any of the events of the afternoon—had meant. After weeks of brooding, though, Elisa had decided that Dr. Rivers' words and actions could have meant one of two things: (1) Dr. Rivers was trying to seduce her, and her parting words meant that Elisa was provincial for not taking the bait, or (2) Dr. Rivers had no intention of seducing Elisa but was so sophisticated she thought nothing of displaying her erotic literature and tattoos. If the second case were true, then her parting words meant that Elisa was an ignorant little hick for making such a big deal of innocent actions.

Regardless of which was true, Elisa was in an awkward position, and she had no idea how her mentor would treat her when she saw her the next morning. Elisa propped up on one elbow and watched Jo sleep. Jo's eyelashes rested on her cheeks, and her blond curls framed her fair-skinned face. She looked like an angel—beautiful, androgynous and at peace. Elisa wished she could find the peace that seemed to come to Jo so easily, but it seemed there was always something to worry about.

There were a couple of familiar faces in Women in Modernism—Thalia and that girl named Liz who looked like a dyke but apparently wasn't one. Elisa sat down next to Thalia.

"Hey!" Thalia said. She was wearing a fisherman's sweater that looked like it had belonged to several fishermen before it had gotten to her. "God, I'm glad to be back. I am so fucking happy fucking Christmas is fucking over."

"I know what you mean," Elisa said, even as she cringed a little at the f-word being used in such close proximity to Christmas. Her discomfort was probably a sign of the provinciality Dr. Rivers had warned her about. Dr. Rivers who would be here any minute, who was on Elisa's mind so much it was hard to concentrate on what Thalia was saying.

When Dr. Rivers did arrive, Elisa hunched over her blank notebook as though it were filled with the secrets of the universe. And when Dr. Rivers called her name on the roll, she said "here" without looking up.

She had no choice but to look up, though, when Dr. Rivers started writing on the board. "THE LOST GENERATION," Dr. Rivers wrote in huge, chalky letters. "A term coined by Gertrude Stein—and sometimes stolen by Ernest Hemingway—to describe the writers and artists in the aftermath of World War One, looking for meaning and identity in a world that bred corruption, violence and alienation." Dr. Rivers was wearing a sage green dress and had ditched her ugly sandals for the winter in favor of a pair of tan suede boots. She looked pretty, and Elisa searched her face for any indications that she was mad at her or disappointed in her or had even noticed she was there.

But there were no indications to be read. When she lectured, Dr. Rivers seemed to enter a trancelike state. She seemed to be looking at her inner catalog of knowledge and discussing the catalog with great enthusiasm, seemingly for her own entertainment.

Elisa knew she would have been exhilarated by Dr. Rivers' lecture if she weren't so nervous. When class was over, she took a deep breath before she had to walk past Dr. Rivers' lectern. She knew she should say hello, but she was afraid her voice would come out as a terrified squeak.

"Elisa, I trust you enjoyed your holiday."

At least now Elisa didn't have to worry about speaking first. "Yes. You?"

"It was lovely. Listen, if you have a moment, could you pop up to my office with me? I have something I want to give you."

"Okay," Elisa squeaked.

"I was in France for most of the holiday," Dr. Rivers said as they walked through the crowded hallway. "As you can probably tell from my increased dress size. All that butter and cheese and wine! And the chocolate—I can't forget the chocolate—which, I suppose, is why I've gone up a dress size."

Elisa smiled, too nervous to laugh. What would Dr. Rivers say to her once they were alone?

"Now . . ." Dr. Rivers said, once she had closed the door of her office. "You mustn't let the other students know I'm doing this, but . . ."

Elisa gulped. Was Dr. Rivers going to take her clothes off?

Dr. Rivers turned to the nearest bookcase and retrieved a stack of paperbacks. "I know the cost of textbooks is ridiculous, and I just happened to have some fairly pristine copies of the books we're using in class. I thought you might have to sign less of your life's savings away to the university if I gave you these."

Elisa looked down at the books: *To the Lighthouse*, *The Collected Works of Gertrude Stein*, *Nightwood*. Every warm feeling she had for Dr. Rivers welled up as tears in her eyes. How much time she had wasted on worry. "Thank you."

"You're very welcome. And by the way, I'm sorry I called you provincial when I last saw you. No one can be as crabby as I can when I'm being forced to attend a stuffy academic cocktail party."

"You don't have to apologize."

"Oh, but I do. And I should have known better than to ask you to shelve the books I keep in my bedroom. I tend to think of my whole house as a library—fiction's in the living room, women's studies and critical theory in the study and human sexuality in the bedroom. I was thinking of getting my books in order instead of thinking about how seeing some of those titles might affect you." She smiled. "But anyway, I hope I haven't scared you away from coming to my house again."

"No, not at all. And thank you for the books."

Elisa left so that Dr. Rivers wouldn't see the tears of shame that streaked her face. How could she have been ignorant and arrogant enough to think that Dr. Rivers would come on to someone like her? Dr. Rivers' motives were pure; it was Elisa who should be ashamed of herself for being such a silly—and provincial—little girl.

Beth

Each girl held a white candle and stood in a circle around Amy, singing,

"Just as this candle bright
Will light up the night
Our love will cast a glow
So all the world will know."

As soon as the song was over, the girls applauded and squealed and crowded around Amy to hug her. The candlelight song was one of Theta's most beloved traditions. It was sung only when one of the girls got engaged, and so when Amy had returned from winter break flashing a one-carat diamond, the girls had broken out the white candles.

Beth stood back and watched the hugging, laughing girls. Some of them were even crying.

"God, I can't believe Amy got engaged before me," one sister whined. "I'm so jealous!"

"I'm not," Quimby said. "I'm still too young and too cute to be tied down to one boy. I don't plan to settle down till my ass gets fat." She nudged Beth. "I'll bet you a dollar that this is the next girl we'll be singing the candlelight song to."

Beth tried to smile, but she felt more like throwing up. So often for the past month or so, she had been in such a deep state of anxiety that she had no idea what her body would do next. Would she pass out like she did at the Festival of Trees? Or throw up like she did right after Christmas dinner? Or would it be one of the old, familiar spells where the room distorted like a fishbowl and everybody seemed to be staring at her so hard they could see right into her? Whatever form it took, her anxiety had been getting harder and harder to hide. When her mother had noticed it over break, Beth had pleaded stress over school and her responsibilities in the sorority.

"I remember that feeling exactly," her mother had said. "Being in a sorority is like working a full-time job and being in college at the same time." She had then packed Beth off to see her doctor, the same one who provided her with a variety of questionable weight loss medications. After a few perfunctory questions, the doctor had written Beth a prescription for some orange pills which helped a little when Beth took them alone and a lot when she took them with vodka.

But she hadn't taken an orange pill since this morning, and she hadn't had a drink all day, and she needed something to help her breathe, to stop this feeling that she was going to fly into a million pieces.

"You know what we ought to do?" Quimby was saying. "We ought to have a bachelorette party for Amy. We could get a keg and hire some of those guys who strip down to those teensy little banana holders . . ."

"Eew!" a couple of girls squealed; another said, "Quimby, you're awful!"

"Oh, come on, Jennifer." Quimby laughed. "I know you've peeled a banana or two in your time."

Beth sat down. She would've put her head between her knees if it wouldn't have called too much attention to her. Everybody was laughing and hugging and talking about where to go for drinks. Would anybody notice if she just left?

She grabbed her bag and stole from the room, walking faster and faster until she finally reached the door. In her room, she shook out an orange pill and chased it with an airplane bottle of vodka.

Later she opened her eyes when she heard the door open. "Well, there you are!" Quimby said too loudly. She was obviously drunk. "What the hell happened to you? You missed two-dollar well drinks at Radar's."

"I . . . I got sick," Beth said. "I had to go."

Quimby kicked off her ballet flats and sat down on the foot of Beth's bed. "Listen," she said. "We need to talk."

"Can't it wait until tomorrow?" Beth's brain was cloudy from the pill and sleep.

"I don't think it ought to wait. Look, Beth, I'm your best friend, right?"

"Right." Beth figured any conversation that started with this sentence had to be heading in a bad direction. Blades of panic sliced through her drug-induced fog.

"Okay, well, as your best friend, I've got to tell you that some of the girls have been talking about you."

Beth sat up as if she had awoken to find a gun pointed at her face. "Really?"

"Yeah. I mean, I'm not going to name names, but over at Radar's some of the sisters were talking about how your heart just doesn't seem to be in the sorority anymore. They said you show up for meetings, but it's like you're sleepwalking or a zombie or something. They said they hoped you'd get better after some rest over winter break, but that you don't seem to be showing any improvement."

"Ouch," Beth said, but in fact she was relieved that it was just her attitude and not her sexual behavior that had been cited.

"Look, Beth, I don't want to trash my sisters, but you know what bitches some of those girls can be. One of them actually said that if you weren't a legacy, your badge would've been jerked a long time ago. You don't want to give them a reason to kick you out."

"I know," Beth said, and the tears started. Quimby cuddled up against her and put her arm around her, which only made Beth cry harder because she knew that if Quimby knew the truth, there was no way she'd touch her like that.

"If something's bothering you, you can talk to me about it," Quimby whispered. "No matter what it is. You're not pregnant, are you?"

The question was so opposite of her problem that Beth laughed even as she cried. "No, Quimby, I'm not pregnant."

"Well . . . are you having problems with Mike?"

"No. Mike's . . . great. We're great."

Quimby stroked Beth's hair. "But something's bothering you."

Beth struggled to find a way to talk about her problem without calling it by name. She couldn't just lie there and say nothing. Quimby was her best friend, and she was obviously worried. "Okay," she said. "Quimby, do you ever just start thinking about your life and where it is and where it's going, and . . . and you just feel like it's out of control and there's just too, too much to think about?"

Quimby's pretty brown eyes were as innocent and blank as a fawn's. She smiled. "No, not really."

Looking at Quimby's trusting but puzzled expression, Beth realized that her friend was telling the absolute truth: For Quimby, there was no anxiety or doubt. Life was a series of parties and cute boys, and as long as she didn't turn up pregnant, she had no worries. Beth did not envy her newly engaged sorority sister, but she sure as hell envied Quimby.

Liz

"Hey, my long-lost friend!" Audrey was bundled up in a vintage fake leopard coat and matching hat. Though she was now in the warmth of the student center, her nose was still red from the cold. "I thought you'd disappeared or been thrown out of school or something. How are you?"

Twenty thousand people enrolled in this school, Liz thought, *and I run into the one person I'm trying to avoid.* "Um . . . good," she managed.

"Say, do you have class now?"

"Um . . . no." Liz was so rattled she forgot to lie.

"So why don't we grab a cup of hot chocolate? It's fucking freezing out there."

Before Liz could answer, she found Audrey's arm linked in hers, and she was being herded off to the student center's coffee shop.

Over Styrofoam cups of instant cocoa, Audrey said, "You know what the problem is with this Swiss Miss shit? These dinky little excuses for marshmallows. If I'm going to have marshmallows, I want the big, gooey kind . . . the kind you use to make s'mores." She blew into her cup. "Of course, Gideon's from up North, and he doesn't put marshmallows in his hot chocolate. He uses whipped cream instead. Blasphemy, I say. Are you okay, Liz? I feel like I'm doing stand-up comedy for an audience of corpses here."

"I'm sorry. I'm just kind of out of it today. Hungover." She was definitely suffering from last night's combination of too much beer and too little sleep, but that wasn't the real reason for her trauma. If she were sitting across from Dan or Todd or even creepy Stu, she would be fine. But she was sitting across from Audrey.

"Hangovers are a bitch, eh? You reckon they'll ever figure out what causes them?"

Liz grinned in spite of herself. "That would be quite a medical breakthrough, wouldn't it? If they could just link the phenomenon to some behavior, say . . ."

Audrey set her cup aside and leaned forward. "Liz?"

Liz felt her stomach lurch in panic. "Yeah?"

"I make you nervous, don't I?"

"No," Liz said, but she found herself avoiding eye contact. "Well, okay, maybe a little."

Audrey smiled. "Thank you for deciding on honesty. So . . . is it because of the kiss?"

"No," Liz said, too quickly.

"You know, it's funny . . . as soon as I said 'the kiss,' your eyes started darting around like you were afraid somebody you knew heard me. When, in fact, there's nothing incriminating about the phrase—I could've been talking about the Gustav Klimt painting called *The Kiss*."

"I know. It's weird. I mean, I've got a boyfriend—"

"I know. Listen, Liz. I want to ask you something. Do you like me? And before you answer, I'm not asking the elementary school mash note version of the question, I'm just asking if personally, as somebody to hang out with, you like me."

Liz couldn't look at her, but she did say yes.

"Okay, well, I like you, too. And I'd like you to stop avoiding me. I'd like you to come over to the house for tea, to grab a sandwich or a beer with me every once in a while. We can just be pals and forget about the kiss. Okay?"

"Okay." Liz exhaled in relief. She liked the idea of being Audrey's pal, of having an actual female friend for a change. But she didn't know if she could forget about the kiss.

Elisa

"We've never been to Moneymaker's," Elisa said from the backseat, where she was crammed in between Jo and Thalia. "We went to that Merry-Go-Round place once, but I didn't like it." After the GLOBAL meeting, Jamal had invited all interested parties to carpool to Moneymaker's, the new and supposedly upscale gay club in West Knoxville.

"The Merry-Go-Round is just nasty," Jamal said.

"The gates of hell can't be scarier than the men's room there," Shaun said from his spot in the shotgun seat.

"The women's room is pretty bad, too," Jo said. "I went in there and kept getting the eye from some old dyke who looked like she'd been cut up in a fight."

Thalia laughed. "What were her intentions toward you?"

Jo shrugged. "I didn't stick around long enough to find out. I didn't even stay long enough to pee."

"I don't know . . . I kind of like the Merry-Go-Round," Thalia said. "It's like a piece of history, you know?"

"Yeah, from the Stone Age," Jamal said.

Moneymaker's was in the back basement level of a red brick yuppie strip mall. Its existence was announced by a neon sign that spelled out the club's name in lavender script.

"Jesus," Thalia said, "I can't believe there's a queer bar in the same shopping center as the Wine Cellar and the Gourmet Grocery."

"It makes sense, though," Jamal said. "They all cater to fags with money."

"And dykes with money," Elisa said, reminding Jamal to be inclusive.

"Honey, dykes don't have money," Jamal scoffed. "Dykes have *principles!*"

Elisa laughed, but she hoped money and principles weren't mutually exclusive. She had grown up watching her mother scraping up pennies to keep them in peanut butter and Hamburger Helper, and Jo's family had been even worse off. She was all for having principles, but she knew they didn't amount to a hill of beans when it came time to buy groceries or pay the light bill.

The entrance hall of Moneymaker's looked like the living room of a luxurious home. There was a camelback sofa and two wing chairs and a gilt-framed mirror hanging on the wall. Other than the insistent beat of the dance music that shook the walls, the only clue that this room wasn't a suburban parlor was the goldfish bowl sitting on the coffee table and filled with colorful condoms.

Beyond the entrance hall, a willowy young blond man stood at a table with a cash register.

"There's my favorite River Phoenix look-alike!" Shaun crowed. "Up for another photo session sometime soon?"

The blonde's smile revealed a mouthful of toothpaste commercial-perfect teeth. "Anytime. And you can go on back. No cover charge for the paparazzi."

"And no need for me to show ID since you know I'm older than God," Shaun said, pecking the blonde on the cheek and flouncing past him.

With Shaun gone, the blonde took on a more businesslike air. "I need to see some IDs, please." He scanned the proffered licenses and pointed to Jamal and Thalia. "Okay, you can drink, and you can drink, but"—he nodded at Jo and Elisa—"you two can't."

"We can still go in, right?" Elisa said.

"It's eighteen to get in and twenty-one to drink. Let's see your hands, please."

Elisa held out her hand, and the young man wrote "NO" on it in neon-green Magic Marker.

Inside the club, Elisa's senses were assaulted by pounding music and flashing lights. The dance floor was packed with writhing couples and singles and groups—mostly male. A well-toned young man dressed only in Daisy Dukes gyrated on top of a speaker. Elisa didn't know the song that was playing, and she was sure that to Jo's country music-loving ears, it sounded like nothing but a lot of racket. "You wanna dance?" Elisa hollered at Jo, knowing full well what the answer would be.

"Not unless they start playing some Hank Junior," Jo hollered back.

"So I guess that's a no," Elisa said. She deplored Jo's musical tastes as far too rednecky. Elisa listened to Top Forty and oldies herself, though lately she had been trying to broaden her horizons by listening to the local classical station even though it lulled her to sleep more often than not.

"Why don't we find a place to sit down?" Jo yelled. She took Elisa's hand and led her, in the maneuver Elisa always thought of as the "butch-femme drag," away from the dance floor, down a narrow hallway and into a back room where round tables were arranged around a thrust stage. Most of the tables had filled up, but Jo pulled Elisa toward an empty one near the stage.

"Oh, so you wanted to be where you could make goo-goo eyes at the drag queens?" Elisa teased.

"Well, I do like looking at 'em," Jo said, "but I've got the good sense to know it's all pretend, like watching a magic show. And I'm happy to be going home with the real thing."

Jo leaned in for a short, soft kiss, and Elisa felt the joy of being able to show affection in public without fear.

The first drag queen wore a big blond wig and lip-synched to Tammy Wynette's "Stand By Your Man" (Jo gave her a dollar); the second wore an aqua sequined evening gown and moved her lips to a Whitney Houston song. The third performer, though, shocked and baffled Elisa. A beautiful passing woman with Stevie Nicks-style blond hair, she wore a black lace mantilla, a rosary and a high-necked, long-sleeved, floor-length black gown. She placed a row of lighted candles in front of her and began to sway with grace and sadness to a song Elisa didn't know about the night belonging to lovers. As the song progressed, the performer became more and more spastic in her movements, finally kneeling in front of the candles and pouring the molten wax over her face. Her mascara and blush blended with the wax and dripped down her cheeks and hardened, creating a mask that, like the face of a weeping woman, was beautiful and horrible to behold.

When the number ended, Jo leaned over and said, "What the Sam Hill was that?"

Elisa, who was halfway between being frightened and being moved, said, "I think it was art."

"Well, it was too deep for me, I'll tell you that. I think I'll stick with Tammy Wynette."

Elisa knew that if something jerked Jo out of her comfort zone, her automatic response was not to like it. But Elisa liked seeing things she had never seen before. If she had wanted things to stay predictable, she would have stayed in Odessa.

When the show was over, Jo said, "I saw a sign that said something about a game room. You wanna see if we can get up a game of pool?"

"Sure." Elisa sucked at pool, but she loved to watch Jo play, to see the confident way she leaned in for a shot, her cocky pleasure when the ball dropped into the pocket.

They were making their way through the maze of tables when Elisa heard a voice call her name. She thought it might be Thalia, who had parted ways with them at the dance floor, but the voice lacked Thalia's raspiness. Elisa turned in the direction of the voice to see Dr. Rivers wearing an elegant little black dress with her customary pearls, sitting next to a muscular woman with short salt-and-pepper hair and wire-framed glasses.

"Dr. Rivers?" Elisa said, not meaning to reveal the disbelief she felt.

"What is it, Elisa? Shocked to see your old professor out on the town?" Dr. Rivers laughed. "It's not all critical theory with me all the time, you know." She smiled over at her companion. "Of course, come to think of it, tonight is kind of about theory, isn't it? My friend Maureen is visiting from out of town. She's working on a project on gender, so she wanted to see a drag show. Maureen, this is Elisa, one of my most gifted students."

Elisa felt herself blushing and hoped it was rendered unnoticeable by the dim lights. "Thank you," she said. "But I don't guess that says much for your other students, does it? Oh, and this is Jo, my . . . girlfriend." She hated how juvenile that word sounded.

"So you're the famous Dr. Rivers," Jo said, holding out her hand. "Elisa talks about you all the time. She thinks you hung the moon."

Dr. Rivers smiled. "Well, I'm afraid I didn't. Would the two of you care to join us?"

"Actually, we were just getting ready to shoot some pool," Jo said before Elisa could answer. "It was real nice to meet y'all, though."

As soon as they were in the game room, Elisa was surprised to see Jo burst out laughing. She laughed so hard she had to wipe her eyes with the hanky she always carried in her pocket.

"What's gotten into you?" Elisa asked.

"Nothing." Jo laughed some more. "It's just . . . I've wasted so much time being jealous of this Dr. Rivers. And then when I get a look at her . . . well, she's about as girly as you are! You want to talk about worrying over nothing!" Jo selected a pool cue, but she didn't stop laughing.

Elisa's mind was still back at the table with Dr. Rivers. And who was that Maureen woman anyway? Was she Dr. Rivers' lover? How strange to see Dr. Rivers out like this and to have her finally meet Jo. And of course, here was Jo, saying she had nothing to worry about because Elisa couldn't possibly be interested in a woman as feminine as Dr. Rivers. And yet when Elisa thought about Dr. Rivers, all cozy at that table with her salt-and-pepper-haired friend, what she felt was definitely jealousy.

Beth

"I can't believe we all have to wear these white shirts and black pants," Quimby whispered to Beth. "We look like a bunch of waitresses."

"Or a bunch of penguins." Beth surveyed her identical black-and-white sisters. "Anorexic penguins."

Quimby giggled. "Drunk anorexic penguins."

The chapter president flashed them a ladylike look that meant "shut up." They were supposed to be listening while she explained—for the umpteen millionth time—the correct proceedings and etiquette for tonight's rush party, during which dozens of hopeful freshmen would descend on the Panhellenic ballroom, all itching to become Theta's newest members. It was up to Beth and her sisters to decide which girls would make the cut.

Ever since her and Quimby's talk, Beth had sworn to throw herself into the sorority's activities. It had been a mistake to assume that because most of her sisters weren't exactly the greatest minds of the twentieth century, they wouldn't notice that she was emotionally distant from the group. It was precisely because so many of the girls thought of little else but the sorority and their frat boyfriends that they could sniff out Beth's indifference. And if they could sniff out her indifference, was it just a matter of time until they sniffed out her difference as well?

She would fix that potential problem by not being different. She would smile and giggle and flirt and do all the things sorority girls were supposed to do. One of the few things (other than the awkwardness with Thalia) that Beth remembered about that God-awful women's studies class last semester was how the professor kept rattling on about women's choices. Women, Dr. Rivers always said, should have the right to choose what kind of lives to lead.

Beth had made her choice. Here, among these girls with their fifty-dollar haircuts and three-hundred-dollar shoes, was where she would stay. The area below her waist had led her astray, but the area above her neck knew that this life was the only reasonable choice. If she chose otherwise, what kind of life could she have? A life like Thalia's? Thalia's future, Beth thought, wouldn't be that different from Thalia's present, except that she would be finished with school and so would spend her days waiting tables or stocking the shelves in a bookstore or doing some other menial task. She'd still live in dumpy group housing and go to every pathetic, pointless political demonstration, never realizing that nobody cared what she had to say.

Fuck that.

Beth would be a partner in her daddy's law firm. She'd drive an aubergine Jaguar and fly to New York twice a year to buy clothes since nothing sold in Knoxville would be good enough. She would live in one of the mansions on Cherokee Trail and have a maid and a cook and a gardener. She would be so rich and so successful that nobody could talk badly about her or hurt her.

At eight o'clock, the rushees rushed in. Beth, like her sisters, wore a wide, welcoming smile, even though it was obvious from the get-go that a lot of the girls were total losers who didn't stand a chance. Nudged by a sister, Beth approached a fat, brown-skinned girl—what was she? Hawaiian? Mexican?—who was wearing a cheap flowered dress that looked like the kind of thing somebody's grandmother would be buried in.

"Hi, I'm Beth Chamberlain, a junior and a proud Theta sister. And you are?"

"Andrea Hill."

"Hill" was a totally unhelpful name when it came to figuring out this girl's ethnicity—not that Beth had anything against people of other races. "It's great to meet you, Andrea. So what's your major?"

"Music." Andrea beamed. "I'm one of the newest members of the WBU marching band!"

A band nerd. Like this girl didn't already have enough strikes against her. Beth had to ditch this girl, and fast. She spotted a sister named Becky and waved her over. "My sister Becky is a music major," Beth said. "Let me introduce you."

Becky smiled widely and shook Andrea's hand, but Beth could see the trapped-animal look in her sister's eyes.

The next rushee Beth met was cute and petite—she couldn't have been more than five feet even, and Beth would have been shocked if she weighed a hundred pounds. The girl's name was Carly, and she wore a Donna Karan dress and Prada shoes. When Carly said she was from Nashville, Beth asked her what part of town. "Brentwood," Carly said, and Beth smiled in recognition of the neighborhood's status. With a Brentwood address, Carly's parents would have no trouble paying their daughter's sorority dues.

Beth would have been fine with talking to Carly all night, but her job was to circulate. She kept her rictus smile as she talked to assorted middle-class strivers, rednecks and nerds. The next girl she liked didn't exactly fit the Theta mold, but she had her own kind of sporty elegance. Her flame-red hair was cropped short, which showed off her devastating cheekbones. She wore a simple, tailored, blue dress, but it was a Ralph Lauren. She wore little makeup, but real diamond studs glittered in her earlobes.

"Anna Stokes," the rushee introduced herself after Beth had run through her spiel. "I'm from Memphis, and I'm a communications major."

"Memphis—what a great city!" Beth gushed. "Where did you grow up?"

"Germantown."

A good address, Beth noted. "So why are you interested in joining Theta?"

"Well . . ." Anna grinned, a little shyly. "To tell you the truth, I'm an only child, and I always wanted sisters. I figure joining Theta could be the way to have the sisterhood I've always dreamed of."

"With none of the sibling rivalry," Beth said, though this wasn't really true. She found herself giving Anna a sincere smile instead of a pasted-on one, but then she felt a wave of panic once she understood the reason for the smile. She liked Anna—liked her in an incestuous desire-for-a-sorority-sister kind of way. She had to get away from this girl. In her frenzy, she spotted a sister whom she knew only vaguely but who was, she was reasonably sure, a communications major. "You know," she said, pasting the fake smile back on, "I have a sister who's a communications major. Let me introduce you."

After the rushees had been herded out, the sisters exploded in tension-relieving laughter. "Omigod, Beth," Becky said, "that band nerd girl you stuck me with! The only way she'd stand a chance is if we decided to adopt the whale as our mascot."

"You know who I liked?" Quimby said. "Carly."

Carly received a chorus of approving statements such as, "I'd kill for those shoes she had on." The sisters tossed around various names, most of them in disapproval.

"This is the most pathetic group of rushees ever," Amy said. "Beth, weren't you talking to that girl with the short red hair?"

"Anna, yeah," Beth said, being careful not to give an opinion until she heard what the other girls thought.

"That girl was a total dyke!" Amy said.

Beth's stomach knotted. "You think so?"

"Totally," Amy said. "I mean, that hair and that outfit—she looked like she'd just come from playing field hockey. She probably wants to get into our sorority so she can prey on all of us beautiful women. God, Beth, did you really not know she was a dyke?"

Beth managed to say no, but the effects of her orange pill seemed to have worn off instantly. The room was starting to fishbowl, and she felt her sisters' judgmental eyes on her.

"Poor little Beth, you really are naïve," Amy said, laughing. "I always know a dyke when I see one."

Liz

It was rare for Liz to be up and dressed and out of her room before noon on a Saturday, but she had promised to stop by Audrey's house around eleven. Her head was throbbing, and her eyes were as light-sensitive as a mole's, but with the help of the coffee and the preservative-laden Danish she had picked up at the campus convenience store, she hoped to be somewhat coherent by the time she knocked on Audrey's door.

"Hungover again, I see," Audrey greeted her.

"Am I that obvious?"

"Oh, come on. The dark sunglasses, the cup of coffee in the trembling hand . . . you're the patron saint of hangovers. Plus, I usually figure that if it's morning, you must be hungover."

Liz bristled at Audrey's last comment. "Thanks for making me sound like a total alcoholic."

"I don't think you're an alcoholic," Audrey said, "but I do think you spend too much time making that vibrantly colored head of yours all muzzy. Of course, that's just my unsolicited opinion."

One of the interesting things about Audrey was that her extreme level of frankness, which would be off-putting in a less pleasant and playful person, was somehow endearing. Plus, Liz knew that Audrey was probably right. "Well," Liz said, "like the T-shirt says, when I want your opinion, I'll beat it out of you."

"Promises, promises," Audrey said, wiggling her eyebrows suggestively. "So . . . I was thinking we might ride downtown and poke around the thrift stores a bit. I've got an extra bike you can borrow."

Liz was sure she was an even deeper shade of red at the prospect of the embarrassing confession she had to make. "Uh, well, see . . . I never really learned to ride a bike."

Audrey clapped her hands over her mouth. "You what?"

"I never learned to ride. I was a very bookish child. I had a lot more interest in going places in my head than in going places with my body."

Audrey laughed. "I was a bookish child, too, but I always stuck a book in my bike basket, and off I went." She clapped her hands. "So that's what we'll do today. I'll teach you to ride a bike."

"No!" Liz almost yelled.

"Why not? There are three things that every red-blooded American needs to know: how to type, how to ride a bike and how to drive a stick shift."

Liz decided not to tell Audrey that she didn't even have a driver's license, lest she add driving lessons to the day's plan. "I'm an excellent typist."

"And by this afternoon, you'll be an excellent bike rider."

"Audrey, you're sweet to want to teach me, but I can't learn out in the open like this. I'll look like an idiot."

"To whom? The street's deserted. Everybody's still sleeping off last night's beer. And even if they weren't, so what? Looking like an idiot can pay off sometimes. Look at Dan Quayle."

"Of course, with him it's not just a matter of *looking* like an idiot."

"True. Appearances are not deceiving in that case. Listen. You wait here, and I'll run around back and get the bikes." She brushed back her hair and flashed a full, dimple-revealing smile. "Okay?"

Liz knew she was beaten. "Okay."

"All right," Audrey said when she returned. "You get on, and I'll hold it steady while you get the feel of it."

"The least you could do is provide me with training wheels."

"Training wheels are for wimps." Draping her arms around Liz's shoulders, Audrey steadied the handlebars. "Now pedal like the wind, girl."

Liz was nothing like the wind. She was more like a wobbly newborn colt trying to stand up for the first time. Audrey's support was the only thing that was keeping her vertical. A dreadlocked white boy in a Bob Marley T-shirt passed them and grinned. "God, did you see him look at me?" Liz said.

"Hey," Audrey whispered, "white guys with dreadlocks don't have the right to tell anybody they look stupid. Now . . . practice steering."

Soon Audrey was holding only one handlebar. Liz veered toward a fire hydrant, then steered away from it. When they reached a downhill stretch, she stopped pedaling and let the incline do the work while Audrey jogged alongside to keep up. "Okay," Liz said, gasping, when she reached the bottom of the hill, "that was fun."

"See, there's something to be said for not living in your head all the time."

"I guess I've never put much emphasis on the physical. I was raised Catholic, so I was always taught to overcome the physical. Plus, I've never really liked my body, so I've mostly tried to ignore it."

"Believe me, Liz. There's nothing wrong with your body."

Liz looked down to hide her embarrassment and nearly drove straight into a tree.

Audrey jerked her to safety. "Although, if you don't watch where you're going, there might be."

They were nearing the park that, eight years earlier, had been the site of the World's Fair. The Sunsphere, a giant gold ball on a tower which resembled a gigantic video game joystick, was in sight. The park was paved and, unlike most of Knoxville, fairly flat.

The pedaling was easier here, and soon Audrey was clapping and yelling, "Go, Liz!"

It was only then Liz realized that Audrey had let go of the handlebar, meaning that she had been successfully balancing and pedaling on her own for several yards. Finally, at the age of twenty, she could ride a bike. At this rate, she might have a driver's license by the time she was forty. She brought the bike to a wobbly stop. By the time she had dismounted gracelessly, Audrey was standing beside her.

"Well"—Liz laughed—"when it comes it remedial bike riding, you, madam, are a master teacher."

Audrey draped her arm around Liz. "Hey, I didn't do anything but tell you to get on the bike."

"Well, then, you must've been the right person to tell me because if it was anybody else, I'd have told them to fuck right off."

"I think," Audrey said, releasing Liz from her half-hug, "that I will choose to take that as a compliment."

"You should." In fact, Liz was amazed that she had gotten on the bike at all, much less ridden it. If she had been with Dan instead of Audrey, she sure as hell wouldn't have done it. She would have been too scared—not so scared of causing herself serious injury as of looking klutzy or moronic. Since their talk over bad hot chocolate, Liz had felt easier with Audrey than she did with Dan. Unlike when she was with Dan, she didn't spend every second with Audrey trying to identify and cater to her every thought and feeling.

"I'll tell you what," Audrey said. "Why don't we head back to the house, and I'll make us some lunch to celebrate your athletic victory?"

"Don't call it a victory yet," Liz said. "The ride back is uphill."

By the time they reached the theater house, Liz was excruciatingly aware of the effects of every joint she had smoked and every beer she had drunk on her feeling-much-older-than-twenty body.

"Oh, God, I forgot there were stairs to your house." She moaned.

"Shall I carry you up them?"

The image of Audrey's lips pressing against hers flashed in her mind. "No, I've got 'em." It was funny; Liz could be so comfortable with Audrey, but the second that kiss popped into her head, she felt like running away. Of course, right now she was too exhausted to run.

As Liz flopped on the couch with a glass of water, Audrey rummaged through the refrigerator. "How do you feel about Gorgonzola? It's made from real gorgons," Audrey called.

"I only like it for Medusa-nal purposes," Liz answered, wincing at her own pun, which was at least as cheesy as the Gorgonzola. Truth be told, she knew Gorgonzola was a kind of cheese but had no idea what it tasted like.

Audrey stood in the kitchen doorway, wielding a wedge of cheese. "You know, I usually refuse to cook for people who make puns that bad. Lucky for you, I'm in a charitable mood. Plus, I have a craving for pasta with Gorgonzola cream sauce."

Audrey set the bowl of steaming pasta on the table. "Would you like a glass of Chianti?"

"I thought you said I drink too much," Liz said, sitting down at the table.

"You probably do, but Chianti goes great with this dish. And besides, we're celebrating your bike-riding triumph. When you're off winning the Tour de France, remember me."

"I'll send you some wine and cheese." The Gorgonzola was totally different from the Kraft products of Liz's childhood. It was creamy and delicious, but in a complicated way. "The pasta sauce is wonderful, by the way."

"Thanks. I've been really into different kinds of cheeses lately. I was a Cheez Whiz kid, so now I'm really enjoying exploring different cheeses' tastes and textures."

"I was a Velveeta girl myself." Liz realized this was something she never would have confessed to Dan—Dan, whose family considered using jarred artichoke hearts instead of fresh ones to be déclassé to the point of vulgarity.

"Oh, that's some interesting stuff." Audrey laughed. "Kind of like cheese-flavored Play-Doh. I'll tell you a secret, though. Sometimes when I've had a bad day, I still pop some Cheez Whiz in the microwave and eat it with Fritos. If you turn into too much of a snob, you can lose out on some good stuff."

When they took their wine into the living room and sat down on the couch, they were suddenly silent. Liz, in her nervousness, knocked back a big slug of wine.

"The last time we sat on this couch together, I kissed you," Audrey said. "That's what you were thinking about, weren't you?"

Staring at her nearly empty glass, Liz nodded. Her mind told her to get up and run away, but her legs didn't seem to be in the mood to obey.

"I know I told you I could just be your pal," Audrey said. "And I can, if that's what you want. But I also want you to know that I'd like to kiss you again if you'd let me."

Liz felt like she might cry. "Dan," she began, but once she got his name out, she didn't know what else to say.

"Liz, since that time you talked to me about him, have you and Dan had sex?"

Liz shook her head no.

"Kissed?"

Tears coming to her eyes, Liz shook her head again.

"What have you and he done?"

Liz shrugged and wiped her eyes. "Talked. Hung out. Drank beer. You know."

"Liz, if that's what constitutes a romantic relationship, then there are billions of straight men who are currently involved in romantic relationships with each other. How can you work so hard at being faithful to a relationship when there's no relationship to be faithful to?"

Angry tears burned Liz's eyes. She couldn't remember the last time she'd been so furious. How could Audrey have presumed to speak about her and Dan's relationship? And how could she have known Liz such a short time and be so absolutely right? Dan didn't want her, Liz knew, and she had spent over two years of her life wanting him all the more for it. For all her espoused feminism, she was just another female masochist. But since she couldn't admit to any of this out loud, she said, "You don't know anything about Dan and me."

"That may be true," Audrey said. "But I do know a woman who needs to be kissed when I see one." She took the wineglass out of Liz's hand and set it on the table. "Who *deserves* to be kissed." She leaned toward Liz and whispered, "If you don't want me to do this, just tell me to stop."

Stop. Liz saw the word in white block letters on a red octagon. She saw it, but she couldn't say it, and soon Audrey's lips were brushing against hers. *Stop*, Liz still thought, but Audrey's lips were full and open, not thin and tight like Dan's. And when Audrey brought her tongue into the kiss, it was with a subtle flick instead of the full-throttle, Pez Dispenser onslaught to which Liz was accustomed.

Liz gave her lips to Audrey in a way she had never given them to Dan, perhaps because Dan had never seemed that interested in her lips unless they were headed south of his navel. But even as she nearly surrendered to the glorious pleasures of kissing for kissing's sake, fear and confusion prodded her. What did it mean that she was doing this with another girl? She broke away from the kiss and found herself saying, in a voice that didn't sound like her own, "Your roommates . . ."

"Are off with their respective boyfriends, probably doing about what we're doing now. You look scared, Liz. Are you?"

Liz nodded, embarrassed by her transparency. "I think I'm scared of what this means."

Audrey rested her hand on Liz's cheek. "It doesn't have to mean anything you don't want it to mean. Do you like it . . . when I kiss you?"

Liz nodded again. It was the fact that she did like it that scared her.

"Good. Then if it's okay with you, I think I might do it again."

Liz fell into Audrey's kisses like Alice falling down the rabbit hole. She kissed and kissed and kissed just like Alice fell and fell and fell, without having any idea how many minutes or hours had passed. The only time measurement Liz could be sure of was that the duration of her and Audrey's kissing session had by far outlasted the duration of any sexual encounter she had ever had with Dan.

After however many minutes or hours, Audrey whispered, "We could lie down . . . if you'd be more comfortable."

"Okay."

The walls of Audrey's bedroom were decorated with prints of Georgia O'Keefe's gynecological-looking flowers. Liz sucked in her breath, teetering somewhere between titillation and terror.

"Listen," Audrey said, "I don't want you to feel pressured. We won't do anything you don't want to do. If you start feeling uncomfortable at any point—even if it seems like a bad time to say anything—just tell me to stop."

"I feel like such a virgin." Liz sat down on the bed next to her.

"Well, you are, aren't you? There are all kinds of virginity." She smiled, then leaned in for a kiss.

Soon they were lying on the bed with Audrey leaning over Liz. When Audrey started pulling at the snaps of Liz's cowboy shirt, Liz felt like her heart was going to pound right out of her chest. With Dan, her desire had always dissipated by the time they were actually in bed, but here, now, with each snap undone, Liz felt her desire double until its intensity was almost unbearable.

"No bra—I didn't think so." Audrey ran a finger from Liz's throat down the middle of her chest and belly where her shirt parted. When Audrey opened the shirt wider and brushed her lips against Liz's breasts, Liz was shocked by the pleasure of it.

Their lovemaking evolved slowly. Unlike with Dan, there seemed to be no predictable script to follow, and Audrey paid Liz's hands and feet the same amount of passionate attention she had devoted to her breasts. Daylight was fading by the time Audrey finally peeled off Liz's panties. Liz was nervous when Audrey parted her thighs. No one, short of the doctor at the student clinic, had ever really looked at her there, and she felt like she should crack a joke to cut the tension.

But when Audrey's tongue touched her there, Liz found herself in a place that was beyond jokes, beyond words of any kind. So this was sex. This was why duels had been fought and vows had been made or renounced. It was as good a reason as any Liz could imagine. In fact, it was better than anything Liz had ever imagined, let alone experienced. This pleasure was so big, it radiated down into her thighs and into her toes, which curled in ecstasy. She panted in time with Audrey's strokes, which grew more and more rapid as the flicker of Liz's pleasure ignited into a flame that shot sparks throughout her entire body, and she heard herself gasping, "Lover!"

They were quiet for a long time. Liz had never felt such quiet.

When she could finally speak, she said, "Thank you."

Audrey laughed. "You know you're dealing with a nice Southern girl when the first words out of her mouth after sex are *thank you*. I guess you'll send me a thank-you note, too: 'Dear Audrey, Thank you for the lovely orgasm. I will treasure it for years to come.' "

Liz laughed. "You're terrible. What I meant was . . . I'd never . . . it's never . . . I mean, I don't know if it's because you're a woman, or because you're older and more experienced . . ."

"Well, there were all those women I fucked in the factories during World War Two. I'm only twenty-five, Liz. Don't make me feel eighty."

"Sorry. I'm just . . . I mean, I didn't know my body could do that."

"Of course it can . . . with the right chemistry. And you and I do seem to cook up a pretty heady brew of pheromones."

"Yes." Liz looked at Audrey's reclining figure. She was wearing only a black lace bra and boxer shorts, which seemed the perfect expression of her quirky brand of femininity. Audrey's figure was fuller than Liz's, her breasts large enough to create a deep cleavage and the kind of hips that are often described as "womanly." She was beautiful, and Liz trembled at the thought of touching her. "I'd like to, uh . . . return the favor," she said. "But I have absolutely no idea what I'm doing."

Audrey smiled a kitty-cat smile. "You're a clever girl. You'll learn fast." She playfully pulled Liz on top of her. "It's just like riding a bicycle."

Elisa

"I reckon we'd better scoot the beds apart before I go," Jo said.

"I guess so," Elisa said. "I hate feeling like a hypocrite, though."

Yesterday afternoon Elisa's mother had called, saying that Elisa's dad had an appointment at the V.A. hospital in Knoxville and so they might stop to see her afterward and get a bite to eat. As a result, Elisa and Jo had to de-dyke the dorm room, separating their beds, shoving any books with overtly lesbian titles into dresser drawers. Elisa's parents knew about her lesbianism, of course, but they considered any physical reminders of her sexual orientation to be "rubbing their noses in it." Jo, the ultimate physical reminder, would be safely away at softball practice by the time Elisa's parents were due to arrive. But Elisa knew that if Jo hadn't had practice, she would have made herself scarce anyway.

When they knocked on the door, Elisa was trying her damnedest to make sense of some Gertrude Stein thing—was it a poem? A story? A random assortment of words?—she was supposed to read for Women in

Modernism. She shoved the book under her pillow before she got up to answer the door.

Elisa's mom, who outweighed Elisa's dad by at least two hundred pounds, was wearing the outfit that always meant she was "dressed up": purple polyester pull-on pants and a royal blue polyester blouse splashed with big purple flowers. Elisa's tiny daddy was wearing a Western shirt and Wrangler jeans and the same hairstyle he had sported in his high school yearbook photo: a "wet-look" black pompadour.

"Hidy, stranger!" Her mom said, but she didn't move to hug her. They weren't huggers, Elisa's parents. Elisa could never even remember seeing the two of them hug each other.

"Hey," Elisa said. "Did your doctor's visit go all right, Daddy?"

Elisa's father said nothing—as Elisa knew he wouldn't—but her mother said, "It went all right. The doctor wants him to try a new lift in his shoe. Your daddy was wantin' to walk down to Krystal's."

Elisa smiled. "Why am I not surprised?" There was no Krystal in Odessa, and Elisa's daddy loved their greasy little hamburgers. "Just let me get my purse."

It was funny; Elisa had spent her childhood and teen years in Odessa dreaming of little but getting the hell out of there, but even as a self-conscious teenager, she couldn't remember feeling embarrassed to be seen out with her parents. Of course, in Odessa, her parents didn't look that strange—there were plenty of overweight women in polyester outfits and men in Western wear with anachronistic haircuts. But when her parents visited her in Knoxville, Elisa was hyper-conscious of how out of place they looked, especially in a university setting. As they walked across the dorm's parking lot, with her mother panting from exertion and her dad nervously sucking on a Marlboro, Elisa could feel the stares of her fellow students, causing her embarrassment mixed with shame about being embarrassed.

Her parents were good people. Once Elisa started elementary school, her mother had taken a job at the dime store so she could afford to order her girls decent clothes out of the J.C. Penney catalog. And despite the fact that they were always short on money, Elisa's mom had always made sure that her and her sister Marie's childhood was not short on celebrations. There were cookouts with cake and ice cream for birthdays and elaborate, hand-sewn costumes for Halloween, including, one year, beautiful sequined mermaid costumes. And during the Christmas season, in Elisa's opinion, her mother went stark raving mad with festivity, outlining the house in lights, making her one-legged husband secure a lighted plastic Santa's sleigh on the roof and playing the Loretta Lynn Christmas album during every waking hour. Elisa knew that her mother had been raised in a home where a day without a beating was a cause for celebration, so Elisa admired her mother's insistence on cheer.

And then there was her daddy—quiet, dutiful, wounded in ways the V.A. hospital could never fix. He never talked about the war—never talked much, period, except to ask someone to refill his coffee or fetch his cigarette lighter. His thoughts were an utter mystery to Elisa, but she did know that he worked hard to provide what he could for his family, getting up for work at six a.m. and not coming home until six at night, when he'd unstrap his prosthetic foot, sit down in his recliner and sigh in relief. Elisa had often wondered what her dad had been like before the war—if he had talked more or laughed more before the damage had been done. Marie used to get furious at him, at his silence and seeming emotional absence. But Elisa was always more patient with him, confident that after all he had been through, he was doing the best he could.

Elisa loved her parents. Even though she was glad every day not to be living with them anymore, she still loved them. And so she felt terrible for hoping she didn't see anybody she knew as she walked with them to Krystal. If they were to run into Dr. Rivers, she was confident she would die on the spot. It wasn't a comfortable feeling, knowing this about herself, but she supposed it was just another manifestation of the emotional truth she had known since she was a little girl: she loved her family fiercely, but she wasn't like them.

In the fluorescent lighting of Krystal, Elisa's dad hunched over his hamburgers, not looking up at his tablemates or the other diners. Elisa knew that public places made him nervous, and he would rather eat alone in his truck.

"Did I tell you Marie's workin' out at the Shell Mart now?" her mom asked, not waiting for a reply. "She likes it better than the burger house. She says this way she don't go around smelling like french fry grease all the time."

In the seven years since Marie dropped out of high school to have Travis, she had worked a succession of dead-end fast-food and convenience store jobs, adding on the pounds that came with spending one's days surrounded by junk food. Elisa periodically tried to encourage her to get her GED and go to vocational school, but Marie always told her to mind her own business, that not everybody could be a genius like her. "That's good," Elisa said.

"And what else . . ." Her mother trailed off, biting into a burger. "Your mamaw's cataract surgery is at the end of the month, so you might want to send her a card or somethin'."

"I will," Elisa said.

While her dad chewed silently, her mom prattled on about people in Odessa who were sick or injured, marrying or pregnant or divorcing. Elisa's mother didn't ask her any questions about her own life, about her classes or her personal life or her plans. She knew that this lack of questions wasn't because her mother didn't care about her. It was just that Elisa's life had grown so different from her mother's that her mother had no idea what kind of questions to ask.

After she and her parents parted ways in the dorm lobby (with her mother slipping her a twenty-dollar bill that Elisa knew was the result of much sacrifice), Elisa stopped in the bathroom on her floor. As she sat down to pee, she heard a girl in the shower say to a friend in the adjoining shower, "Did you see those people walking around the hall today? They were, like, total hillbillies."

The other voice laughed. "Oh, you mean that four-hundred-pound woman and that guy with the Elvis hair who was, like, four feet tall? They looked like they'd escaped from a freak show."

"Yeah," the other voice said. "The fat lady and the world's shortest Elvis impersonator."

Elisa's first impulse was to storm into the shower and snatch both girls bald-headed for talking like that about her mother and daddy. But then she thought, if she wasn't from a little place like Odessa and she saw a couple that looked like her parents walking around campus, her reaction would probably be the same: *Who are these people?*

Beth

Beth had never been to the Merry-Go-Round without Mike, but he was off doing something manly with his frat brothers, and she had to get away from sorority activities for a while and blow off some steam. Girls who weren't in a sorority could never understand how exhausting this time of year was. The Theta sisters had picked their favorites from the rushees, who had now become pledges. Beth had heard of some sororities that practically tortured their pledges, doing things like making them strip down to their underwear and crawl on their knees and elbows on uncooked rice until they bled. The Theta sisters weren't that mean, though they weren't above making new pledges do their laundry, give them pedicures or do numerous vodka shots while reciting Theta rules from memory.

The thing that made pledge period so tiring was that Beth had to be in Panhell all the time. Every minute she wasn't in class, it seemed like she was in some organized sorority activity. But she was giving it her all; she really was. Ever since Quimby's warning, she had been the model sorority sister, aided by the orange pills that made it so much easier to smile. This rush period was really giving her the opportunity to shine. She was stern or sweet with the pledges, as the occasion warranted, the embodiment of a big sister.

But God, she was worn out, and tonight she deserved a little fun. It was two for one well drinks, and she held a vodka collins in each hand. She knocked back the first one in a hurry and reserved the second one for sipping as she made her circuit of the club.

Where were the cute dykes? The women at the pool table were cute enough, but they were obviously a couple. The audience watching the Taylor Dayne-loving drag queen was made up of gay men and their straight, or at least straight-looking, women friends. Straight and straight-looking women were of no sexual interest to Beth; the sorority was full of them.

At the downstairs bar, she ordered two more vodka collinses, one for chugging and one for sipping. Once she had downed the first one, she carried the second onto the dance floor, which was covered with sweaty, shirtless boys. No cute dykes to be seen, but "Groove Is in the Heart" was playing, and she was feeling a buzz, so she shook her hips and twirled through the sea of sweaty boyflesh. She was lost in the music until she felt a hand on her arm.

"So how come you sorority and frat types always dance with a drink in your hand?"

It was Thalia, and Beth found that, thanks to vodka collins number four, she wasn't unhappy to see her. The girl was damned cute, that was for sure. "It's all about efficiency," Beth yelled over the music. "If you don't drink while you dance, you lose out on valuable drinking time."

"But you can't be as free with your body with a drink in your hand."

"Oh, but I can be very free with my body," Beth said, "as you might remember."

They were walking away from the dance floor. "I remember," Thalia said, peeling the label off her beer bottle. "But you're not so free once you've sobered up, are you? Then you ran so fast you left skid marks on my hardwood floors."

"I'm sorry." Beth reached out and toyed with the zipper pull on Thalia's leather jacket. "Do you still like me, though?"

Thalia took a long swig of beer. "Yes, God help me, I still like you. And in that red dress, I really like you."

Beth leaned over and whispered, "I bet you'd like me even better out of it."

Thalia shook her head. "Okay, you got me. I'm absolutely helpless in the face of your high-femme seductiveness. Let's go to my place."

When Thalia flipped on the living room light, she said, "Thank God nobody else is home. Dee Dee says I only took you to bed because I was deprived of Barbie dolls as a child. Chloe, though, she says that you and I are playing out some kind of Stanley Kowalski/Blanche DuBois dynamic, if you get my reference."

"I get your reference. I'm not stupid."

"No," Thalia said, encircling Beth's waist with her arms. "You're too damn complicated to be stupid. Besides, I'm never attracted to stupid women. You are beautiful and intelligent and probably much too fucked up for me to be involved with."

"So don't get involved. Just fuck me." She leaned over and whispered in Thalia's ear, "Here. Now."

"What if my roommates walk in?"

"Let 'em."

Thalia did what she was told, as Beth had known she would, first up against the living room wall, so hard they knocked a picture down, then leaning over a worse-for-wear armchair. Tears sprang to Beth's eyes as she spasmed around Thalia's hand.

Once their breathing steadied, Thalia said, "That was fun."

"Yeah." Beth was still leaning against the armchair.

"So," Thalia said, "why don't we move to the bedroom and slow things down a little?"

Beth thought of waking up, sober, in bed with Thalia. "No, I'd better not. I . . . I think I should go."

Thalia grabbed her wrist. "Why? Are you afraid you might feel something besides just a rush of endorphins? Are you afraid I might want you to talk to me . . . or worse, touch me?"

"It's nothing like that." Beth freed herself of Thalia's grip. "I just can't be up all night. I've got stuff to do tomorrow—it's pledge season. I can't be all free-spirited like you; I've got responsibilities." She hitched up her panties, pulled down her skirt and slammed the front door behind her.

Liz

Liz wondered if Dan could tell how awkward she felt around him. She tried to act normal when they were together, but of course, the fact that she had to try was a sign that things were far from normal. Saturday afternoon with Audrey, their kisses, their naked embraces, that moment when Liz had felt like her molecules were being pleasurably ripped apart . . . this was the one thing on her mind, just as surely as it was the one thing she hadn't spoken about to Dan. In fact, Liz wasn't sure she had spoken of Audrey to Dan at all. He probably wasn't even aware of her existence, let alone the fact that Audrey had caused a physical reaction in his "old lady" that in over two years of sexual activity, he had never been able to effect.

This was the word in Liz's mind that connected what happened between her and Audrey, *this* as in, "What does *this* mean?" and "How am I going to tell Dan about *this*?" She wasn't having success answering either of these questions; in fact, all these questions seemed to do was beget other questions, such as, "Does this mean I'm a lesbian even though I was always attracted to guys before? And if this does mean I'm a lesbian, does it mean that all the people who have 'mistaken' me for a lesbian since I came to college were able to see something in me that I couldn't see myself? And is this better or worse than if I cheated on Dan with a guy, if, in fact, it was cheating since Dan and I haven't had sex in eons?"

Still, Dan was her partner and her companion, so she had to tell him. Telling him might put an end to their relationship, but at least she wouldn't feel like she did now, that she was in a constant state of deception, like one of those big-haired, shoulder-padded, pathologically lying women on the soap operas she used to watch when she stayed home sick from high school.

He was sitting next to her in a booth at the Sagebrush, her blue-jeaned thigh pressed against his. Stu was across from her, wearing his customary leer, and Todd was across from Dan. It was three-dollar pitcher night, and they were polishing off their second.

"Hey, I know you." A girl with long blond, hippie-chick pigtail braids had come up to their table.

It took a couple of seconds for Liz to recognize her as the slow-talking stoner from Thalia's short-lived women's group. Shit, what was her name? Mimi? Fifi? "Hey."

"You're a friend of Audrey's, right?" she said in a cannabis drawl.

What had Audrey told her? Best to change the subject. "I'm a friend of Thalia's, too. We're in Women in Modernism together."

"Oh, yeah. Thal bitches about that class all the time. 'Fucking Gertrude Fucking Stein,' she says. My name's Dee Dee, by the way, so you can quit searching your brain for it."

Now that it was clear that Dee Dee hadn't come up to talk about Audrey, Liz could breathe again. "God, was I that obvious? I suck with names."

"Which is probably why you haven't introduced us," Dan said. Liz made the round of introductions, and Dan said, "So, Dee Dee, why don't you grab a mug and have a seat?"

"I might sit for just a minute." Dee Dee said. "There's this dude I'm supposed to meet here, but I guess I can hang with y'all till he shows up."

She disappeared for a minute, then returned with a mug and another full pitcher, which she poured all around.

Liz grinned as the blond pigtailed, peasant-bloused woman served her beer. "You look like the Saint Pauli girl . . . you know, on the beer label."

"Nah, too flat-chested," Dee Dee said, filling her own mug. "Swiss Miss is more like it. But I tell you what . . . if I was Swiss Miss, I wouldn't put those pissy little marshmallows in my cocoa. Those things piss me off, man."

Who else had Liz heard bitch about the marshmallows in instant cocoa? Audrey. She decided to keep her mouth shut.

"So this dude you're meeting," Stu asked Dee Dee, "is he your boyfriend?"

Stu never quit, Liz thought.

"No, man," Dee Dee said. "He's just some dude that's supposed to sell me a bag. I don't do the boyfriend thing."

"What?" Stu said. "Are you a nun or something?"

"Fuck, no. I'm a dyke."

Liz was amazed by the seeming ease with which those words rolled off Dee Dee's tongue—how confident she seemed of who and what she was.

Stu and Todd looked like they'd been pole-axed, but Dan said, "I've long been an admirer of the daughters of Sappho. I can scarcely believe that when there are other options, any woman would want to share her bed with creatures as distasteful as menfolk."

"Hey, don't get me wrong," Dee Dee said, gesturing with her beer mug. "I've fucked some dudes, and it was all right. And hey, I might fuck a dude again someday . . . I don't know. But see, because a woman has a woman's body, she knows how what she's doing feels to the other woman . . . she knows what penetration means."

"Whoa," Stu said. "So you're saying that even with dicks, guys don't measure up?"

Dee Dee grinned. "Give me the choice, and I'll take a dyke over a dick anyday."

"Wow," Todd said, "that's really depressing."

"We, gentlemen, are obsolete," Dan said. "The dinosaur of heterosexuality is sinking into the tarpits."

"I'm not saying all women feel that way," Dee Dee said. "I mean, some chicks are totally straight. And then, like my roommate Chloe, she doesn't care what sex somebody is. She says she likes the person, not the gender. And man, she does like . . . people."

"And I'd like her phone number," Stu said.

"So how about you, Liz?" Dee Dee turned away from Stu. "I know Dan here's your old man, so are you, like, straight as an arrow, or what?"

Here it was. Her opportunity to not exactly confess to Dan, but to test the waters a little. And she was drunk, which increased her courage. "Well . . ." Liz said, "my arrow may be a little bit . . . bent."

"So you're bi?" Dee Dee said.

"Yeah. Yeah, I guess I am." She looked over at Dan, expecting to see a look of shock or horror, but instead he gazed at her with a level of admiration usually reserved for people who rescue children from a burning orphanage.

"Wow, Liz," Dan said. "You never told me that."

Or anybody else. Even myself, Liz thought. "Yeah . . . well . . . I didn't want you to think that if I was out with you, I was . . . you know, looking at girls all the time."

"But see," Dan said, "you can look at girls. I'm not possessive, you know that about me. So . . . do you see any girls here you find attractive?"

"Oh, there's my dude," Dee Dee said, nodding toward a dreadlocked white guy at the bar.

"Say," Stu said, "I've been looking for a new source. Maybe you could introduce me?"

"Sure, man."

Stu followed Dee Dee to the bar.

"Typical Stu," Todd said. "If he can't get any pussy, he'll at least get some weed. Speaking of pussy . . . I think I'm going to excuse myself to the little boys' room while you two cruise for chicks."

"So," Dan said, scooting in closer to Liz. "See anybody you like?"

Liz scanned the bar. There was a biker chick with bleached hair and blue eye shadow, a Goth girl with black hair and black eye shadow. The truth was, Audrey was the only woman she was interested in, but she couldn't exactly say that to Dan, so she said, "Well, Dee Dee's attractive."

"See, I thought you liked her." Dan took her hand. "I feel really close to you right now, Liz."

Dan was looking at her the way she'd always wanted him to look at her, with adoration, with—was it desire? "I really appreciate you being so supportive . . ."

"Liz, would you like to come back to my room with me?"

So this was what it took to make him want her? A confession of lesbian tendencies? The human psyche was a complex thing. But maybe, she thought, some time in bed with Dan was what she needed. It had been so long since they had been together—maybe it had been desperation that had driven her into Audrey's bed. Maybe if she and Dan went back to his room and had a nice time, her life could return to some kind of normalcy, and she wouldn't spend all her time asking herself difficult questions. "Sure, okay."

On the way back to the dorm, still holding her hand, Dan said, "So . . . have you ever . . . been with another woman?"

Liz's stomach knotted, but she heard herself telling at least part of the truth. "Yeah. One time."

"What was it like?" His voice was heavy with wonder, as though she had told him she'd once walked on the moon.

"It was great." She, of course, didn't add a key piece of information: it was last week.

In his room, Dan locked his lips to hers with an urgency she'd never felt from him. Soon they were naked in his narrow bed, with him on top of her. How different his body felt from Audrey's. Audrey was soft and padded, as comfortable as an armchair, while Dan was all hard lines and angles, as Spartan as a piece of Shaker furniture. "I want . . ." he whispered in her ear, "to use my mouth on you . . . like a woman."

He used his mouth, all right, but it wasn't like a woman. Or at least, it wasn't like Audrey. While Audrey had focused the tip of her tongue on the exact point that gave Liz the most pleasure, Dan lapped at the entire surface area with all the finesse of a hungry dog licking out a gravy boat. After several minutes of this, she had to make him stop. But saying "stop" seemed rude, so instead she said "ooh!" and then "ah!" and finally sighed with feigned satisfaction and said, "Thanks. You can stop now."

Dan rose from between her legs, as drooly and pleased with himself as a just-fed baby. "Liz," he said, laying his cheek on her breast. "I don't suppose I've ever said it to you because I'm hardly the hearts and flowers type, but you . . . you do know I love you, don't you?"

Liz was sure that from where Dan was lying, the terrified thudding of her heart must be deafening. There they were . . . the words that she had longed to hear, but now their only effect was to make her feel even more confused. Tears welled in her eyes. "No, Dan, I didn't know." She knew she was supposed to let him know his feelings were returned, but at the moment, she didn't know how she felt. Soon, though, it didn't matter because Dan had rearranged himself on his back and was pushing her head downward. At least with her mouth full, she wouldn't be expected to say, "I love you, too."

Elisa

Ever since her parents' visit, Elisa had been depressed. She did her reading and went to her classes like the dutiful little student she was, but as soon as her last class of the day was over, she went back to her room, put on her pink pajamas and crawled into bed. Many nights she didn't make it over to the cafeteria for dinner. She just made do with whatever was in the room—a packet of Pop Tarts, a sleeve of saltines. Jo's softball practices had increased in length and frequency what with the season starting up, so she wasn't around enough to pick up on the fact that her usually bubbly girlfriend was about as cheery as the protagonist of *The Bell Jar*. Not that Jo had ever read *The Bell Jar*.

Tonight she was sprawled in bed, coated in Oreo crumbs, reading *The Waves* by Virginia Woolf, yet another depressed woman. The door swung open, and there was Jo, dripping wet in her softball uniform. "They called practice off on account of the rain," she said.

"As wet as you are, it looks like you kept right on playing."

"You know me and umbrellas don't get along." Jo kicked off her cleats. "Say, the way your teeth look after them Oreos, you oughta be smokin' a cigar outside the Pig."

Elisa grinned, but held up her hand to cover her teeth, which apparently bore a temporary resemblance to those of Ted Hoskins, the black-toothed bum (supposedly a millionaire because of an inheritance from his coal company executive daddy) who was always smoking stogies and loafing outside the Odessa Piggly Wiggly. "I've got to stop eating so much junk. I think I've gained five pounds in the last week."

Jo had stripped down to her boxers and sports bra. "You could put on fifty pounds, and you'd still look good to me."

"You're nicer to me than I deserve." And just like that, the tears started, accompanied by big, racking sobs—the hard, ugly kind of crying.

"Hey now," Jo said, and she crawled into bed beside Elisa, brushing away tears and Oreo crumbs. "What's the matter?"

"I don't know. I'm a wreck, and I'm not even sure why. I have been ever since I saw Mommy and Daddy."

"Did they say anything bad to you?" Jo was stroking Elisa's hair.

"No. You know Daddy never says anything. And Mommy, well, she talks all the time, but she never says anything either. It was just being with them . . . it made me feel weird. Walking across campus and seeing people's eyes on them and knowing they were thinking, 'What rubes,' you know? And then, that night, I heard a couple of girls in the bathroom—sorority types, from the sound of them—laughing about these hillbillies they'd seen in the hall."

"And why should you care what those Susie Sorority types think about your momma and daddy? Those are the same girls that go around talkin' about how fat they are even though they weigh eighty pounds."

"I don't care what they think, not really," Elisa said. "It's just that I'm having a hard time reconciling where I've come from with where I'm going . . . or where I'm trying to go, anyway. I mean, I see somebody like Dr. Rivers, and I think, that's the kind of life I want. But then I see my parents and know that's a big part of who I am, too. So how can I be a sophisticated university professor, living the life of the mind, when all I am really is little Bitsy Ricketts from Odessa, Tennessee? I'd be a fraud, and everybody would know it. I can't fit in that world, but I can't fit in my parents' world either."

"I know what it is not to fit, that's for sure," Jo said. "Always wantin' to do the boy stuff, but never bein' let to because I wasn't a boy, but never bein' enough of a girl to be accepted by the girls either."

"But see, that's about being gay," Elisa said. "And I have no problems with being gay. I wouldn't choose to be any other way if I could. What I'm worried about is my future . . . if I can become what I want to become."

"See, that's where you and me are different, lady." Jo wasn't stroking Elisa's head anymore. "I came to college for two reasons: to be with you and to play ball. With you, it's always meant something bigger, like getting away from Odessa and getting educated is going to change you from a lump of coal to a diamond. But, lady, you were already a diamond in the first place."

"Jo . . ." She reached out to touch Jo's arm.

"Wait. I've been wanting to say this for a while, so I'm gonna go ahead and get it said. See, I could live in a trailer in Odessa for the rest of my life as long as I could live there with you. That's the way I love you. But I don't think you could say the same thing about me."

"I do love you, Jo." The words came out as sobs.

"I know you do. But you're enough to make me happy, and I'm not enough for you."

It wasn't wholly true. Jo could and did make her happy often, but unlike Jo, she craved something from life other than love and a ball to knock around. And Elisa knew, as much as she'd like to deny it, that she wouldn't stay with Jo forever if it meant living in a trailer in Odessa. Even though she loved Jo as much as she could ever imagine loving anyone, she didn't love her enough for that.

Beth

The theme of tonight's mixer was "the Fabulous Fifties." Beth had decided to go all out and have a costume made for the occasion—a mid-calf-length pink wool skirt decorated with a fuzzy gray poodle on a leash. A charcoal gray sweater set matched the poodle, and her ponytailed hair was tied in a pink ribbon. Most of the girls hadn't done much besides rolling up their jeans and snatching their hair back into ponytails, so the extra effort Beth had put into her outfit really showed.

Mike looked good, too. He had modeled his style after James Dean in *Rebel Without a Cause*—white T-shirt and red jacket, blue jeans and white canvas Converses, hair swooped into a fairly impressive pompadour. He looked, Beth thought with a secret giggle, like a cute, boyish dyke.

The mixer itself was being held in the rented-out top floor of a restaurant called Arnold's, which had been chosen for its *Happy Days* connotations. An old, neon-lit jukebox, stocked with Fifties hits, had been brought in for the occasion, and a bunch of girls, some with drinks in their hands, were engaged in a woefully inept Hula Hoop contest to the tune of "Shake, Rattle, and Roll." People were already pretty drunk. The open bar was specializing in two custom drinks, Pink Poodles and Blue Suede Shoes. Beth didn't know what was in a Pink Poodle, but having already drunk two, she could attest that it had substantial bite.

"Have you noticed," Mike whispered to her, "how all the girls are drinking pink drinks and all the boys are drinking blue drinks? It's as color-coded as a nursery in here."

"Well, don't go ordering a Pink Poodle just to be different," Beth said. "Besides, they're so full of grenadine that it's like drinking cough syrup. Omigod, that was pathetic!" she said after Quimby dropped her Hula Hoop again without even making it start to spin.

"I bet you couldn't do better," Mike said.

"I bet I could. When I was ten years old, I lived to Hula Hoop."

"Well, go for it, then," Mike grinned.

Beth looked at how ridiculous the Hula Hooping girls—grown women, actually—looked. "Nah."

"Come on. I double-dog dare you."

Beth thought for a minute. Silly fun and games were part of being a real sorority sister. And she was trying to be the best sister she could be. She knocked back the dregs of her third Pink Poodle and handed the empty glass to Mike. "Okay, watch this."

She lifted her Hula Hoop as the first notes of "Good Golly, Miss Molly" blasted from the jukebox. When "Miss Molly" ended, her hoop was still spinning, and it spun all the way through "Whole Lotta Shakin' Goin' On." No one else had been able to keep her hoop aloft for as much as a minute, and Beth was declared the winner, to the wild applause of the group.

Chad, Quimby's former short-term boyfriend, presented Beth with a trophy of a ponytailed bobby soxer and said, "Congratulations, Beth. With pelvic action like that, Mike must be a happy man." The crowd whooped and laughed, and Beth, blushing though there wasn't much to blush about, took her trophy to show Mike and kissed his cheek.

"Clearly you're a girl with many hidden talents," Mike said, winking.

The pink and blue beverages continued to flow, and everybody kicked off their saddle oxfords or penny loafers or sneakers for the "sock hop" portion of the mixer. Beth was always impressed by Mike's dancing, which was the envy of many sisters whose boyfriends danced badly or not at all. But it was extra fun to watch him twist and shake to the '50's tunes; he sported some surprisingly Elvis-like moves.

At midnight a projector and screen were brought in for a showing of *Grease*. Beth and Mike settled on a couch in the corner; as the Frankie Valli theme song began to play, she laid her head on his shoulder. It was strange—even though she felt no physical desire for Mike, she still liked to be close to him. To cuddle with him, to hold hands with him was comforting somehow. Safe—not like when she was with a woman. The two times she'd been with Thalia, she had felt excited and passionate, but not safe. The depth of such desires—the way she could lose control entirely—was too scary to be safe.

About half an hour into the movie, which was being watched with a "Rocky Horror" level of audience participation, Mike whispered, "Why don't we go out and get some air?"

Beth followed him down the stairs and out of the restaurant. Once they were outside, sitting on a bench, she asked, "Are you okay?"

"I'm fine. I just didn't think it would be wise to let my frat brothers see that I burst into tears when Olivia sings 'Hopelessly Devoted to You.' I already have to worry that they think I'm too good of a dancer. See, you're lucky. You don't have these problems."

"Don't worry; I have plenty of problems of my own."

"You mean besides thinking that Stockard Channing is cuter than John Travolta?"

"Shh!" She play-slapped his arm.

"Nobody's around. It's okay."

Beth looked around to confirm that they were indeed alone. "I went to the Merry-Go-Round the other night."

"Without me?"

"You were off with your brothers, and I was desperate. Anyway, Thalia was there."

Mike's eyes widened. "The bulldyke? Did she see you?"

Beth looked around again, then whispered, "She saw all of me. I went home with her."

"What? Are you suicidal or something?"

Tears welled in her eyes. "Maybe—I don't know. I just . . . I like the way she makes me feel."

"Well, I like the way a whole bottle of Jack Daniels makes me feel, but if I drink one, I know there'll be hell to pay in the morning. You need to think of the consequences of having a relationship with this woman. They could be way worse than a hangover, I'll tell you that."

"I know. I shouldn't have been so careless."

Mike took her hand. "And I shouldn't lecture you, especially since I have no room to talk." He looked to the left and right. "There's this guy—Jeff—I've been playing racquetball with, but we've started to turn into something more than just racquetball partners, if you know what I mean. But he's not like your dyke—he's quiet, conservative—hell, he's an officer in the Student Republicans, so he's capable of being discreet. Still, like you said, we can't get careless."

Beth snuggled against Mike's shoulder. "It's hard, huh?"

"Yeah."

They sat in comfortable silence for a while. Really, Mike was the only person she could feel wholly comfortable with because she knew he was the only person who really understood her. "Mike," she said finally, "I've been thinking about something that could, you know, give us extra protection."

"You sound like a deodorant commercial."

Beth laughed. "Not that kind of protection, you goofball. I mean . . . protection so that nobody doubts that we are . . . what we say we are."

"Okay, now I'm thoroughly confused."

"You know Amy got engaged, right?"

Mike rolled his eyes. "The way she's shoving that ring up against everybody's eyeballs, it's kind of hard to miss."

"Well, after we sang the candlelight song to her, Quimby said she bet I'd be the next girl they'd be singing that song to."

Mike laughed. "Are you proposing to me?"

"No, I'm just saying that if sometime we decided to take that step, then everybody would take our relationship really seriously."

"And start planning our wedding." Mike shivered.

"Not necessarily. It could be a really long engagement. I mean, I'll have three years of law school after I graduate, and you want to get your MBA. And of course, we wouldn't think of actually tying the knot until we had completed our educations . . ."

"And until you pass the bar and we both get settled in our careers." Mike rubbed his chin thoughtfully. "Yeah, I can see how this engagement thing could drag out for a long time. And God, it would make my parents happy. And my brothers would rag on me about it, but it would . . . remove any doubt, wouldn't it?"

"Exactly."

Mike laughed like he had just heard the world's funniest joke. When he recovered, he said, "So should I order your ring from Tiffany's, then?"

Beth squealed. "You're kidding!"

"Nah, might as well do this right. White gold, Tiffany setting . . . how many carats?"

Beth laughed. "Oh, I don't know . . ."

"Don't be shy. My parents will foot the bill."

Beth thought. "Well, less than a carat looks chintzy, obviously. But more than two can look kind of vulgar."

"One and a half, then?"

"Perfect." Beth knew that Amy's tacky little diamond had been bought at a chain store in the mall. When Amy saw Beth's engagement ring, she would just die.

Liz

Liz had actually dozed off for a moment in her stupefyingly dull intermediate French class. The class met right after lunch, the time of day when Liz had the least energy. No matter how hungover she was, she could usually stay alert during her morning classes through a combination of interest in their subjects and sheer force of will. But intermediate French, in which dowdy, kindly old Professeur Clement tried to guide a group of uninterested and mostly East Tennessee-accented students through inane conversations *en français*, always sent Liz into a stupor, even though she had begun taking the precaution of drinking an extra cup of coffee at lunch.

Today when her eyes drooped shut, Professeur Clement had called on her. "Babette?"

They had all been assigned French aliases for use in class, and Liz had gotten saddled with Babette, a ridiculous pink poodle of a name. It was a miracle that when Professeur Clement addressed her as Babette, she actually regained consciousness and recognized the name as her own. It was even more of a miracle that when she answered it came out in French: "*Pardonez-moi, Professeur Clement. Je suis tre s fatigue e.*"

And of course, Professeur Clement had simply beamed at her. It didn't matter what you said to the woman as long as you said it in French.

Liz wished she had Dan's gift for foreign languages. A French major and a German minor, he spent his spare daytime hours in the library reading Alexandre Dumas *en français*. Liz knew she would never progress much beyond being able to puzzle out a French restaurant menu.

Her admission of tiredness in class had provoked a typically inane discussion, *en français*, of the various activities one might perform as a result of being tired, the result of which was to intensify her desire for a nap. Now, walking back to the dorm, she was completely focused on the sleep she was soon to enjoy. But when she entered the dorm's lobby, she tensed up so much that sleep became unimaginable. There was Audrey in her witchy striped tights, on the house phone. "Hey," she said, putting the receiver back in the cradle. "I was just trying to call you."

Liz hadn't called or seen Audrey since she had gone home with Dan. She felt a little bad about this, of course, but she and Audrey didn't have a history like she had with Dan. And in a way, through no fault of her own, Audrey had messed things up for her with Dan by becoming a complicating factor. If it weren't for Audrey, Liz wouldn't have felt so confused when Dan confessed his feelings to her. She would have just felt happy, which was how she had wanted to feel. But the look on Audrey's face told her she was not in for a happy time. "Um . . . hey."

"Can we go up to your room?"

Liz looked around uncomfortably. "It's kind of a mess."

"Not as big a mess as I am." Audrey blinked hard. "Look, I just need to talk to you, okay?"

Audrey looked from Liz's cluttered side of the room to Martina's neat one. "Your roommate's not going to walk in while we're talking, is she?"

"My roommate never walks in. Sometimes I think she's a figment of my imagination."

Audrey stood by the window, gazing out, not looking at Liz. "So the last time we were together, we were joking about being proper Southern ladies and everything. I didn't really expect a thank-you note from you, Liz, but I did think maybe you'd call me or come by for tea or something."

"I've just been . . . busy," Liz said, hardly believing how lame her words sounded. "And plus, you said what happened between us didn't have to mean anything I didn't want it to mean."

"I did say that, but I still hoped it would mean . . . something. So just out of curiosity, what did it mean to you?"

Liz searched for words. How could she answer this question for Audrey when she hadn't been able to answer it for herself? "I don't know . . . I guess it was like . . . an experiment."

"Oh, that sounds so passionate. Like we were stirring together baking soda and vinegar or something."

"That's not how I meant it . . ."

"But the experiment was a success, wasn't it? I mean, I definitely caused a reaction in you." She laughed, but it was bitter laughter.

Liz felt her face go hot. "Audrey, I guess I ought to tell you that Dan and I are back together . . . in the full sense of the word. And . . . and he told me he loves me."

Audrey shook her head. "Let me guess. You were naked at the time."

Liz bristled. How dare Audrey be so judgmental? Where did she get off acting like Liz was simple-minded and utterly predictable? "Well, we were, but it's not like you make it sound. We were . . . finished when he said it. It wasn't like it was in the heat of the moment or anything."

"So that was all it took, huh? Almost three years of emotional distance and neglect, and those three magic words are all it takes to make everything all better. One word for each year, I guess."

"Like I've told you, Dan isn't an emotionally demonstrative person. It's taken him a long time to be sure of his feelings."

"Other people are sure of their feelings much sooner."

Liz waited for Audrey to say something else, but Audrey just stared out the window until Liz finally prompted her with a "what do you mean?"

When Audrey turned around, her eyes were full of tears. "Okay, so you're going to make me state the obvious, are you?" She took two steps toward Liz. "Liz, I was sure of my feelings for you the night I met you. I could have told you right then that I'm crazy in love with you. I should have told you a long time ago, but I kept hoping that if I didn't acknowledge my feelings, they'd go away. Because you're younger than me. Because you were allegedly straight and have a boyfriend. But, well . . . I seem to lose all self-control when I'm with you. Thus, what happened between us. Thus, me standing here, blabbering and blubbering. God, say something, Liz, just to shut me up."

"I . . . I don't know what to say." What Liz really wanted to do was run—away from Audrey, maybe away from Dan, too, away from everybody and everything that made her feel so overwhelmed. Was being a hermit a career opportunity anymore? She could see herself isolated in a cabin in the mountains, where no one could touch her or talk to her or make her feel anything. Then she would be safe.

"Listen, Liz." Audrey sat down on the corner of Liz's bed, an action that, bizarrely, struck Liz as too intimate. "I've been with a couple of girls before who were just experimenting—straight girls who wanted to see what the girl-girl thing was like. And with each of them, the sex was tentative and exploratory, almost clinical in a way. It was like the whole time they were thinking, 'It's a nice place to visit, but I wouldn't want to live here.' You, though . . . you were passionate. I guess what I'm saying is, you don't strike me as an experimenting straight girl."

"So are you trying to tell me I'm a lesbian?"

"Of course not. You can't tell somebody else what they are. All I'm saying is, you say Dan's sure of his feelings, and I know I'm sure of my feelings. You just need to be sure of your feelings, too."

Hot tears spilled down Liz's cheeks. "How can I be sure of anything when everything's so damn complicated? Before I met you I had always liked guys. I mean, when I was in high school, I had posters of James Dean and Jim Morrison on the walls of my room."

"Maybe you just like dead guys."

"No, there were living guys I had crushes on, too . . . and then there was Dan. But then I started noticing that when I was around you I'd feel all weird and nervous and then later I'd wonder when we'd see each other again. And then there was what happened."

"Don't make it sound like a natural disaster. You mean we had sex."

"Yes. And so what does it mean? Does it mean that everybody who's ever called me a dyke was actually right? But then there's Dan and my feelings for other guys, too. Does that mean I'm bisexual? Or with you and me is it like when Djuna Barnes said she didn't love women, she just loved Thelma? Not that I'm saying I love you, though, because right now I'm too confused to know if I love my own mother. I mean, what kind of lifestyle am I supposed to be having here?"

Audrey stood up and rested her hands on Liz's shoulders. "I don't think you're asking yourself the right questions. It doesn't matter what label you choose to stick on yourself. What matters is who you love. I'm not asking you to choose a lifestyle, Liz. I'm asking you to choose *me*."

For a moment, Liz looked into Audrey's blue-gray eyes, but Audrey's gaze was too intense, and Liz had to look away.

"Don't feel like you have to say anything," Audrey said. "I'm going to leave now, and I don't want you to call me or visit me until you're ready to talk. Really talk. But you do owe me at least one conversation, Liz, so don't try to avoid me indefinitely just to save yourself the awkwardness. Do you promise you'll talk to me when you're ready?"

Liz nodded.

"Okay. I'm going then."

Even after Audrey had closed the door, Liz stood, sobbing, in the same spot, afraid to make a move.

Elisa

"Let me get you a cup of tea," Dr. Rivers said as soon as she shut the door of her office. "I know tea always helps me if my nerves are rattled. Is Earl Grey all right?"

"Sure." Elisa knew as little about tea as she did about wine and imported cheese and all the other things on which Dr. Rivers seemed to be an authority. The only tea Elisa had drunk growing up was iced Lipton with lots of sugar. She suddenly remembered her manners. "Thank you. For the tea and for letting me come talk to you."

Dr. Rivers plugged in a hot pot and got out a mug decorated with a caricature of Virgina Woolf. "There's no need to thank me in either case. Boiling water for tea isn't enough effort to earn a thank you, and as for coming to talk to me, you know you're always welcome. I'm your advisor and—at least I like to flatter myself—your friend."

"You are my friend," Elisa said. "And I'm the one who should be flattered."

"Nonsense," Dr. Rivers said, riffling through a cabinet drawer. "The flattery is all mine. Ah! Here we are. I knew I had some chocolate cookies in here somewhere. Chocolate is a known mood elevator, you know."

"Well, my mood could use some elevating." Ever since Jo had speculated that Elisa didn't love her enough to be happy with her in a trailer in Odessa, things had been strained between them. It wasn't in Jo's nature to be angry or hostile, but she was distant, and when she came back from softball practice, she claimed to be too tired to make love.

Elisa knew what was happening to Jo—she was hiding beneath the hard shell she'd had to grow in order to survive as a small-town boyish lesbian. In Odessa, Jo had spent most of her time in her shell, untouched by the jeers of the mean high school girls and the whippings by her drunken father. Only two loves could coax Jo out of her shell back then: softball and Elisa. Elisa felt terrible knowing that she had hurt Jo enough to push her back into her old hiding place.

"So talk to me," Dr. Rivers said, setting a steaming mug and a napkin of cookies in front of Elisa. "You seem quite distraught."

"I am." Elisa felt the catch in her voice and prayed that the tears wouldn't start. "And some of it's about my career and studies and the kind of stuff we usually talk about, but a lot of it is girlfriend stuff, too."

Dr. Rivers smiled. "Well, I've had a girlfriend or two in my time, so perhaps I can be of some help. And of course, I've met your girlfriend . . . that evening at what passes in Knoxville for a nightclub."

"Yes," Elisa said. "You were there with your girlfriend, right?"

"Ex-girlfriend. Very ex." Dr. Rivers laughed. "In that grand lesbian tradition, Maureen and I spent six miserable months as lovers followed by six blissful years as friends. Your lover, though . . . Jo is her name?"

"Yes."

"She's handsome. She has that young Marlon Brando swagger about her."

"She does swagger, doesn't she? I used to tell her she walked like Popeye."

"But you, of course, are much better looking than Olive Oyl."

"Well, that's some compliment, isn't it?"

"Damning you with faint praise, eh?" Dr. Rivers sipped her tea. "But as pleasant as all this kidding is, I know you didn't come here for my dazzling wit. Are you and Jo having problems?"

"No. Yes. Well, really, I'm not sure. I guess it depends on what you mean by problems." Elisa set down her mug. "Jo and I are different . . . real different. And that's never been a problem in the past . . . actually, it's been good in a lot of ways."

"Polarity can generate a powerful attraction."

"Yes, and lack of attraction has never been an issue for Jo and me," Elisa said, feeling embarrassed at coming so close to discussing her sex life with a teacher. "But now that we're getting older . . ."

"Twenty?" Dr. Rivers laughed.

"Well, I don't mean we're ready for a nursing home or anything. I just mean that we're getting to an age where we need to be figuring out what we're gonna do with our lives. Now our differences feel like more of a problem. Like Jo, she's not that ambitious. As long as she can play ball and have enough money for basic needs and be with me, she's happy."

"Jo lacks ambition?" Dr. Rivers said.

"But I don't mean that in a bad way. She's just content . . . content in a way I'm not. Actually, I'm kind of jealous of her. I mean, sometimes I just want so many things I feel like I'm going to explode from all the wanting."

"What kinds of things?"

"Well, I don't really mean things like money or fancy cars or anything like that, although I would like to be more comfortable than the way I was raised. The things I really want, though, are knowledge and sophistication and travel and a career. Really, in a lot of ways, I want to be like you, Dr. Rivers."

Dr. Rivers smiled. Was she blushing a little? "Trust me. I'm not anybody's role model." She looked Elisa in the eye. "Listen. If I were to ask you what's the most important thing in the world to Jo, what would you say?"

"That's easy. She's told me. It's me." Elisa felt tears spring to her eyes at the thought of Jo's devotion.

"And if I asked you what's the most important thing in the world to you?"

Now Elisa was crying for real. She knew her runny mascara and eyeliner were making her look like a suicidal raccoon. She hated for Dr. Rivers to see her in such a state. "I . . . I don't know the answer to that question. I mean, I love Jo, but my head is so full of things that are important to me—"

"As it should be at your age," Dr. Rivers said. "You're supposed to be passionate and bursting with ideas and dreams and desires. That's one of the things I love about students like you. I can look in your eyes and see new ideas and inspiration exploding like kernels of popcorn." Dr. Rivers got up and leaned on the edge of her desk near Elisa. "Elisa, even though I'm your advisor, I'm not here to tell you what to do with your life. But I will say that sometimes for young women with real aspirations, some types of romantic relationships can hold them back."

"Hold them back?"

"The classic example, of course, is the kind of heterosexual relationship where the man wants the 'little woman' to cook his meals and clean his house instead of improving her mind and pursuing a career. But some lesbian relationships can be stifling, too, especially is your partner isn't your intellectual equal or doesn't share your dreams."

Elisa's stomach knotted. "Are you saying I should break up with Jo?"

"Of course not. It's not my place to make such a suggestion. All I'm saying, Elisa, is that you're a brilliant woman. You should never sell yourself short. And you should never let anyone hold you back." Dr. Rivers bent down and gave Elisa a quick kiss on the forehead. "I'll tell you what," she said, brushing back Elisa's hair with her fingers. "I have one of those wretched cocktail parties this Saturday, but how about if next Saturday evening I come get you and take you back to my house for dinner? I know the cafeteria meals on Saturdays are nothing but scraps from earlier in the week, so why don't you let me make you a decent Saturday night dinner for a change? Maybe by then you will have had some time to think, and we can talk more."

Elisa looked up at Dr. Rivers, touched by her kindness. "That would be nice. Thank you."

"One warning, though." Dr. Rivers comically wagged her index finger. "I'm issuing this invitation as your friend, not as your advisor."

"Okay." Elisa smiled and—she hoped—wiped away some of her smeared mascara.

"I know it's easy to get intimidated by all the choices you have to make at this age," she said as Elisa stood up to leave. "But how fabulous it is for you to have all your adult life spread out before you like a sumptuous buffet. Enjoy it, and make good choices."

Beth

"Just as this candle bright
Will light up the night
Our love will cast a glow
So all the world will know."

As soon as the girls blew out the white candles, they descended on Beth, squealing their congratulations. Beth hugged so many girls she lost track of whom she was hugging. Squeezed by arm after arm after arm, she felt like she was being attacked by a giant octopus.

The biggest hug of all came from Quimby, who said, "Just so you know, I'm going to be your maid of honor."

"By the time we actually get around to getting married, you might be my matron of honor," Beth said. "It's going to be a long engagement."

"Don't worry. It'll be an even longer time till I'm a matron."

Of course, if the state of being a maid still depended on virginity, it had been an exceptionally long time since Quimby had filled that bill.

"I can't believe he actually ordered your ring from Tiffany's!" Jennifer said. "I mean, really, what guy do we know besides Mike who'd have such good taste?"

None, Beth thought. *Because all the guys you know are straight.*

She was amazed by the amount of joy and goodwill that announcing her engagement had generated. She'd told her mother and daddy over Sunday brunch at the country club, and they had burst into tears and ordered champagne. And now here were her sisters, laughing and crying and hugging her.

Apparently Mike's announcement of their engagement had generated a similar level of approval, especially from his parents who had, according to Mike, wept with what sounded a lot like relief. His frat brothers weren't huggy and squealy in their approval, but they did chuck him on the arm and buy him beers and joke about bachelor parties and the perils of becoming pussy whipped.

"Drinks are on us tonight," Amy said, touching her engagement ring to Beth's in a kind of toast.

"Yeah," Quimby said. "You soon-to-be-married girls better have fun while you still can."

Beth smiled because she was supposed to. What was the deal with marriage anyway? People congratulated you on your engagement like it was the best thing that was ever going to happen to you, and in the same breath they started teasing you about how miserable and boring married life was going to be. She wondered how many people entered marriage without really wanting to, only doing it because it was a tradition, like eating turkey on Thanksgiving even if you didn't care for it much.

It was warm enough to sit on the patio at Radar's, and Quimby and Amy ordered pitchers of Long Island iced tea.

Beth would have to be careful. L.I.T.s were lethal, and she had taken two of her orange pills in order to survive the candle singing. Not that mixing pills with alcohol didn't make you feel pretty fabulous, but you had to control the amount of alcohol, or fabulousness would give way to unconsciousness.

"So have you picked out a gown yet?" Jennifer asked, after drinks had been poured all around.

"God, no," Beth said. "We haven't even thought ahead to the wedding. We've got degrees to get first—bachelor's and professional school."

"But you must have some plans for your wedding," Amy said. "I've had my wedding planned since I was six years old."

A chorus of "me too's" followed such that Beth was afraid she might appear abnormal if she admitted she hadn't spent her entire childhood dreaming of being a bride. "Well, I planned out my wedding when I was little, too," she lied. "But I think I'd better scrap those plans since it had a Barbie theme."

"Oh, but you shouldn't!" Quimby laughed. "You could have a Barbie Dream Wedding. You look like Barbie anyway, and Mike could look like Ken if you slicked his hair down with styling gel."

"Quimby, you're my best friend and I love you, but if I tried to sell my daddy on the idea of a Barbie Dream Wedding, he'd disown me." *Unless I told him it was a choice between a Barbie Dream Wedding and a lesbian daughter*, she thought, in which case he'd start ordering the hot pink bridesmaids' dresses immediately.

After three L.I.T.s, Beth was feeling pretty l-i-t, and the pills mixed with the liquor were causing some interesting sensations. It took a good deal of effort to sit upright in the socially sanctioned sorority girl perky posture because she felt like her bones had turned to linguini and her muscles to pudding. Pasta and pudding—she hadn't allowed herself to eat those two favorites since when . . . high school?

Another effect of the booze and pills was that everything struck her as absolutely hilarious. The image of herself in a white gown walking down the aisle of the First Presbyterian Church while Mike waited for her at the altar . . . nothing was funnier. Well, nothing except these fawning sisters cooing over how Beth had found "true love." God, why had she wasted so much of her life worrying that everyone would see through her? People were so easy to fool it was ridiculous. When they looked at other people, they were so desperate to see a mirror image of themselves that unless there was screamingly obvious evidence to the contrary, that was exactly what they saw.

"Well, girls," Beth said—it came out as "girlsh"—"thanks for the drinkies, but I'd better run. My fiancé is waiting for me."

"Oh, so that's how it is," Quimby said. "You get engaged, and then you don't have time for girls anymore."

"Don't worry," Beth said. "I'll always have time for girls." And to stifle the giggle she felt bubbling up out of her throat, she bit her cheek until it bled.

After another round of hugs, she waved good-bye, blew kisses and staggered on her linguini legs in the direction of Mike's frat house until she knew she was out of sight. Then she made a left and another left, all the time letting out the wild laughter she'd had to stifle while she was out with the girls. Anybody who saw her would have thought she was a crazy person, but she was just happy—happy because her engagement had made her so socially acceptable that nobody would ever suspect she might have a secret life. She steadied herself on the railing as she walked up the porch steps. Then she took off her engagement ring, dropped it in her purse and knocked on Thalia's door.

Liz

Some nights, when another evening at the Sagebrush seemed like too much of a grind, Liz and Dan would go listen to local music—to Smokin' Dave and the Premo Dopes when they played downtown or to Scott Miller, who played every Saturday night at Radar's. She always looked forward to these shows, but tonight, even as Scott Miller sang his locally famous sarcastic song about sorority girls, Liz was having a hard time focusing, let alone laughing at the witty lyrics. How could you laugh when you were in the middle of an existential crisis?

Because that's what it was. She wasn't just torn between two lovers; she was torn between two identities, one of which was familiar and comfortable if somewhat unfulfilling, the other of which might be potentially fulfilling but was terrifying in its unfamiliarity. There was no denying how Audrey made her feel, and yet here was Dan beside her, bobbing his head in time with the music like one of those toy dogs people put in the back of their cars. She knew Dan had no clue about her existential crisis.

It was funny . . . she had been chasing Dan for so long, and now that he had finally told her his feelings, she was reminded of the old joke about the dog who finally catches the car but has no idea what to do with it. Still, she knew what her life was like when she was with Dan, but she had no idea what her life would be like if she were with Audrey.

How would a life with Audrey affect Liz's writing, for example? Would she embrace Audrey as her muse and finish all those stories she'd started? Would she become a weird lesbian poetess, composing villanelles about her armpit hair? Or would she be unable to write at all?

"You want another gin and tonic?" Dan asked after Scott Miller had announced he was going to take a short break.

"Sure." Liz was just about to grab her wallet when her eyes caught a figure across the room. She hoped it was a hallucination, but the hallucination looked back at Liz with a look of horror that probably mirrored her own. They weren't supposed to talk or see each other until Liz was ready. And Liz was definitely not ready.

Dan turned around, no doubt to see if Liz's expression was due to a madman who'd just walked into the club with a machine gun. The next words out of Dan's mouth made Liz come as close to fainting as she ever had in her life. "Audrey!" he yelled across the room. "Hey!"

Audrey smiled stiffly, yelled, "Hey yourself, Dan!" and began the approach to their table.

Liz couldn't breathe. How could she when her whole life had just collapsed to the size of a matchbox? The only thing that had been keeping her even moderately sane was her ability to keep her relationship with Dan and her relationship with Audrey separate. And now here the two of them were, not only in the same room, but apparently great friends from way back. Why the hell hadn't Audrey told her she knew Dan?

After the hour it seemed to take for Audrey to get to their table, Dan said, "Liz, do you know Audrey?"

"Yes," Liz managed to say, opting not to add, *at least I thought I did*. "So," she said, trying for breezy and casual but sounding shrill and hysterical, "how do you guys know each other?"

"You know the French Table I go to every month?" Dan said.

Liz nodded. The French Table was a student group that met at different restaurants near campus to practice their conversational French.

"Well, Audrey is a French Table compatriot of mine," Dan said. "As a matter of fact"—he nodded to Audrey—"I think this is the first time we've conversed *en anglaise.*"

"*Oui,*" Audrey said.

"Please join us," Dan said. "I was just about to get us some drinks, but first I must visit *le pissoir.*"

Audrey said something back to him in French, and they both laughed. God, they were like those creepy identical twins who develop a secret language they use with each other. Liz was shut out entirely.

After Dan disappeared to the bathroom, Audrey sat down next to Liz in the seat where Dan had been. "So . . . this isn't awkward," she said.

"Why didn't you tell me you knew Dan?" Liz said through clenched teeth.

"I didn't know I knew him." Audrey knitted her brow. "What I mean to say is . . . yes, I know Dan from French Table, but I never knew his last name and never really gave him any thought except when I spoke French with him and lots of other near strangers once a month. When you mentioned that your boyfriend's name was Dan, it never occurred to me it would be the same Dan. I mean, how many Dans do you think there are at William Blount? Dozens, at least."

"And you've never talked to him about me?"

"God, no. My French isn't good enough for me to use it to discuss my personal life."

When Dan returned with the drinks, the tape that was playing during Scott Miller's break began to blast "Jumpin' Jack Flash."

"If you spectacular ladies would excuse me for just one more moment," Dan said.

Liz winced, knowing what was coming. One of the unfortunate effects of Dan's obsession with the Rolling Stones was that if a Stones song came on when they were out drinking, he had to dance to it then and there, even if nobody else was dancing.

Dan found an open space in front of the stage and began thrusting his torso back and forth while keeping his hips perfectly stationary. A few people glanced at him in apparent curiosity, then resumed their conversations. After continuing his torso thrusting a few moments, he raised his arms over his head, lifted one leg up with knee bent and hopped. The dance, as best Liz could tell, was the dramatization of a rooster transforming itself into a whooping crane.

"No offense intended," Audrey said, "but if you reject me in favor of a man who dances like that, I may kill myself."

"Don't even joke about that. I'm freaking out enough as it is."

"Okay, sorry," Audrey said. "I joke when I'm nervous. Listen, Liz, you're not ready to talk to me yet, are you?"

Liz looked down, blinking back tears, and shook her head no.

"Well, you know where to find me when you are. I'm gonna take off now. Enjoy the second set." She looked toward Dan, waved gaily and called, "*Au revoir!*"

Elisa

"Oh, this is so beautiful. You shouldn't have gone to all this trouble." The table was set with a white linen tablecloth, and lavender candles glowed in silver candle holders.

"It wasn't trouble; it was a pleasure," Dr. Rivers said. "When I have a guest over for a meal, I like to turn it into an occasion."

Elisa wished she had known dinner was going to be an occasion. She wouldn't have worn jeans. Dr. Rivers was wearing a gorgeous black sheath dress with her ever-present pearls. The fact that Dr. Rivers feet were bare, though, made Elisa feel slightly less underdressed.

"If you'll remember," Dr. Rivers said, "I invited you tonight as your friend, not as your advisor, so it would make me very happy if you would call me Angela. After all, none of my friends call me Dr. Rivers."

"Okay, Angela," Elisa said, trying it out. Angela was a nice name, and it suited Dr. Rivers well enough, but it still felt strange on her tongue.

"Thank you." Dr. Rivers beamed. "Well, I, for one, am ravenous. Shall we have dinner?"

"Is there anything I can do to help?"

"Of course not. You're my guest. Your job is to sit down and let me wait on you. Here, let me pour you some wine."

Elisa hadn't drunk wine other than what was in wine coolers, but out of politeness, she let Dr. Rivers fill her glass.

"Now," Dr. Rivers said, "let me just scurry into the kitchen to get the first course."

"The first course? How fancy!"

"What, you were expecting a bag of burgers from McDonald's?"

The first course was soup, a tomato-basil bisque, Dr. Rivers called it. Elisa watched Dr. Rivers sip her soup from the side of her spoon and did likewise. "This is delicious," she said, and it was the best soup she'd ever tasted. Of course, her anxiety over spillage, thanks to her new soup-eating technique, did dim her enjoyment somewhat.

"It's sinfully easy to make. The key is the freshness of the ingredients—fresh tomatoes and fresh basil, never dried."

"There's nothing better in the world than a fresh tomato," Elisa said. "We always grew tomatoes in the summer when I was a kid, and I'd pick them off the vine and eat them like apples. They'd still be all warm from the sun, and the juice would run down my chin." She sipped some of the wine, which tasted better the more she drank of it. "And then in the winter when there was nothing but those pink grocery store tomatoes, it would always be such a disappointment, you know?"

"Yes. And how sad that those grocery store specimens are all many people know as tomatoes. People lose out on so many of life's pleasures out of ignorance or lack of opportunity . . . or fear."

"I don't know why anybody would fear a tomato." Elisa laughed.

"I wasn't just thinking about tomatoes," Dr. Rivers said. She smiled. "Are we ready for our entrée?"

The main dish, Dr. Rivers explained, was gnocchi in pesto cream sauce. Elisa was relieved to find that she liked it and didn't have to poke it down out of politeness as she had done with the sushi during their long-ago first lunch together. After Dr. Rivers refilled Elisa's wine and took away her pasta plate, she returned with a salad, of all things.

"A salad for dessert?" Elisa asked.

"It's how they do it in Paris—the salad comes after the entrée. But there's always dessert, too, as there will be tonight."

Elisa dutifully munched her way through the salad, although the dressing was too vinegary for her taste, and imported and fancy or not, the green crumbly cheese on it had surely gone bad. When Dr. Rivers replaced her salad plate with a dish of chocolate mousse, it felt like a reward for good behavior.

As they finished the mousse, Dr. Rivers said, "I have an idea for after dinner if you're interested."

Elisa hoped Dr. Rivers wasn't going to ask her to shelve more of her books. "Let's hear it."

"I have a hot tub on my deck. On these cool spring nights, it's heaven to soak in it and stare up at the stars."

"Well, uh . . ." Elisa wasn't sure how Jo would react to her being in a hot tub with another woman, even if the woman was her teacher and a femme to boot.

"Now don't get all prim on me, Elisa. I happen to have an extra swimsuit that should fit you just perfectly. And I'll wear one, too, of course."

Elisa grinned, embarrassed by her provincialism. "Well, I guess that would be all right, then. I've never been in a hot tub before."

"You'll love it. It's amazing how it works the knots out of your muscles."

The suit Dr. Rivers loaned her was a black two-piece, a little skimpier than something she would have picked out for herself. If she'd known she was going to be wearing a swimsuit, she would have shaved her legs and armpits. Not that she looked like Thalia or anything, but still, she was a little stubbly.

When Elisa emerged from getting changed, Dr. Rivers was in the living room in a lavender two-piece. Her body, Elisa noticed, was in excellent condition—toned arms and legs and a flat belly. Dr. Rivers had once told Elisa that she got up early every morning to run, and the results definitely showed. "Why don't we take the rest of the wine out on the deck?" Dr. Rivers said.

As soon as Elisa sank into the steaming, bubbling water, all her anxieties were forgotten. She looked up at the stars and imagined a future where such pleasure and sophistication would seem as normal to her as it apparently did to Dr. Rivers. Dr. Rivers refilled her wineglass, and Elisa sipped and soaked and smiled.

"You look like a kitten full of cream," Dr. Rivers said.

"I'd purr if I could. This is all so nice."

"I wanted to give you a nice evening," Dr. Rivers said. "When you came to me the other day you were so upset."

Elisa was touched. "Thank you."

"So," Dr. Rivers said, "are things any better with Jo?"

"Some. But I don't know . . . there's still more distance than I'd like." Lately she had noticed Jo amending her statements with disclaimers like, "But what do I know? I'm just an ignorant hillbilly." She seemed hyperconscious of Elisa's intellectual aspirations and even more conscious of her own lack thereof.

"Elisa, may I ask you a personal question?" She smiled. "Or perhaps I should say *another* personal question."

"Sure." The combination of wine and hot water was making her feel loose and floaty.

"Is Jo the only woman you've ever . . . been intimate with?"

Elisa giggled at her professor asking such a question. "Yes. She's the only person I've ever been with, actually. No boys, no other girls . . . just Jo since we were in tenth grade."

Dr. Rivers shook her head. "Amazing . . . it's like you were a lesbian version of an Appalachian child bride. Have you ever thought about other women?"

"Sure, I've *thought* about them." Elisa sipped her wine. "I mean, when I watch Jo play ball, I'll notice how some of the other girls fill out their uniforms, you know. But I'd never actually *do* anything about it."

"That's interesting . . . how you're so tied to the idea of monogamy. Even when I was married and thought I was straight, I felt like monogamy was just society's way of putting chains around the human heart."

"Huh," Elisa said, sipping her wine. "I never thought about it like that."

"Because society has conditioned you to believe monogamy is the only way. It's funny how many lesbians embrace the rules created by straight society when it seems they should be making their own rules . . . or dispensing with rules entirely." She shook her hair over her shoulder. "So, Elisa, when you find a woman attractive, is she always . . . masculine?"

Elisa grinned. "Well, I guess that tends to be what catches my eye first."

"Once again," Dr. Rivers said, "so much like heterosexual society . . . that same polarity of sex roles. Have you ever thought of being with a more feminine woman just to see what it's like?"

"I guess I've thought about feminine women a time or two." Elisa thought she would probably be uncomfortable if this conversation were occurring outside a hot tub while she was sober, but the more she soaked and drank, the more unreal the world outside the hot tub seemed.

"Have you ever thought about me?"

The question caught Elisa so off-guard that she said yes before she had a chance to think. But as soon as the word was out, she started backpedaling desperately. "I mean, you're the most brilliant woman I've ever met, and you've had more impact on my life than anybody I've met since I've been here . . ."

"You don't have to explain," Dr. Rivers said. "I just wanted to hear you say yes."

And then Dr. Rivers—Angela—was coming toward Elisa, holding Elisa's face in her hands, leaning her head toward Elisa's—and then everything went black.

Elisa woke up still in her damp bathing suit but wrapped in a blanket, on Dr. Rivers' couch.

"Oh, thank God. I was just about to give up and call nine-one-one," Dr. Rivers said.

Elisa looked around groggily. "Did I . . . faint?"

"You passed out, yes. I've heard of that happening to people sometimes when they drink alcohol in hot tubs, but only when they're drinking to excess . . . not after just a couple of glasses of wine."

"For me, that was drinking to excess. That's the most alcohol I've ever drunk in my life."

"Really?" Dr. Rivers patted Elisa's knee. "You really are a *good* girl, aren't you? I'm so sorry that happened. If I had thought there would be any danger . . ."

"It's okay. I'm fine. I could use some water, though, and maybe a couple of aspirin."

"Of course." When Dr. Rivers returned with a glass and pills, she said, "It's a good thing you're so tiny, or I don't know how I would have gotten you out of that hot tub."

"How long was I out?"

"Not long. Ten minutes or so."

Elisa felt overwhelmed and exhausted, partly because of passing out in the hot tub but mostly from what happened right before. If she hadn't passed out, what would have happened? Would she have kissed Dr. Rivers back? Would their bathing suits have come off?

Yes, probably. The tingle had been there, the desire, along with curiosity about what it would be like to be with another woman besides Jo, a woman with more age and experience. But could she have made love with Dr. Rivers and then gone home to wait for Jo to get back from her away game as if nothing had happened? And what would it have been like to go to Women in Modernism on Monday and listen to a lecture by a professor who had made love to her in a hot tub just hours before? "I'm awfully tired. After I get dressed, can you take me home?"

"Of course."

In the parking lot beside the dorm, Elisa turned to face Dr. Rivers. "Thank you so much for a lovely evening. I honestly think that was the best dinner I've ever eaten."

"Elisa." Dr. Rivers almost whispered her name. "I know we were kind of . . . interrupted, but in regard to what we were talking about in the hot tub, my offer still stands."

"Thank you." Elisa couldn't make eye contact with her. "I'll think about it."

"Do. And please, don't think all I want from you is a one-night stand. We already have a relationship, Elisa. This would just add another dimension to it. And I know that given our age difference, it probably wouldn't last forever. Eventually you'd gravitate toward someone younger.

But I feel I have a lot to offer you. I could be the warm cocoon where you, over time, transform yourself into a glorious butterfly. And when the day comes for you to break out and fly away, I'll be sad, of course, but also proud . . . and glad of our time together."

Elisa was trembling. This was what she wanted, wasn't it? For someone worldly and sophisticated to take her hand and lead her down the path of transformation.

"I do adore you, Elisa."

"I adore you, too, Dr.—Angela." And she did. She had adored Dr. Rivers since her first day of Women in Lit class fall semester. She felt a little strange saying those words out loud, but telling Dr. Rivers she adored her wasn't really the same thing as telling Jo she loved her, was it?

They hugged. It was a long, lesbian hug, torsos pressed together, arms tight around each other. Elisa breathed in Dr. Rivers' strawberry shampoo, her lavender perfume and the spicy natural scent of her body. She was entranced, but then she worried that Dr. Rivers' scent would be transferred to her so that Jo would smell the other woman.

Elisa broke the hug first. She said good night and got out of the car. When she reached the door of her room, she didn't get the key into the keyhole until the third try because she was shaking so hard.

Beth

Mike pressed the BMW's keys into Beth's hand. "You drive, okay?"

"Okay." Mike had never asked Beth to drive his car before. Even when he'd drunk too much, he still insisted on taking the wheel.

Something was wrong. The fact that he didn't want to drive was a sign of it, as was the fact that he had started his earlier phone call with the sentence "We need to talk." "We need to talk" always signaled bad news in a relationship, even in a fake relationship like hers and Mike's.

"You want me to drive to the park?" she asked.

"Sure," he said, and Beth noticed that his eyes were red and puffy, perhaps from lack of sleep. Her eyes always looked like that when she'd been crying.

She drove to the park while Mike sat in uncharacteristic silence. She felt her anxiety building, and when she stopped at the park, she noticed she was gripping the steering wheel with the force of a drowning person holding a life preserver. "Okay, what is it?" she said. "You have to tell me now, or my head's going to explode."

"Maybe it would be better if your head did explode." A tear trickled down Mike's cheek. "Shit, I said I wasn't going to cry."

Beth grabbed his hand, and he squeezed back, hard. "Cry all you need to, but talk."

"Okay." He wiped his eyes with his free hand. "I told you there was this guy I was seeing, right? Jeff, my racquetball buddy?"

"Yeah." Beth's heart felt like it was going to pound right out of her chest.

"Well, he and I had been playing one day, and he dropped me back at the house. But I had made him this tape that I forgot in my room, and he asked if he could come up and get it, and I said sure. The house was pretty quiet, and even if any of my brothers did see him, it would be cool. They know I play racquetball with Jeff, and Jeff's from a really good family." Mike took a breath that was punctuated by a sob and another swipe at his eyes. "So anyway, we're in my room, and Jeff starts going on about how the whole house smells like hot guys and how he's always had this fantasy about doing it in a frat house. And the door to my room is shut, and we didn't see anybody coming in, so within seconds his shorts are down, and I'm on my knees—"

"Oh, Mike." Beth had taken her hand out of Mike's so she could press it against her diaphragm. She was having a hard time breathing.

"So you know what happened next. Chad comes by, swings the door open and yells, 'Hey, asshole, what are we drinking tonight?' But then he says, 'Jesus Fucking Christ,' because he sees what we're doing."

"Stop." Beth opened the car door, leaned out and vomited. Even once her stomach was empty of its meager contents, she still spasmed and gagged.

When she closed the door and leaned back in her seat, Mike said, "Are you okay?"

Beth just looked at him.

"I know, stupid question. But I guess I'm stupid all around. You know, if it had been Jeff sucking my dick, at least I could claim I was drunk and in a weakened state. But it was him with his dick in my mouth. And you know the old joke, bake one cake, and it doesn't make you a baker, but suck one cock, and you're a cocksucker all your life."

"So they're pulling your badge."

"You bet they are. I'm as kicked out as hell. All my shit's packed up in boxes on the porch of the house. Of course, the worst part was telling my dad."

Beth's mouth fell open. "You told him? Why?"

Mike shrugged. "Because I knew if I didn't tell him, somebody else would. Besides, who else could get me out of a situation like this?"

Beth's eyes overflowed, for Mike, for her, for the fact that so much could be lost because of a moment of passion and an unlocked door. "What are you going to do?"

"For now, I'm going back home with my tail between my legs. And then I'll find a new school to start at in the fall." He smiled a joyless smile. "Dad says he'll pay for me to go somewhere else on two conditions: the school can't have a Greek system, and it must be religiously affiliated."

"Shit." She was crying so hard she was shaking.

Mike handed her a tissue. "I'm so sorry, Beth. I've fucked this up for you, too."

"Yeah," Beth said. "I'm not mad, though. It could have been me who got caught just as easily."

"Yeah, we've both taken some risks, huh?"

"Yeah." Beth took Mike's hand and squeezed it. "God, now I guess I need to figure out what's going to happen once news of this gets out . . . which it will, fast."

"No," Mike said, brushing back her hair. "There's nothing for you to figure out. You're the innocent victim. You had no idea I was a queer . . . though, now that you think of it, I was an awfully good dancer, and I always noticed your outfits. This doesn't have to blow your cover. All you have to do is give me that ring back."

Beth looked down at her hand. The diamond was glittering in the sunshine that streamed through the car windows, making tiny rainbows on the ceiling.

Liz

Thalia had torn into her falafel sandwich as soon as the waitress set it in front of her, but Liz just scooted her fried eggplant around on her plate. "So the reason I invited you to lunch . . . other than the fact that I like you . . . is that I need to ask you about a friend of yours."

"Okay," Thalia said around a mouthful of falafel. "Who?"

"Audrey."

Thalia grinned. "Audrey's great. She's one of my favorite people. The only reason I don't ask her to marry me is that she feels too much like a sibling. What do you want to know about her?"

Liz gave up on her eggplant; her stomach was already full of butterflies. "Well, the thing is . . . and I'm telling you this in total confidence . . . Audrey and I have been kind of . . . involved."

Thalia's eyebrows shot up. "Romantically?"

"Um, well, kinda."

"Goddamn it, Liz, that's great!" Thalia hollered. "I knew you were a dyke the second I saw you!"

Liz looked around and was relieved to see that the restaurant was populated only by strangers. "Well, to be honest, I don't know if I am a real dyke. I just know that I like Audrey."

"Well, that's a start. A really good start, actually. And hey, if it turns out you're straight except for where Audrey's concerned, that's cool, too. It's not like some representative of the Lesbian Nation is going to show up at your door and make you sign a lifetime contract."

Liz smiled. "Really? I thought you had to sign it in your own blood and everything."

"No," Thalia said, "that's for becoming a Republican."

Liz's smile faded when she thought of Dan. "There is another issue, though. I have a boyfriend."

Thalia shrugged. "So? Dump him."

"You make it sound so easy."

"Listen." Thalia nodded her thanks at the waitress who refilled her iced tea. "If it were anybody else but Audrey, I'd say you could stay with the dude and see the woman, too, as long as they both knew what was going on. But Audrey wouldn't agree to that. She'd want more, and she deserves more." She leaned forward. "Can I play therapist with you for a minute?"

"Please do."

"Okay. Can you tell me what it was that first drew you to Audrey?"

It was an easy question. "I'm drawn to her sense of humor. And her intelligence and social conscience. And she looks great, too, but that wouldn't matter if it weren't for all that other stuff."

"Now the dude. What's his name?"

"Dan."

"Okay. Tell me what it was that first drew you to Dan."

"Well, I met Dan my first semester in this God-awful honors history class. The professor was a total prick, and Dan wasn't afraid to call bullshit on him, which I admired. I thought Dan was the smartest guy my age I'd ever met, and we liked a lot of the same music and books and laughed about a lot of the same things. Plus I liked how he wasn't into macho posturing and had a little beaky nose and wire-framed glasses like John Lennon."

"Hmm." Thalia sipped her tea. "Did you notice how everything you said about Dan was in the past tense and everything you said about Audrey was in the present?"

Liz hadn't noticed. "No shit?"

"No shit. Sister, you've gotta dump him."

Liz put her head in her hands. She would walk across a mile of hot coals in order to avoid an emotional confrontation with somebody. How was she going to initiate a breakup? "Dan loves me. This is really going to hurt him."

"Look, you're not going to be doing the dude any favors if you stay with him in body when your heart's really with Audrey."

Liz knew it was true, but the thought of actively hurting someone who had been the focal point of her life for almost three years was more than she could stand. "You're right."

"I know I'm right. Dump him. Do it now if you can . . . before you have the chance to think too much and fuck things up."

"Now?"

"Yep."

The waitress appeared with the bill. "Well, at least let me pay for your lunch first," Liz said. "It's a small price to pay for a therapy session."

"Thanks." Thalia grabbed her hand. "And listen, if you're free tonight after you've dumped the dude, you ought to come hear Wanda Bledsoe read at the library. She's a totally kick-ass lesbian writer, and if you're gonna be a dyke, you've gotta study up on the literature."

"Why?" Liz said. "Is there a test or something?"

Thalia grinned. "From the sound of things, you've already passed it."

Liz forced her feet to keep walking in the direction of Dan's dorm. All the while her anxiety about Dan's emotional reaction was growing. Would he cry? She'd never seen him cry, but that didn't mean he couldn't. Or would he get angry? She had cheated on him, after all. And what of the long-term emotional consequences? Would his heartbreak turn him into a full-fledged alcoholic instead of just a heavy recreational drinker? Was she a terrible person for doing this to him?

And yet if she was going to call herself a feminist, she had a responsibility to herself, too. And the self she was with Audrey was her natural, true self—the self she was with glimmers of the self she aspired to be. And for whatever reason, with Dan, she was always shape shifting, trying to mold herself into the person she thought he wanted.

She picked up the phone in the dorm lobby and prayed that Dan wouldn't be in his room. He picked up after two rings.

"Hey," Liz said, her voice tight. "What are you up to?"

"Smoking a bowl. You want to come up?"

"Yeah."

When Dan opened the door, Liz's nose was assaulted by the odor of marijuana masked by Lysol. She slipped in quickly to prevent the fumes from wafting down the hallway. Once she was in, Dan locked the door and replaced the rolled-up towel at its base. He held out a wooden pipe. "Can I offer you a toke?"

She was tempted, but she remembered what Audrey had said about her spending too much time muzzy-headed. She needed to be clear when she did this. "Actually, not right now. There's something I need to talk to you about."

Dan held the pipe to his lips and lit it. "Yeah," he said in the guttural voice of someone holding in a double lungful of smoke. "I suppose I need to talk to you about something, too."

"Really?" Liz sat down on the edge of the bed, her heart pounding. "You go first." She couldn't break up with him until she found out what he needed to tell her. What if he was dying of cancer or something? She couldn't dump him then.

"Well . . ." He emptied out the pipe, pinched up a bud from a plastic baggie and loaded it in. "It appears that come fall semester, I won't be in school . . . or in Knoxville, for that matter."

For a moment Liz was so shocked she forgot the reason she had come to talk to Dan in the first place. "But why?"

"According to the powers of the university, I am not making satisfactory progress toward my degree."

"I . . . I don't understand. You're an honors student."

"I entered the university as an honors student, yes. But last semester I didn't pass any of my classes."

"Why?" Right now, Liz felt like *why* was the only word in her vocabulary.

"I attended class fairly regularly, contributed to class discussions and did quite well on tests. But when it came to writing papers and course projects, well, I simply didn't do them. I had already proven my knowledge to the instructors, so why should I have bothered with their petty little busywork assignments?"

"To pass the class?" Liz tried.

"They should have passed me anyway because of my level of knowledge and intelligence. And this semester I just kind of lost interest in attending classes. Why should I when I can learn so much more spending my days in the library? As you know I've already read my way through Dumas in French. Right now I'm on the third volume of *The Education of Henry Adams*. I intend to finish it before I leave school."

"And where will you go . . . when you leave?"

"Back to Nashville. My parents have said I can live with them for a year, provided that I hold down a steady job. So I'll work, and in the fall they want me to take a couple of courses at the community college, though I'm not sure I can bring myself to."

Liz felt like she'd been hit in the head with a sledgehammer. "So how long have you known that you wouldn't be coming back?"

Dan rubbed his chin thoughtfully. "What is this . . . April? I guess I've known since mid-February."

"And when were you going to tell me?"

Dan surveyed her with a puzzled expression. "It never occurred to me to tell you until now. I didn't think it was a big deal as far as you were concerned. I mean, I'll call you from time to time, and I'll visit when I make enough money for a car."

For Dan, Liz realized, this relationship hadn't been much of a relationship at all. She had spent years obsessing over Dan's every gesture and utterance, but she could not say with any degree of certainty that when she was not in Dan's range of vision, he had ever thought of her at all. "Dan, I want to break up with you. That's what I came here to tell you. It's not your fault or anything, but I don't think you're good for me anymore, and I've met someone—a woman—and I think she is."

"Oh. Well. All right." He lit the pipe again and inhaled. "I suppose I'll be able to cadge lots of sympathy beers at the Sagebrush when I tell folks my old lady's left me to become a lesbian."

Liz searched his eyes for a sign of sadness or regret. She saw nothing.

"Well," he said, "before you go, shall we smoke the peace pipe?"

Under the circumstances, it seemed rude to refuse. She took the pipe, lit it, sucked on it and passed it back to him. He went to the stereo, took out his *Sticky Fingers* LP—an original one with the zipper and one of his most prized possessions—and put it on the turntable. He let the needle drop onto "Wild Horses," and Liz knew this was the closest he'd ever come to expressing sadness at their relationship's demise. She sat with him and smoked until the song was over, then she rose and left without a word, softly shutting the door behind her.

Elisa

Dr. Rivers adjusted the microphone on the podium in the library's lecture hall. "Wanda Jean Bledsoe," she enunciated into the mike, "first came on the scene as a feminist poet in the late seventies, when her work appeared in such journals as *Sister Sojourner* and *Bluestocking*. In nineteen eighty-two, her poems were collected to form her first book, *Woman Been Down*. In nineteen eighty-eight, her book of short stories, *Sorry as Bluejohn*, won the Radclyffe Hall Award for lesbian fiction and blew the doors open on the subject of social class in lesbian culture. And next year, her novel, *Scar Tissue*, will be published by St. Martin's Press. Wanda will follow her reading with a reception and signing in the library lounge. Thank you for coming, and please join me in welcoming the spectacular Wanda Jean Bledsoe."

Elisa looked around the audience as she applauded. She saw Thalia and a couple of other girls from Women in Modernism, but the majority of the audience was made up of women she didn't know. Or, to be more specific, dykes she didn't know. Elisa's gaydar was in overdrive as she looked at all the women—a few her age, but most of them older, who were obviously "together," quite a few of them in butch-femme pairings.

A fortyish woman with a broad face and long, straight auburn hair stepped up to the mike. "Hey, y'all," she said. "I'm Wanda Jean Bledsoe, and I'm a white trash femme dyke from the coalfields of West Virginia." Her accent was as sweet, slow and Southern as molasses poured on a biscuit, and Elisa was amazed that anybody who sounded like she did would get invited to speak at a university.

And then Wanda Jean read a story—a story about a family with a teenaged tomboy daughter that lived in a tarpaper shack—a family that owned nothing but their dignity. The father in the story, like Elisa's father, had been wounded in war, but it was Korea, not Vietnam. The real war being fought in the story was a war within the characters—to survive, to keep hope alive. The message of the story cut right into Elisa's heart: These people—these poor, uneducated, rural people who were so much like her family and Jo's family—mattered. She had never heard such a message before, let alone read in a university lecture hall in an honest Appalachian twang, and she found it impossible to hold back her tears.

At the reception, Dr. Rivers draped an arm around Elisa's shoulder. "Have you talked to Wanda Jean yet?"

"Not yet." Elisa looked over at the signing table where any view of Wanda Jean was blocked by legions of adoring dykes. "I'm waiting for the line to thin out . . . and to get my nerve up."

"There's no need to be nervous," Dr. Rivers said. "She's quite charming."

"She's amazing," Elisa said. "How she's so smart and down to earth at the same time, how she's not ashamed of where she came from . . ."

"Yes, yes," Dr. Rivers said, a little distractedly. "It's an effective persona, isn't it?" She wrinkled her nose at a butch woman whose hair was spiky on top and long in the back. She wore a Harley-Davidson T-shirt, as did her bleached blond femme girlfriend. "So, Elisa," Dr. Rivers whispered, "Where do you think some of the women at this thing *came from*?"

Elisa looked at Dr. Rivers with her real pearls and her small, soft hands untouched by hard labor. "From the same kind of place I did, probably," she said.

"Maybe so," Dr. Rivers replied, "but you're coming along quite nicely."

The crowd had finally parted enough so that Elisa could see Wanda Jean. "Excuse me," she said to Dr. Rivers. Elisa, knowing that she was going to feel the pinch of spending the money, picked up a copy of *Sorry As Bluejohn* and handed it to Wanda Jean. She wanted to say something articulate, but all that came out was, "I think you're great."

Wanda Jean grinned. "Well, you're sweet to say so. Who should I sign this to, hon?"

"Elisa," she said, then reconsidered. "Actually, maybe you should make it out to Elisa and Jo."

When Elisa left the signing table, she almost ran smack into Thalia, who was also holding a copy of *Sorry As Bluejohn*. "Heya," Thalia said, "doesn't Wanda Jean kick ass?"

"She sure does."

"Say"—Thalia looked around and lowered her voice—"you've been hanging out with Dr. Rivers a lot, huh?"

"Yeah, some."

Thalia grinned. "That's familiar territory for me. I was her little pet last spring. She has this thing, you know, about mentoring little dykes she thinks are 'diamonds in the rough.' It's like she's starring in a production of *My Fair Lezzie* or something. Don't take that the wrong way, though. I still like her. She's cool as hell. I had a great time with her, and I learned a lot, and not just about literature, if you know what I mean. Say, has she made that speech to you about the butterfly and the cocoon yet?"

"No," Elisa said, not because she wanted to lie, but because she couldn't bring herself to admit that she had listened to the speech rapturously and thought it was just for her.

Beth

Beth lay sprawled on the king-sized bed, watching a stupid comedy she didn't know the name of on HBO. Her bottle of orange pills and a screwdriver she'd mixed courtesy of the mini-bar were on the nightstand within easy reach. She held a half-empty jar of macadamia nuts, also from the mini-bar, between her knees. The fat content in macadamias was off the charts, and normally she wouldn't let herself eat them, but since the waves of anxiety that swept her up every half-hour or so resulted in her puking in the bathroom, she figured the calories didn't count anyway.

As soon as she got out of Mike's car after their fateful talk, she had found herself walking away from campus. She couldn't go back to her room, where Quimby probably was, and she sure as hell couldn't go to that night's sorority meeting. And so she had walked to Walgreen's, where she purchased a toothbrush and a plastic package of panties so cheap she wouldn't ordinarily have let them touch her body. Walgreen's bag in hand, she had then walked all the way downtown, where she used her daddy's credit card to check herself into the Bentley, Knoxville's oldest and most expensive hotel.

And here in her room she had lain for three days, avoiding her classes, her sorority sisters, her family. She couldn't go on like this, she knew, safe from questions and suspicion. But whenever she thought of returning to campus, of facing Quimby or calling her parents, the force of her nausea propelled her back to the bathroom.

What time was it? Hotels had such a timeless, placeless quality it was easy to lose track. Five forty-five p.m. She swallowed a pill with a slug of screwdriver and picked up the phone.

"Hello?"

"Thalia?"

"Yeah?" Her voice showed no sign of recognition.

"This is Beth."

"Beth? Oh, hey! I'm sorry I didn't recognize your voice. You've never called me before. You sound different."

Beth probably sounded different because she hadn't spoken to another soul in three days. Her voice had grown scratchy from disuse. "Yeah, well, listen, I've got a room over at the Bentley, and I was wondering if you might maybe come over?"

"Are you there alone?"

"I'm alone," Beth said, a statement that struck her as painfully true. "Room three seventeen."

"Okay, well, I'll be there in an hour or so, I guess."

Beth ran herself a bath with the almond oil bath foam the hotel provided. She lay in the tub, sipped her screwdriver and soaked, then wrapped herself in the hotel's fluffy white bathrobe when there was a knock on the door.

Thalia was wearing a T-shirt that said *Black Flag*, and Beth was puzzled why anybody would buy a T-shirt advertising roach killer. "Hey," Thalia said, looking around the room. "Wow, and I always thought the Holiday Inn was plenty fancy. Why are you staying here anyway?"

"I . . . I just needed a little getaway for myself." A tiny voice inside Beth said *tell her everything*, but she ignored it.

"In the middle of the week?"

"Sure, why not? Listen, I thought maybe we could order dinner from room service." Beth held out a leather-bound menu.

"I don't have enough money."

Beth laughed. "Don't worry about money. Daddy's credit card is taking care of it."

Thalia raised a doubtful eyebrow. "It that okay with, uh, Daddy?"

"It will be." Beth knew this was true. Once her daddy heard about the broken engagement, he would pity her enough to cut her some slack when he saw the credit card statement.

"Well, okay, why not? I mean, you guys are rolling in it, right?"

They sat on the bed and pored over the menu. "Fettucini Alfredo!" Beth practically moaned. "That's what I'm having, calories be damned."

"So it's really true you sorority girls worry about calories all the time?"

"Not all the time. Not tonight. So what are you having? Pick anything you want."

"The salmon."

"And for dessert?"

"I haven't even thought about dessert."

"I can't decide between the cheesecake and the chocolate torte. Should we get a slice of each and share?"

"I guess so."

"And how about a bottle of champagne?"

"Fuck, are you serious?"

They ate sitting on the bed. Until now Beth had forgotten the sensual pleasure of stuffing food into her mouth, had forgotten how divine a creamy sauce combined with a comforting carbohydrate could be. The champagne popped pleasurably on her tongue.

Thalia was laughing.

"What is it?" Beth said.

"I was just thinking," Thalia said, spearing a morsel of salmon. "I've fucked you six ways to Sunday, but this is the first time we've eaten a meal together. This is a very strange relationship, Beth."

Beth touched Thalia's hand. "You like me, though, right?"

Thalia laughed. "Yes, I do. My friends think I'm totally insane, but I really do like you."

"I like you, too."

The chocolate frosting on the torte was quite useful for smearing on one's partner's body and then licking off. Thalia first put a dollop on Beth's neck, then proceeded to her collarbone, then her breast, each time presenting her finger to Beth so she could suck off the remaining chocolate.

When Thalia had finally worked her way down between Beth's thighs, Beth whispered, "Are you going to put chocolate there, too?"

"Nope, can't put anything too sugary there . . . bad for the woman parts. Besides, it would sort of be gilding the lily, wouldn't it?"

Beth didn't know if it was because of all the tension that had built up in her body, but when she came, she was pretty sure the walls and windows shook. She wouldn't have been surprised if the whole room had collapsed around them.

Once Thalia was lying beside her again, Beth said, "Now you."

"What?"

"Now I want to do . . . things to you."

"Really? You never have before."

"Is it okay if I do?"

Thalia grinned. "It's more than okay."

It was the first time since with Gina in high school that Beth had been an active giver of pleasure. She undressed Thalia and touched her gently, almost reverently, with her fingertips, her tongue, touching and tasting each lovely hill, mound and valley. She wanted Thalia to be in her senses—for Thalia's taste to live on in her mouth, for Thalia's smell to be buried deep in her olfactory center. She wanted to be able to close her eyes and still see the olive cast of Thalia's skin, still hear the sounds of her gasps in her ears. She had to soak all of this in because she knew it would be the last time.

In the morning, Thalia was already up and dressed and fiddling with the coffeemaker when Beth opened her eyes.

"Hey," Thalia said. "You know, my parents' deli is just up the street from here. You want to go get some breakfast? I figure I ate compliments of your dad last night, so maybe I can return the favor."

"I can't. You go without me." Beth swallowed hard. "Actually, maybe you should go now. Last night . . . it was my way of saying good-bye."

"Good-bye? What—like, we're not going to see each other anymore? You just wanted me to come to your hotel room like I was some kind of expensive whore?"

Beth winced. "I didn't mean it like that. I . . . I just wanted to be with you. I still do, really, but I can't."

"Why? Because somebody might find out and tell one of your sorority sisters or your daddy? You're a really fucked up girl, Beth."

Beth wiped her eyes. "You're better off without me."

"Hell, I don't know. Maybe I am."

"So go."

Thalia headed toward the door, then stopped. "Listen, if I leave, you're not going to, like, do something stupid, are you? I mean, you're all holed up in this hotel by yourself with your pills and your booze. I can handle us not seeing each other anymore. It stings, but I'll handle it. But if you were to . . . I don't know . . . take all those pills or something." She rubbed her eyes. "Before I go, I want you to look me in the face and tell me you're okay."

Thalia's face looked blurry through Beth's tears. "I'm okay," she said with a catch in her throat.

Thalia sighed. "Well, I hope you're telling the truth."

After Thalia shut the door, Beth shook out the contents of her pill bottle and counted the tablets in her hand. Fifteen. Was that even enough? And who would find her if she did it? The maid? The maid? The maid would scream, and the management would call the police, and for the rest of their lives her parents would be known as those people whose daughter killed herself after her fiancé was caught in a homosexual scandal. No. She couldn't do that to them or herself either.

She swallowed one pill and put the rest back in the bottle, went in the bathroom and turned on the shower. She scrubbed the sticky spots where Thalia had frosted her with chocolate and washed her hair for the first time in days. She toweled off, brushed her teeth and carefully applied some foundation, mascara and lip gloss. There was nothing to wear but the Walgreen's panties and the clothes she'd had on when she arrived, so she put those on and took the elevator to the lobby.

Next door to the Bentley was a dress shop that was frequented by ladies older than Beth's mother. The quality of the clothing was excellent but a little on the matronly side for a girl Beth's age. Today, though, it would have to do. She selected a tan sundress that would look okay with the sandals she was wearing. She changed in the fitting room, where she dumped her old clothes in the wastebasket. She paid for the dress with her daddy's credit card and asked the elderly clerk if she could cut the tags off for her. The lady looked incredulous but obliged.

The sorority's Spring Into Brunch event had been scheduled to start at eleven. Beth managed to arrive at the Panhell Building by a quarter after. When she walked into the ballroom, dozens of girls, also in sundresses and sandals, were congregating around a buffet table spread with muffins, bagels and fruit.

Quimby saw Beth first. She shrieked, threw her muffin in the air and ran to Beth with her arms open wide. "Omigod! Beth! We've been so worried! You've got to call your mom and dad. I finally broke down and called them last night. They're hysterical. They called the police . . ."

Beth pulled back from the hug. "Do they know about Mike?"

"God," Quimby said, "everybody knows about Mike."

The girls swarmed Beth, hugging her and offering their sympathies, all of which overlapped in Beth's ears: *What a shock you must have been furious is your daddy going to kill him the least the little faggot could have done was let you keep the diamond.*

Mike had been right. In the girls' minds, Beth was the innocent victim of his deception. They might have thought of her as a dupe, but not as a dyke. She let them hold her and fuss over her and bring her fruit, and as she sobbed, she knew they thought she was crying over Mike. But every tear she shed was because she knew that now she could never again risk another night like the one before.

Liz

As Liz stood on Audrey's front porch, the most amazing thing happened: an idea for a whole story popped into her head. Not just an idea for some characters in an opening scene, spouting some clever yet empty dialogue, but a whole story.

She knocked on the door.

When Audrey answered, Liz was rendered breathless. She didn't know if it was the way the sun was lighting the golden streaks in Audrey's hair or the way her eyes crinkled at the corners when she smiled or the way Audrey stood there perfectly framed by the door, but Liz felt this was a picture she'd carry with her a long time, like a treasured photograph.

"Hey," Audrey said.

"Hey." Liz looked down, suddenly shy. "Um . . . I think I might be ready to have that talk now."

Audrey's smile was luminous. "Well, then, let's talk." She took Liz's hand and led her through the open door.

Elisa

Elisa was still panting even though Jo had finished making love to her five minutes ago. "You know," Elisa said, laughing. "Maybe I do love you enough to live with you in a trailer in Odessa. Not that that would be my first choice, mind you."

Jo propped up on her elbow. "Hey, it wouldn't be my first choice either. We've got to live in a town that's big enough to support a women's softball team. Like, I can see us"—her voice softened into dreaminess—"living here or maybe someplace bigger. We could have a little house with a yard so I could putter around and plant tomatoes in the summer. And while you finish up graduate school, I could teach P.E. and coach somewhere. And then maybe after you get all settled in your career, we could have a baby."

"A baby?" Elisa laughed. "Where would we get a baby?"

"Oh, there's this article in one of them magazines Thalia gave you about lesbians having babies. They buy sperm from these banks, you see—"

"And who would carry this baby?" Elisa liked children, but she had never thought of having one of her own.

"Well, I would."

"You?"

"Sure. I mean, I'm good at physical things, and havin' a baby's about as physical as it gets, right? And see, while you teach college, I could maybe stay home with the baby a couple of years, until he's ready to start preschool. I could teach him to play ball."

"And if it's a girl?"

"Then I'll teach her to play ball. I'll be damned if I'm gonna be the only athletic one in this family."

"Wow," Elisa said, shaking her head. "A baby, huh?" She looked at Jo—really looked at her—for the first time in a long time. "You know," she said, "I wandered away from you a little while there. I didn't cheat on you or anything, but I wasn't with you the way I should've been. I'm sorry."

"It's okay," Jo said. "I knew you'd come back."

Beth

Beth had excused herself from lunch with her parents to use the ladies' room. Actually, her use for the ladies' room was to stand in it and take one of her orange pills in hopes of curtailing a particularly potent panic attack. The Sequoyah Country Club thoughtfully provided little paper cups in the ladies' room, many of which, Beth suspected, were used by the ladies of the club to wash down their tranquilizers.

Beth was giving herself a quick once-over in the mirror when Suzanne Foster walked in, stately with her tailored sky-blue jacket and bobbed silver hair. Beth's stomach clenched. Mrs. Foster was a very active alumna of William Blount's Theta chapter who always wanted to chat her up about Greek life and to ask about that nice young man she was dating.

"Beth, dear!" Mrs. Foster took both of her hands and leaned in to touch her cheek to Beth's.

"Nice to see you, Mrs. Foster," Beth said, making her way to the exit.

"Just a moment, Beth, dear." Suzanne Foster held up her index finger.

Beth knew she was trapped. Suzanne Foster was born into Knoxville's second richest family and had married into the first richest. Before she retired, she had run Knoxville's most elite real estate firm, and she still served as the president of the Knoxville Women's Club. When Suzanne Foster told you "just a moment," you stopped in your tracks until you were told to do otherwise. "Yes, ma'am?"

Mrs. Foster surveyed the room. "Good. We're alone. I just wanted to let you know that your mother told me about the unfortunate incident with your young man."

"Yes, ma'am." Beth's words came out as a gasp. She wished the orange pills worked faster.

"Discretion," Mrs. Foster said, fussing with her hair in the mirror, "is so important." She fished a cosmetic case out of her Louis Vuitton handbag. "You know, when I became engaged to my dear, late husband, so many people wondered why James would choose a gawky girl like me when I had two beautiful sisters who were also of marriageable age." She touched up her lipstick. "James married me because he knew I could be discreet. And I knew the same thing about him. Mutually agreed upon discretion—it is key."

Beth thought she must surely be reading too much into Mrs. Foster's words. "So you're saying . . ."

"That Miss Benson, who has lived under my roof for the past twenty-four years, might be something more than my personal assistant? Perhaps." She smiled. "But no one would ever say so because I have four generations' worth of money and connections, and I have a 'Mrs.' in front of my name, which I'll carry with me to my grave. You have two out of three of those, Beth. And I would advise you to pursue the third sometime before you're out of your twenties. But when you do, you must find someone who knows when to keep his zipper zipped." She dusted her nose with powder. "I'll tell you what. I'll keep an eye out for a discreet young man of our kind. I have been known to . . . make such arrangements." Her nose powdered, she snapped her compact shut. "Well, delightful to see you as always, dear. Have a lovely lunch."

Beth had always wondered why there was a sofa in the ladies' room, but right now she was grateful to be able to sink into it. Mrs. Foster and Miss Benson? Beth wondered how many of the women in the club, playing bridge, drinking tea, gossiping over chicken salad, were members of another secret club as well. And how many men, after practicing their manly swings on the golf course, were casting secret, longing glances at their peers in the men's locker room? Perhaps Beth wasn't as alone as she had thought. Suddenly she could breathe again. It was time to go back to her family's table.

Publications from Spinsters Ink

P.O. Box 242
Midway, Florida 32343
Phone: 800-301-6860
www.spinstersink.com

A POEM FOR WHAT'S HER NAME by Dani O'Connor. Professor Dani O'Connor had pretty much resigned herself to the fact that there was no such thing as a complete woman. Then out of nowhere, along comes a woman who blows Dani's theory right out of the water.   ISBN: 1-883523-78-8 $14.95

WOMEN'S STUDIES by Julia Watts. With humor and heart, Women's Studies follows one school year in the lives of these three young women and shows that in college, one's extracurricular activities are often much more educational that what goes on in the classroom.   ISBN: 1-883523-75-3 $14.95

THE SECRET KEEPING by Francine Saint Marie. The Secret Keeping is a high stakes, girl-gets-girl romance, where the moral of the story is that money can buy you love if it's invested wisely.
                          ISBN: 1-883523-77-X $14.95

DISORDERLY ATTACHMENTS by Jennifer L. Jordan. 5th Kristin Ashe Mystery. Kris investigates whether a mansion someone wants to convert into condos is haunted.   ISBN 1-883523-74-5 $14.95

VERA'S STILL POINT by Ruth Perkinson. Vera is reminded of exactly what it is that she has been missing in life.
                          ISBN 1-883523-73-7 $14.95

OUTRAGEOUS by Sheila Ortiz-Taylor. Arden Benbow, a motor-cycle riding, lesbian Latina poet from LA is hired to teach poetry in a small liberal arts college in northwest Florida.
ISBN 1-883523-72-9 $14.95

UNBREAKABLE by Blayne Cooper. The bonds of love and friend-ship can be as strong as steel. But are they unbreakable?
ISBN 1-883523-76-1 $14.95

ALL BETS OFF by Jaime Clevenger. Bette Lawrence is about to find out how hard life can be for someone of low society standing in the 1900s.
ISBN 1-883523-71-0 $14.95

UNBEARABLE LOSSES by Jennifer L. Jordan. 4th in the Kristin Ashe Mystery series. Two elderly sisters have hired Kris to discover who is pilfering from their award-winning holiday display.
ISBN 1-883523-68-0 $14.95

FRENCH POSTCARDS by Jane Merchant. When Elinor moves to France with her husband and two children, she never expects that her life is about to be changed forever.
ISBN 1-883523-67-2 $14.95

EXISTING SOLUTIONS by Jennifer L. Jordan. 2nd book in the Kristin Ashe Mystery series. When Kris is hired to find an activist's biological father, things get complicated when she finds herself fall-ing for her client.
ISBN 1-883523-69-9 $14.95

A SAFE PLACE TO SLEEP by Jennifer L. Jordan. 1st in the Kris-tin Ashe Mystery series. Kris is approached by well-known lesbian Destiny Greaves with an unusual request. One that will lead Kris to hunt for her own missing childhood pieces.
ISBN 1-883523-70-2 $14.95

Visit

Spinsters Ink

at

SpinstersInk.com

or call our toll-free number

1-800-301-6860